In the Spotlight

What Reviewers Say About Lesley Davis's Work

Playing With Fire

"Strong, mature characters embracing their feelings (good, bad and indifferent). An awfully attractive African-American MC, Takira Lathan. Dealing head-on with stereotypes. Good chemistry. A lovely relationship wherein the MCs talk to each other about themselves, their insecurities, their feelings and even what they like sexually. This book has a lot going for it."—*Reviewer@large*

"First of all, this book is a total geek dream. …This book was packed with tropes, like seriously all the best ones, and had everything from references, to cute moments inspired by making sure we all believe in a little bit of magic. It was uplifting and just added a little something extra to this story, like the right ingredients in a secret sauce."—*LESBIreviewed*

Raging at the Stars

"*Raging at the Stars* is a very entertaining and engaging read. The alien invasion storyline—with a twist—is very original and the plot is very well developed. The two leads are very likeable and the supporting characters are equally interesting. The author's style of writing is very engaging, especially the witty dialogue."—Melina Bickard, Librarian, Waterloo Library (London)

"A Sci Fi book with a side of romance and a hint of aliens (Or is there really a hint? What else could be going on?). Anyway, it's basically my perfect book, and I thought it was totally awesome." —Danielle Kimerer, Librarian, Nevins Memorial Public Library (MA)

"I am 800% here for this book. It reminded me of a fun mashup of *X-Files* and *Independence Day*, with lesbians, and honestly, I can't think of anything cooler at this moment. …I'll definitely track down more of Davis's titles. Definitely recommend."—*Kissing Backwards: Lesbian Book Reviews*

Playing in Shadow

"*Playing In Shadow* is different from my typical romance reading, but at the same time exactly the same. I loved the two main characters and the secondary characters. The issues they all face were realistic and handled really well. …I do not often read LGBT romance, but thus far every time I have I have been thrilled with how fantastic the writing is. I guess I need to read more!"—Sharon Tyler, Librarian, Cheshire Public Library (CT)

"Overall, this was an amazing read, great and engaging story, and as it progresses adding layers to the characters and the complexity of their struggles it starts to consume a little bit of your heart making you wish this was a Saga and not just one story."—*Collector of Book Boyfriends*

"The story is emotional and feels very honest. You won't miss out on the romance either, with equal parts of 'Awe, that's so sweet!' and 'Whoa, Steamy!'"—Katie Larson, Librarian, Tooele City Public Library (Utah)

Starstruck

"Both leads were well developed with believable backgrounds and Mischa was a delight. It was nice to 'run into' Trent and Elton from the author's previous book."—Melina Bickard, Librarian, Waterloo Library (London)

Truth Behind the Mask

"It is rare to find good lesbian science fantasy. It is also rare to have a deaf lesbian heroine. Davis has given readers both in *Truth Behind the Mask*. In her tightly wrapped novel, Davis vividly describes the feeling of the night wind and the heat of the fires. She is just as deft at describing the blossoming love between Pagan and Erith, two of her main characters. *Truth Behind the Mask* has enough intriguing twists and turns to keep the pages flying right to the exciting conclusion."—*Just About Write*

Playing Passion's Game

"*Playing Passion's Game* is a delightful read with lots of twists, turns, and good laughs. Davis has provided a varied and interesting supportive cast. Those who enjoy computer games will recognize some familiar scenes, and those new to the topic get to learn about a whole new world."—*Just About Write*

Pale Wings Protecting

"*Pale Wings Protecting* is a provocative paranormal mystery; it's an otherworldly thriller couched inside a tale of budding romance. The novel contains an absorbing narrative, full of thrilling revelations, that skillfully leads the reader into the uncanny dimensions of the supernatural."—*Lambda Literary Review*

"[*Pale Wings Protecting*] was just a delicious delight with so many levels of intrigue on the case level and the personal level. Plus, the celestial and diabolical beings were incredibly intriguing. …I was riveted from beginning to end and I certainly will look forward to additional books by Lesley Davis. By all means, give this story a total once-over!"—*Rainbow Book Reviews*

Dark Wings Descending—***Lambda Literary Award Finalist***

"[*Dark Wings Descending*] is an intriguing story that presents a vision of life after death many will find challenging. It also gives the reader some wonderful sex scenes, humor, and a great read!" —*Reviewer RLynne*

By the Author

Truth Behind the Mask

Playing Passion's Game

Playing in Shadow

Starstruck

Raging at the Stars

Playing with Fire

In the Spotlight

The Wings Series

Dark Wings Descending

Pale Wings Protecting

White Wings Weeping

In the Spotlight

by

Lesley Davis

2021

IN THE SPOTLIGHT

ISBN 13: 978-1-63555-926-2

This Trade Paperback Original Is Published By
Bold Strokes Books, Inc.
P.O. Box 249
Valley Falls, NY 12185

First Edition: May 2021

Credits
Editor: Cindy Cresap
Production Design: Susan Ramundo
Cover Design By Tammy Seidick

Acknowledgments

Thank you as always to Radclyffe. This story marks my 10th book with BSB, and I still couldn't be prouder of my stories bearing that logo.

Thanks to Sandy Lowe, for your "spirited urging" for me to write a sequel to *Starstruck*. Here it is! Thank you for getting the tiny cogs in my brain whirring and firing to set this tale in motion.

Cindy Cresap, you totally and utterly rock. Best editor ever. Best remover of my overabundance of adjectives ever. Thank you doesn't begin to cover it. You're the 13th Doctor level of awesomeness and genius in my eyes. You're Han Solo and Princess Leia rolled into one…no, wait, that makes you Kylo Ren. Hell no! Can you edit that piece out, please?! ;)

Tammy, thank you for creating the gorgeous cover that graces this book. It's fantastic!

And always, a huge thank you and much love to my friends and readers who never fail to spur me on to write more, even when my health is totally crappy, or when I can't bear to tear myself away from the game I'm playing:

Jane Morrison
Pam Goodwin and Gina Paroline
Kim Palmer-Bell and Tracy Palmer-Bell (thank you for the Gamer face mask! xx)
Cheryl Hunter and Anne Hunter
Annie Ellis and Julia Lowndes
Donna Chidley-Gosling and Jools Chidley-Gosling
Kerry Pfadenhauer

A special thank you to Natalie Sussenbach. See? I do, sometimes, manage to write in between my gaming!

And to Cindy Pfannenstiel, for your support in my writing, your enthusiasm for my stories, and for keeping me as sane as I'm ever likely to be through this crazy pandemic. x

Dedication

In memory of Jacky Morrison Hart
My self-proclaimed "Number 1 stalker"
(of the very best kind)
May the afterlife be a source of endless adventure for you

Prologue

The large magnifying lens enhanced every spring, gear, and screw inside the old pocket watch with a sharpened clarity. Hollister Graham wielded a pair of jewelers' tweezers as she carefully lowered a bright red jewel into place.

"Seems to me a dreadful waste of a pretty gem, hiding it away inside a Hunter's casing," Emily Brown said, leaning over Hollister's shoulder as she watched her work.

"It has a very important role to play. Each little jewel is used as a bearing to lessen the friction…" Hollister held her breath as the jewel found its rightful setting. She let out a sigh of relief. "They're really awkward to work with though."

"It's a good thing you have such steady hands, my love."

Hollister looked over her shoulder at Emily who strove to keep a straight face. Hollister playfully narrowed her eyes at her and rose from her seat to take Emily in her arms.

"These hands would rather be exploring you than messing with some old watch." She ran her hand down Emily's back and tugged at the blouse tucked neatly into her long skirt. She pulled until she could finally reach bare skin. Emily gasped as Hollister's fingers brushed up and down her spine. "You're a distraction, Emily Brown, and you know it." Hollister traced patterns across Emily's skin then nipped at her full bottom lip before kissing her. Emily's arms tightened around Hollister's shoulders and she clung to her as the kiss deepened. Hollister couldn't get enough of her, from the softness of her mouth, to the small sounds that escaped Emily as the kiss made them both breathless. Emily finally drew back, but didn't let go of Hollister. Instead, she rested her head on Hollister's chest and laid a kiss over her heart.

"I'm nearly finished, then I can devote the rest of the evening to you as we'd planned. I can wrestle you from that ridiculous buttoned-up blouse and you can get me out of these pants…" Hollister paused and corrected herself. "Sorry, *trousers*. I never dreamed when I came to England from America I'd have to learn a whole new language."

"Well, I for one am glad you took the risk and traveled here. I can't imagine what my life would have been like without you." Emily held her closer.

"You'll never have to worry, my love. We were fated to be. I'm certain of few things in life, but that I know for sure." Hollister kissed Emily sweetly. "Now let me finish with this watch so we can shut up shop and retire for the night."

She turned back to finish laying the last pieces needed to get the watch back in working order. How easy it would be to give in to temptation and just push the watch aside for another day. But Hollister was someone who could never leave a puzzle unsolved. She'd found the old watch mysteriously tucked away in her suitcase. The only person it could have belonged to was her father. Something vaguely resembling his initials appeared worn into the golden casing. They were her initials too, but she'd never owned a pocket watch in her life. She'd put it aside while she and Emily had settled into their new life together, but lately it had been niggling at the back of her mind. Calling to her, almost.

"Your father would be so pleased you're getting the watch working again. He'd be so proud of you and all you've accomplished here."

"It just needed some new innards and a thorough cleaning. It's an old timepiece, but I managed to save some of the original pieces." Hollister drew back from the table and let her eyes adjust from staring too long through the magnifying lens. She carefully picked up the watch and cradled it in her palm. She watched the workings perform their magic, each tiny piece moving the hands to count away the minutes. "It's just curious that I don't remember my father ever owning a pocket watch like this. But it has to be his. After all, it was his suitcase I used when I left home."

"Well, I can't think of a more beautiful way to mark the passage of our time together," Emily said, resting her head against Hollister's before drawing back to deposit a kiss on Hollister's cheek.

"We have all the time in the world, my love." Hollister caught Emily's hand in her own and pressed a kiss into her palm, folding Emily's fingers over it to hold the kiss safely inside. "I feel like I waited a lifetime to find you, and now I just want every second of every minute of every day spent in your company."

Hollister turned back to the watch and gently placed the glass cover over its face. Finally, she attached the ornately engraved golden casing that would snap shut to keep the watch protected and spring open to reveal the time. It was finished. Hollister stood up to thread the thin chain from the watch through a buttonhole on her waistcoat, and with a flourish, she snapped the watch case closed.

The sudden violent shock of electricity slammed through her body like a bolt of lightning. Dimly, she could hear Emily screaming, but she couldn't move a muscle to reach for her. She watched helplessly as Emily tried to touch her, but another crack of electricity struck, visibly searing Emily's flesh and knocking her back on her heels.

"What's happening?" Emily asked, terrified and shaking, cradling her damaged hand to her chest. She kept a safe distance away as the light growing around Hollister crackled and snapped like an angry beast.

"I don't know." Hollister barely got the words out from teeth gritted in pain. She looked down at the watch still resting in her hand. It seemed to be fusing itself *into* her hand. An eerie glow emanated from the shut case, pulsating to a strange beat. The rhythm hypnotized her until she realized it was synchronizing to the exact tempo of her terrified heart. She startled as she began to see right through her hand where the watch lay. Her body was slowly fading as she stood immobile, still cradling the damnable watch whose ticking grew louder and louder with every second passing.

"What's happening to you?" Emily tried desperately to reach for Hollister again but was forcibly repelled by the electric field rapidly growing in size to envelope her. "Hollister! You're fading away!"

Hollister could only stare at the watch. It seemed to be bleeding her of her physical form, wiping her from existence with every tick of the clock.

"Hollister!" Frantic, Emily rushed to grab the poker usually used to stoke the fire in the room. She swung it wildly, trying to break her way into the electrifying shell that was forming around Hollister. Sobbing, screaming, Emily fought to free her.

It was all in vain.

Hollister begged her to stop. She couldn't bear to see her suffering and so distraught. She looked into Emily's beautiful eyes. Her tears broke Hollister's heart. But she couldn't comfort her now, or draw her close, or hold her tight. She was adrift from the physical world.

"I think I have to go," Hollister said. She felt it. She *knew* it. "I love you, Emily. Whatever happens, don't you ever forget that. You are, and have always been, my life, my love, and my reason for being."

"Don't you leave me!" Emily tried again to grab hold of Hollister to pull her out of the light that encompassed her. The second her hand touched the electrical field there was an almighty cracking sound. The power from it threw Emily clear across the room. She crumpled to her knees.

"I don't know where I'm going, but I'll come back to you, I promise. You have my heart, my love. I am forever yours, in each and every lifetime we'll share. I *will* find you again. I'll just follow the beat of your heart." Hollister felt herself disappearing, the room was fading fast, and with it her last sight of Emily. "I love you!"

"And I love you, Hollister Graham. You find a way back to me. Find your way *home*." Emily sobbed and reached out a hand to her. "Come back to me. I'm lost without you."

"I will, I promise you." She spared one last look at the watch. The lid popped open, the hands froze, and all ticking ceased.

"I'm out of time," Hollister whispered as everything she loved disappeared.

Chapter One

"And cut!"

Cole Calder snapped out of the emotional fog she had been acting in. The old-fashioned room Hollister and Emily inhabited, that Cole had imagined for them, was gone. Instead there was a soundstage and a group of onlookers staring at her, critiquing her performance. She wiped at her eyes, brushing away the tears she'd involuntarily shed at the powerful performance from the other actress auditioning. Eris Whyte. Her visible heartbreak in the scene they had performed had taken Cole out of the act and transported her into the reality of what the characters were facing. She'd tested with a few other actresses, replaying this scene over and over, but no one else had captured the devastation of it all quite like Eris had. Her intensity had made Cole raise her own game, and she'd felt the scene come to life in a whole new way.

Eris grinned weakly at Cole, wiping at her own eyes and taking deep breaths to take a step back from her performance. They both reached for each other's hands and squeezed, seeking comfort after such a grueling scene and recognizing how well they had performed it.

"That was awesome," Cole whispered, frightened to break the spell she and Eris had created. Eris nodded and they both turned toward the audience who had been watching and filming their audition. Cole was heartened to see more than a few struggling to hide their emotions.

Except for one who let out a loud, body-wracking sob.

"Oh, Mischa," Cassidy Hayes said, sniffing back her own tears. She shoved a handful of tissues at Mischa Ballantyne who grabbed them gratefully.

"Thank God I wore the waterproof mascara today or I'd look like Alice Cooper," Mischa said, dabbing at her eyes.

Cole sought out the one person's view who mattered the most. Aiden Darrow, the writer of the scene they'd just performed, sat staring at them with something that looked like stunned awe on her face. It made Cole want to punch the air in jubilation. Instead she committed that look to memory to replay over and over.

"Thank you so much for coming back to read again, Cole. And, Eris, thank you for delivering such a masterful performance that you reduced Mischa into the sobbing mess you see before you." Aiden patted Mischa's knee in comfort.

"She's Emily, Aiden. These two could be your characters literally ripped from the page." Mischa took in a shuddering breath to calm herself. "And damn, Ms. Whyte. When you put your heart and soul into a performance you pierce the audience to their very core. Brava." Mischa bowed her head to Eris in respect, one actress to another.

Cole was delighted to see Eris's pale cheeks redden at the praise. She'd received her own compliments from Mischa at a previous audition. It had been heartening to hear that no one else could fit the role of Hollister quite like Cole from someone of Mischa's fame and caliber.

"This opening scene is the most important part of Hollister and Emily's story because if we don't care for the characters right from the start, then their whole story is meaningless." Aiden looked around at the people beside her. "We've seen a lot of actresses doing that exact same scene, but when I watch you two together I can see the characters I created come to life." Her voice broke a little and she coughed to cover her obvious embarrassment. "I wrote this story, I'm also in a position to produce this movie, and I'm consulting on it because I'm determined to see my story come to life as I want it to be told." She looked again at her production team who all gave her emphatic nods. "Because I'm still new to all this I'm going to do things a little differently." Aiden walked over to the makeshift stage they had set up in the soundstage. "I'd like it very much if you two would let me cast you in the leading roles for *A Pocket Full of Time*."

Eris's hand shot to her mouth in shock. "*Really*?" she mumbled through her fingers, her eyes filling again with tears.

Aiden nodded. "We'll work out all the details with your agents, but I want you two on board with this, if you're interested?" She raised an eyebrow at Cole who had been fighting passionately for the coveted role in over a month's worth of auditioning. Cole was stunned at the opportunity that had just opened up for her.

"Oh God, yes! Yes, please!" She had to temper down the urge to hug the life out of Aiden and instead held out a shaking hand and shook Aiden's vigorously instead.

Aiden turned and gestured grandly to the room. "Ladies and gentlemen, we've found our Hollister and Emily."

There was loud applause and cheers from Aiden's crew. Darrow/Hayes Productions was the new company Aiden and Cassidy had started together. Its small independent movies were already garnering awards and recognition for them. Producing *A Pocket Full of Time* was a huge step into mainstream cinema. Cole was thrilled to be a part of it and to get the opportunity to work with people she admired.

Especially Eris. Cole had seen every episode of her TV series *Code Red* and had fangirled enough to check into Eris's bio to learn more. She knew Eris was British born but, like Cole, lived in New York. She was twenty-eight, which was four years younger than Cole. And the bio hadn't lied when it described Eris as pretty. That was a gross understatement. In person, Eris Whyte was breathtaking.

Nonchalantly eyeing both Eris and Cassidy, Cole couldn't help but notice similarities between them. Both were brunettes, wearing their hair long and free. Both had dark brown eyes. And both were exquisitely beautiful, but it was Eris who captivated Cole's attention. Cole smiled to herself ruefully. Having a crush on a costar before she'd even met her wasn't something Cole had experienced before.

But she couldn't argue the fact that Eris was beautiful, and talented, and seemed genuinely sweet. If nothing else, Cole had the chance to make a marvelous friend on the set of her first foray into the movie business.

"Darling Eris, I hope you realize the role you're going to be playing should have been mine." Mischa sighed dramatically as she sashayed over and playfully hip-checked Aiden out of her way so she could address Eris.

Eris laughed. "Yes, you might have mentioned that once or twice in the casting process."

Cassidy came to join them. "I have it on good authority from the author herself that the role of Emily was modeled off *me* so she was always going to be cast with someone who had a proper English accent and be…" Cassidy paused deliberately, "*younger*."

Cole had to bite her lip to rein in her laughter at the glare Mischa gave Cassidy at that pointed dig. She'd witnessed this double act at previous callbacks when auditioning for Hollister on her own. She wondered how Aiden put up with these two very feisty females.

"I can do an English accent. I've hung around with you long enough to pick up the difference between toe-*may*-toe, toh-*mah*-toh, and to-*mar*-ta." Mischa made everyone laugh as she affected a gruff British accent on the last one. "And I've seen every episode of *Downton Abbey* to have perfected Maggie Smith's stiff upper lip inflection. I would totally have rocked as Emily."

Aiden laughed at them both but directed her comment to Cole and Eris. "Hard to believe when I started this company Mischa was listed as a 'silent partner.'" She chuckled as Mischa blew her an air kiss and then went back to glaring at Cassidy, albeit playfully.

"I'm still getting a cameo somewhere in this movie," Mischa pointed out. "I was a fan of your work before your fiancée even cracked open a book of yours."

"You will, I promise, and you'll steal the scene because you are Mischa Ballantyne and all other actresses fall aside in your wake."

Mischa leaned her head on Aiden's shoulder. "I do love you, Aiden. Probably way more than Cassidy does so I think you should just dump her and run away with me."

Cassidy whipped out her phone and began scrolling through the screens. "I'm calling Joe. You pair get the kids, but he and I get Aiden's car."

Aiden just shook her head as she watched the playful bickering between Cassidy and Mischa continue as they headed toward a small craft table to avail themselves of coffee. She turned her attention back to Cole and Eris. "Don't worry, they're extremely professional when they need to be. I just think they love having a new audience to play to."

"How do you cope?" Cole whispered. Eris leaned in to hear Aiden's reply.

"Well, I love Cassidy to death so whatever she says goes… within reason." Aiden winked. "But Mischa is like a work wife. I just threaten her with not babysitting her two children and it works like a charm. You'll be safe from their madness. I like to think I can keep them in line."

Cassidy came back and slipped an arm around Aiden's waist. "Keep telling yourself that, sweetheart. It's never going to happen."

Mischa sidled up on Aiden's other side and kissed her cheek noisily. "I love being in business with you two. There's so much fun to be had." She looked Cole and Eris over. "You two are going to be perfect for this movie. I've read all the novels. I know the characters intimately. You've both got this. You're going to be stars, mark my words."

Cole was surprised how quickly Mischa switched from her teasing personality to a much more sincere one. Mischa gently caught some of Eris's hair in her hand and played with it.

"You, my dear, are going to light up the screen with your beauty and heart." Mischa turned to Cole. "And you are going to break a million lesbian hearts with that handsome face of yours and whatever they'll let us get away with in the PG-13 love scene." Praise imparted, she walked away again, making a beeline toward Olivia Todd, the movie's director, who pretended to hide from her before they hugged tightly and started conspiring.

"*That's* the real Mischa Ballantyne," Cassidy said softly. "You're going to love her."

"I still can't believe I've got this role. But how about you, Aiden? Are you excited to be bringing your book to life on the screen?" Eris asked.

"Yes, but it's going to be a lot of hard work. We've only produced smaller movies so far. But I couldn't see anyone letting me have the final say in the movie unless I produced it myself. I know what I want for my story, and I've been involved in enough screenplays to know what translates to the screen and what doesn't."

"And for what she doesn't know she's found a woman in the business who does," Cassidy said.

"Yes, I'd heard you're hiring as many women as possible," Cole said. "That's going to make for a marked change on set."

"I was inspired by Patty Jenkins who is *my* idea of a Wonder Woman. The future is female, after all, and so many talented women in this business are getting pushed aside and ignored." The noise of a multitude of messages hitting Aiden's phone broke into their conversation. She apologized and quickly ran through the texts. "Looks like I have meetings with your agents lined up. Gabby, my invaluable assistant, has been getting the ball rolling already. Once we've dealt with all the legalities we can get going. We've had set designers working both here and abroad and you're going to be amazed by what they have created. And I can't wait for you to get your costumes fitted. Cole, we're going to have to cut your hair, but you already knew that. Oh, and I hope you'll be ready to see London. We've scouted some marvelous locations there, though they can't promise us it won't rain."

"I'm squeezing in a quick trip with you over there for my role when I'm not working here," Cassidy said, squeezing Aiden's arm. "Forget everyone else's schedules, just work around mine so I can be with you."

"I know you two have other commitments at the moment." Aiden shared a pointed look with Cole. "But we'll work out logistics once we have everything in place. For now, congratulations on landing the leading roles for *A Pocket Full of Time*. I can't wait to get the cameras rolling and see you bring my characters to life."

Chapter Two

Eris stepped out of the soundstage first but waited for Cole to catch up with her. Cole gave her a curious look, but Eris waited until Cole closed the door behind her before she let out a loud whoop of joy and proceeded to break out into a happy dance that hit on every era of crazy dance steps she knew.

Cole laughed at her exuberance. "Wow. That pretty much expresses how I feel too. If I knew how to do cartwheels I'd be busting a few out all around the lot."

Eris couldn't help herself. She grabbed Cole's arms and squeezed. "We got the parts! I've been praying for this opportunity."

"It's a great project," Cole said.

"It is, but I've been desperate to work with Aiden Darrow. The second they announced *A Pocket Full of Time* going into production I begged my agent to get me an audition. I never expected one of the leading roles though." She hugged herself and barely suppressed a squeal of delight. "I'm going to be *Emily*! God, I can't take it all in! I'm teetering between screaming, cheering, or quite honestly, throwing up."

"I know, right? A lesbian story written and produced by a lesbian, with lesbian leads." Cole smiled at Eris. "Gay roles written without courting a gay agenda. Just a fantasy love story that happens to be gay. I'm more than ready to tell that tale."

"Have you read the books themselves?"

"What self-respecting lesbian hasn't? I loved them. I can't wait to see how they're translating them to the screen."

"Is this your first movie? Am I right that I recognize you from *Fortune's Rise*, the family drama that doesn't stint on breaking your heart?" At Cole's nod, Eris added, "How are you going to work the movie into your TV schedule? Your show has what, twenty-two episodes a season? That's a lot of shooting."

Eris was intrigued to see Cole hesitate for a brief moment. In those few seconds, Eris glimpsed a shadow of something painful cloud Cole's face before she skillfully masked it and pushed the emotion down. Eris decided never to challenge Cole to a card game. Her poker face was something carefully crafted because now there was no sign of that fleeting emotion on Cole's face.

But Eris knew it was still there, under the surface.

Eris had grown up in a mentally abusive household. Her father had used words to punish his children instead of his fists. Her mother had thankfully divorced him and gone on to marry a much kinder man. Eris's stepfather had raised the girls with a more loving hand. The cruel and deliberate damage had left its mark though, burned through her psyche. Eris had learned from an early age to recognize the slightest changes in someone's demeanor by the tell-tale emotions that their face gave away. It was even something she'd been able to employ in her acting career. She used those subtle nuances herself that revealed a character's weakness or strength, their fear or their fury.

But Cole's emotion hadn't been anger. It had been *grief.*

"What? Oh God, has your show been canceled? It was doing so well." Eris felt awful that she'd asked.

Cole shook her head. "No, the show's still running and we're coming to the end of filming the third season now. The producers have been very helpful in letting me skip out to audition for this movie." She shrugged. "I might as well tell you, it's bound to be leaked soon enough. I'm leaving the show."

"Really? But you're one of the main leads, aren't you? And an original cast member. Tell me they haven't brought new writers in and there are going to be casualties in a show that's as popular as that is. I had that on my last show. They decided to 'better' the storyline and my character got killed off in the process as they swept house. I'd like to think it only lasted one more season because of my demise, but I know it was because they ruined the premise of the whole show and people just stopped watching."

"I asked not to renew my contract for another year and to be written out."

Eris knew there was something more behind Cole's clearly rehearsed words. She chose not to call her on it. "Wow, bold move. I binge watched the show. You're great as Chris Moore. You and the one who plays your neighbor, Nat Porter. Marie..." Eris tried to remember the actress's name.

"Maria Ramos."

"That's her. Oh, you and Maria generate sparks off each other, even though you both play straight characters." She saw something again dim the light in Cole's eyes. There, then gone. It intrigued her, but she respected Cole's hesitance to divulge what was happening.

"Let's just say it was time for me to move on. We're finishing the last few episodes now so filming will be over well before this movie starts. I couldn't have timed it better. Then I get to take my first steps onto a movie set." She looked around her then performed her own happy dance.

Eris couldn't believe what she was seeing. It was so out of character to see the usually calm and restrained Cole acting so... unrestrained and silly. She loved it. But Cole's dancing was terrible and Eris cracked up at her.

"Oh, you've got to share those moves, Magic Mike! Do it again! I'll film it and post it to Twitter."

Cole shook her head swiftly. "Hell no, my movie career will be over before it even starts. Somehow I don't think I'll need to rely on my gopher dance for Hollister."

"No, she's much more serious than goofy." Eris grinned at the look on Cole's face.

"Who are you calling goofy? I'll have you know I'm a classically trained actor," Cole told her in her haughtiest tone.

"Classically goofy then." Eris jumped as her phone dinged in her purse. "Alas, my other job awaits. I'm filling in at *Andinos*, my sister's restaurant, while I'm filming a series of commercials for

Seiko. Otherwise I am 'resting' between jobs. It's great pay and I get to eat all I want so this artist isn't starving, thankfully." She began scrambling in her purse and handed Cole a card. "If you're ever in the area, come have a meal with us. My sister is an awesome chef. She married a Greek American and they offered me a place to stay while I tried to get work over here and I just never moved out. When I'm not filming I'm waitressing for them." She snapped her purse shut. "I promise you, they make a mean lasagna."

"I'll bear that in mind." Cole carefully pocketed the card.

Outwardly, Cole looked cool and calm, but she began wringing her hands together in a decidedly nervous gesture that made Eris desperate to reach out and ask what was wrong. To be honest, there was a part of Eris that just wanted to reach out and touch her again. The final chemistry test they had just run through had proved to Eris that she and Cole were perfect for the roles they were to play. Meeting Cole, interacting with her, it struck Eris just how incredibly attractive she was. Cole was tall enough to make Eris feel small and protected in her arms as they'd played through the scene. Currently, Cole's blond hair was just shy of reaching her shoulders, but Hollister's hair was a "short back and sides," to fit in with the post World War II setting where *A Pocket Full of Time* began. Eris knew that the severe cut would only emphasize the soft butch air that Cole embodied. Her strong jawline, angular face, and blue eyes had captivated Eris's attention and she'd found herself all too easily distracted by Cole's intense nature when she began to act.

Eris had kissed others on screen before, but she'd be lying if she didn't admit that Cole's kiss had rocked her to her very core. Emily was head over heels in love with Hollister, and Eris found herself unashamedly intrigued by Cole Calder.

That should make for an interesting shoot.

"Well, I'd better go don my apron and help my sister out while I still can. I'm told I'm an awesome waitress."

Cole smiled at her. "I doubt there isn't anything you don't excel at. I saw you in *Out of Reach*. You were fantastic."

Eris was surprised that Cole had seen her in that. "Oh, Betty the drug addict. Yes, I did play that a little too realistic, didn't I? I had so many people offering to help me 'get clean' once it aired that it bordered on ridiculous."

"Yeah, some people can't separate the character from the actress sometimes, can they?"

Eris heard something underlying Cole's words. Cole seemed to realize Eris was staring at her and she began jingling the keys in her pants pocket in agitation. That only served to make Eris's curiosity rise even more. She was an actress, trained to study people's idiosyncrasies. She desperately wanted to lay bare all of Cole's.

"Do you need a ride anywhere?" Cole asked as they started walking toward a small parking lot.

"No, thank you. I brought my car." Eris's eyes widened when she saw the motorcycle Cole was heading for. "Okay, next time I am definitely taking you up on the offer. What a beautiful machine."

Cole ran her hand lovingly across the curves of her black-and-white Harley Davidson. "It's my baby. A Heritage Classic Softail twin engine…rides like a dream. I bought it once my fortune began to rise from *Fortune's Rise* gaining a steady audience. I like to just gear up and ride away from the city confines."

"I know that feeling," Eris said wistfully. "Sometimes the city gets very loud and the need to see something green and leafy calls." Her phone dinged again. "A lot like my sister who is now probably pestering me to learn all the gossip from my audition. I'll get her marvelous Tiramisu cake tonight. She always likes to mark every part I get by something sinfully delicious."

"She sounds wonderful. I'm an only child so the thought of siblings is something of an enigma to me."

"Melanie can be a pain in the ass when she wants to be, but she was my protector as a child as much as an older sibling by four years can be. I love her, and she found a good man in Georgio Andino. I hope I can afford at least a slice or two of her cake before I get fitted for Emily's Victorian attire and have to get used to wearing corsets." Eris made a face. She wasn't looking forward to that piece of the costume at all.

"I guess I'll see you in a few months for the start of our adventure." Cole picked up her helmet.

"Just don't open any pocket watches before then," Eris said.

"I won't. I don't want to miss a moment of this experience. I can't wait for it to start." She donned a pair of mirrored aviator glasses, then slipped her open-faced helmet on. "I'll see you soon, Emily Brown."

Eris curtseyed. "I look forward to it, my sweet Hollister." She all but melted at the rakish grin Cole tossed her before she started her engine. The bike purred deep and throaty like a caged animal ready to pounce. Eris watched Cole ride off the studio lot, handling the large machine with ease.

She walked over to her car giving herself a stern talking to for letting herself even entertain the cliché of falling for her costar. She ran her fingertips across her lips where the ghost of Hollister's kiss to her beloved Emily lingered.

She rushed off a text to her sister to break out the best cognac for her dessert. *I'm going to be eating my feelings tonight.*

"And that's the last shot on *Fortune's Rise* for Cole Calder."

Cole didn't know whether to release a sigh of relief or let go of the sob that was burning a big hole in her chest. She didn't have time to do either before her castmates descended to smother her in hugs.

"I can't believe you're leaving us," Charles Walsh said, "You've been my neighbor for so long." He hugged her again and whispered in her ear, "It won't be the same here without you."

Cole's eyes filled at his sincerity. "It's going to be strange not coming here every day too."

"You're still coming to my birthday party?"

"Of course. You're not sixty every day, and I know Eric's cooking is to die for. I wouldn't miss that for the world. I'm leaving the show, Charles, but I'll stay in touch. You've been a fantastic mentor to me."

He looked around furtively and whispered, "You'd better score me tickets to this movie role you've landed."

"I'll do my best, I promise. Now go." She batted him away. "You're going to ruin your makeup if you cry. You'll still look beautiful whereas we both know I'm an ugly crier. It's not going to be as pretty a sight if you set me off."

Charles kissed her cheek and stood back to let her other friends all crowd in and say their good-byes. By the time the director had his say, Cole was crying, and she gratefully received the tissue Maria Ramos held out for her. Cole could hardly bring herself to look at her. Maria had been her firmest friend on the set from the first day of shooting. Their parting was going to be the hardest. She sobbed as soon as Maria's arms wrapped around her.

"You know I'm going to miss you more than I can say." Maria rubbed at Cole's back and gently led her aside from prying eyes. "And, although we haven't talked about this, I think I know why you're really leaving."

Cole wouldn't open her eyes until Maria cupped her chin and shook her gently. Cole saw the same anguish she felt mirrored on Maria's face.

"This show gave us both a marvelous rise to fame, but it's become a double-edged sword. I'm sorry you're the one who's falling on it."

Cole didn't feel she was being that noble.

"Rico says he's sorry," Maria added.

"Well, he knows where I am when he wants to say that to my face and not relay it via his wife." Cole barely managed to curtail the bite in her words. *He was quick enough to get in my face and scream at me to stay away from his wife.*

Maria nodded. "He realizes now how much of an ass he was over some of the publicity and what the fans were stirring up."

"I never gave him any cause to think I would ever want to break up your marriage." Cole was furious and still desperately hurt at how Rico had threatened her when there was no reason whatsoever for him to do so. "You and I were never like that, Maria, and he knows it."

"I know and I told him to grow the hell up. But he's a man…"

"That's not a great excuse in this day and age, Maria." Cole was somewhat mollified by the ashamed nod Maria gave her. Cole wiped at her cheeks and took a step back. "I hope you get a great new neighbor in the show next season."

Maria's face crumbled. "Oh, Cole. I had the best with *you*. No one could ever take your place. Just promise me you'll keep acting. Don't let the crazy fans out there stop you from what you're so great at doing."

"I won't." Cole looked around her carefully for prying eyes and ears. "I've just landed a movie role."

Maria's eyes widened comically. "You never said anything."

"I've had to keep it quiet in case I couldn't be released from the show." She didn't mention that Charles had known all along because Cole had confided in him. She'd desperately needed someone to talk to. She and Maria had lost that closeness once Rico had caused tension between them with his woefully misplaced jealousy. He'd made her lose her best friend. And, sadly, Maria had let him.

"Can you tell me about it?"

Cole shook her head. "Not yet, but you'll see the press release very soon."

"Are you supporting cast?"

Cole grinned. "No. I got the lead instead."

Maria's mouth dropped open, then she dragged Cole to her and squeezed her tight. "That's fantastic news. I'm so proud of you. You go show everyone how talented you are. I can't wait to see whatever it is you're doing. You're going to be amazing." She paused a moment. "Is it a straight role?"

"It's decidedly out and proud."

Maria squeezed her again with a little squeal. "Tell me they are going to cut your hair."

Cole laughed. Maria knew how much she hated the longer length she'd had to endure playing Chris. "Yes, the straight girl bob is being all cut off and I can't honestly wait for that to happen."

Maria ruffled Cole's hair. "As long as they don't cut all of it off. You're gorgeous, but only Charlize Theron can rock a Furiosa cut."

The sound of the set getting ready for the next scene broke into their silence.

"I'd better go," Cole said. "I know you're due back on set in a while and I need to go see the bosses upstairs so I can say good-bye to them and thank them for letting me go on such short notice."

"I'm going to miss you so much." Maria's eyes welled with tears. "You've been my best friend on here since the start."

"And I'm still that friend. I'm just moving out of the neighborhood."

"The fans will follow you."

Cole heard the underlying warning in Maria's voice. "I know. The genuine ones I welcome. The rest I hope find something or someone else to obsess over."

"I bet they're going to replace you on here with a man," Maria said, not looking too happy about it. Male characters already overpopulated the show and not all were gentlemen.

Cole bit her tongue to hold back a snarky comment about Rico really having something to worry about then, but she wisely kept her mouth shut. She hugged Maria one more time. "Take care of yourself please."

"You too, Cole. The show won't be the same without you but the big screen will let you spread your wings."

Cole took one last look over the *Fortune's Rise* set. The little street lined with fabricated houses had been her home and her learning ground. She'd miss it terribly.

She retrieved her cell phone from her pocket and switched it off silent. A flurry of text messages dinged out as she made her way off the set. One from Aiden Darrow made her smile.

The minute you get your hair cut we're taking a group shot to announce the cast. Just to warn you, Mischa wants to film it and post it to the official movie Twitter account. See you Friday, 10 a.m. sharp at the office. Hollister awaits.

Cole turned back to take one more look at the set and everyone carrying on without her.

Time to bow off this particular stage.

Chapter Three

Brooke Harman scrolled through the screens on her phone while she waited for her drink and her friend to arrive. She looked up to see Ava Riley heading her way, desperately trying to keep her large purse over her shoulder as she weaved between the patrons of the busy little diner. In her bright polka dot dress she reminded Brooke of Wonder Woman's Etta Candy. Ava was blond, full figured, slightly ditsy, and loyal to a fault.

Brooke didn't bother with a greeting. "Did you see *Fortune's Rise* last night?"

Ava sat down with a thump. "I did. God, Cole Calder is so sexy. She and Maria just elevate that show to another level. I wish they'd just let them kiss. The tension is electrifying."

"I think they cut some of the scene out. The direction looked choppy."

Ava nodded. "It was Derek Gould, you know when he's directing an episode they don't always have the same production management. We tried to trend *#DropDerek* the last time he took the helm, but it didn't garner much traction. We could try emailing the show again."

"I just hate how short the scene was. They know the fans love Moore and Porter, our beloved *Morter* ship. They wouldn't have a show on air if it wasn't for the fans of those two boosting the ratings. It would be just another drama series, but Cole and Maria set it alight."

The waitress brought over Ava's drink and they both ordered something to eat.

"Your hair looks great today, by the way," Ava said.

Brooke ran a hand through her hair, pleased with the compliment. "I'm thinking of dying it. Do you think Maria's color would suit me? I might have it styled that way too."

"You're seriously considering dying your dark hair fifty shades lighter and losing all that length for a much shorter style? That's a bold move, especially for someone who complains when I just trim the ends off." Ava eyed Brooke critically for a moment. "But yeah, I think you'd look great. Just call me when you want it cut and dyed. I'll always fit you in among my clients." Distracted by a notification ringing out, Ava checked her phone. "There's a weird vibe on Twitter today. I'm sure something big is going to drop."

Brooke shrugged. "It's probably another Marvel movie. That's all it ever seems to be." She changed the subject back. "I'm thinking we need to promote our couple, have a weekend posting videos of their scenes, and some of the not-so-safe-for-work fan art. The fan fiction is really gaining in numbers too. We have a very talented fan base. Let's get a hashtag trending of Morter to keep the fans busy."

"Cole and Maria deserve it."

"They do such a great job. They deserve our loyalty. We stan two marvelous women."

Ava giggled. "*Stan*. I can't believe that phrase comes from an Eminem song about an obsessive fan. It makes us all sound crazy."

Brooke barely looked up from her phone. "*Devoted*. We are devoted fans. There's a difference. We stan a particular couple who give us the content we crave."

Ava took a quick drink from her glass. "It would be better if they were actually a couple in the show though and then we could really—"

Brooke's head snapped up. "They *are* a couple."

Ava sank down in her seat at Brooke's angry response. "Well, technically, they aren't," she muttered. "They're not a canon couple. They aren't actually together in the show and we just wish they were." Her voice trailed off at Brooke's glare.

"The show baits us with their scenes. They know they have an audience for that coupling, and it's just a matter of time before they put them together properly. They know the show is nothing without the Morter fans watching. Their ratings would plummet if we all jumped ship." Brooke gave Ava another dirty look before starting in on her food. Her phone dinged and she glanced at it. She slammed down her fork. "Oh my God, Cole is back on social media. She's tagged in a video." She quickly brought the video up and she and Ava crowded over the screen.

"Mischa Ballantyne posted it. Isn't she the one from *The Alchemidens*? She's a total MILF."

Brooke shushed Ava and turned up the sound. She watched as Cole sat in a makeup chair and had her hair washed.

"What's she doing?" Ava whispered, her eyes never leaving the screen.

The skillfully edited video speeded up to reveal the spectacle of Cole Calder having her long blond hair cut off quite dramatically. When it was finished, Cole's hair was very short on the back and sides while the top was a little bit longer and fell naturally into a side parting.

Brooke's mouth dropped open. Cole looked amazing, rakish even. "Maria is going to cream herself when she sees Cole step on the set with that cut. I wonder why they did it. Do you think Cole got tired of them trying to make her look straight? Are they butching her up so Morter can finally happen?" She quickly sent a desperate prayer up.

The video ended with Mischa's voice. "Oh, you look gorgeous! Time for the reveal!"

Ava looked at Brooke. "Reveal of what?"

Brooke shrugged. A nauseating pool of dread began churning in her gut. Cole didn't look like Chris anymore.

The video switched to outside the production studios of Darrow/Hayes where a huge poster displaying the book cover of *A Pocket Full of Time* hung.

"Oh my God," Ava squealed. "I love that book!" She gasped dramatically. "Are they actually filming it?"

Brooke recognized Eris Whyte. Eris was grinning at Cole's new haircut and teasingly tousled it. Aiden Darrow stepped between them and announced that *A Pocket Full of Time* was due to start filming that summer and that Cole's big screen debut would be in the role of Hollister Graham and Eris would be Emily Brown. They gave out the movie's official website and promised more videos and behind the scenes exclusives once they started the production.

Ava clapped as the video finished. "Oh my God! Oh my God! That's perfect! I can't wait!" She fumbled for her phone. "I have to follow that site. I don't want to miss a thing."

Brooke was silent for a moment. Her phone dinged again, then began rapidly dinging one after another after another as her fellow Morter fans began messaging her.

Ava checked her own phone. Her face fell and she looked up hesitantly at Brooke. "Oh no. I thought this was just a rumor started by our rival fans. I'm sorry sweetie, the Twitterverse has just exploded with the news." Her eyes shone as she teared up. "Cole has left *Fortune's Rise*."

No.

Pain, intense and burning, seized Brooke and, for a moment, rendered her totally incapable of reacting. She gasped for air like a drowning man.

"Are you having a panic attack?" Ava reached across the table and grabbed for Brooke's hand. "Brooke? Do you have medication for it? An EpiPen? Oh geez, I've never stuck anyone with an EpiPen before, but you're frightening me." She furiously waved to attract the attention of a waitress. "Can you get us some water please?"

Brooke's head was spinning, her heart pounding in her chest. Her world was ripping apart and all she wanted to do was scream until she was hoarse and her throat bled. *What am I going to do? She can't leave. I need her in that show. I need to see Cole with Maria.* She dimly heard the sound of her phone receiving more messages. For a moment, she bordered on blacking out, a thin veil of darkness crowded over her vision. Her head scrambled to make sense of what was happening in her carefully crafted make-believe world.

Then she saw red.

Her fury swept over her as swiftly as her desolation had. Brooke channeled all her anger, disappointment, and betrayal into a seething ball of hate. She stared at Ava and roughly shook her hand off.

"She can't leave," Brooke said. Her jaw was so tight she could hear her teeth grinding together.

Ava hesitantly held up her phone. "The studio has confirmed it. They've written a very nice piece about her and their sadness in losing her and wishing her well for her movie debut."

"Has Maria posted anything?" Brooke knew Maria had been oddly silent on social media for months now. She'd hoped it was because she was finalizing a divorce with her husband, but the rumor mill still had them very much together.

Ava nodded and turned the phone around so that Brooke could see the post. It featured a picture of Maria and Cole on set, laughing.

"That's what we should have seen in the show." Brooke picked up her own phone and searched for the tweet. She saved the photo automatically for her collection. "We have to fight to get her back. I am not losing Morter."

"I don't think she wants to come back, Brooke. Cole's just posted her own thank-yous to the show. She's moving on to bigger and better things. She's got the leading role in a movie. The book is a best seller. The movie of it could be a blockbuster. She deserves this chance."

"She deserves Maria."

"Well, let's be honest, we knew that little fantasy was never going to really happen. Maria is straight and happily married while Cole is a lesbian, foot-loose and fancy-free. Nothing ever comes of shipping a real life couple. It's the TV characters that are ours, no matter how much they screw up their storyline in a show. They're ours now, we can continue to give them their happy ever afters in our fan fiction."

Brooke stopped listening. She knew all the platitudes. Don't get so involved in a make-believe world and make it your reality. Don't think the actresses really care about you or how much you love them or how you want to die at the thought of them not being together in the show. And yes, even if they're together on the screen, don't ship them together in real life. She'd heard them all, read them all in hateful tweets from fans of other shows that endlessly bully other fandoms because their couple alone is the One True Pairing.

Ava reached across the table to touch Brooke's arm. "Cole's going to be amazing as Hollister. And her new haircut lets her just scream 'lesbian' loud and proud. That's the kind of representation we've been dreaming of from her. I'm so excited for her."

"Aren't you even a little disappointed our favorite couple has just been ripped apart?" Brooke glared across the table at Ava. Why wasn't she mourning the loss of them like Brooke was? Brooke's whole world was crashing down and Ava was spouting banalities.

"The show says they've got a space for her should she ever want to return."

Brooke scoffed. "So did the ones at *Supergirl* concerning Maggie Sawyer, but we all know how much they lied through their teeth over that."

Ava conceded that point. "Yeah, but that actress gained an intensely loyal fan base that stopped supporting the show the second she left. They raised a load of money for homeless gay kids in Maggie's name, for God's sake. Cole's not in the same boat. She decided to leave and, to be honest…" Ava hesitated and Brooke stared at her.

"What?"

"The show was never going to give us what we hoped and dreamed for. Chris and Nat weren't going to become a couple no matter how many tweets we sent calling for it or how many conventions *Fortune's Rise* did and Cole and Maria's photo ops sold out first. They were *never* going to be canon. They weren't ever going to be written of that way in the show. We're going to have to move on. Find our representation in another show that actually has two women together in it."

Brooke stopped listening as Ava prattled on. She picked at the crust of her pizza, before brutally shredding it to pieces.

But I'm not done with this *show or its leading ladies yet. They are my endgame.*

They are not over until I say they are.

❖

Eris was thankful she was able to blend into the sea of faces at the airport and go relatively unnoticed. She peeked over the rim of her sunglasses as she watched Cole signing autographs and happily posing for photos with a group of women who had surrounded her before she even got a chance to take a seat in the lounge. Eris was impressed how Cole handled the clamor of voices, the push and shove of everyone wanting their moment with her. Cole spotted her and gestured for her to come on over. Eris shook her head frantically, but one of the women saw the exchange and squealed out Eris's name.

Busted.

Eris waved at the women who all began calling for her to join in the impromptu selfie session.

"You're going to have to get used to that now," George, a security guard assigned to her and Cole by Aiden Darrow, nudged her to go join the madness. "Your and Cole's lives are now in the spotlight and it burns hard and fast there. Taking selfies and signing autographs with a bunch of squealing folk is the price you pay for fame today." He held out a hand. "Give me your coffee cup and go court the masses. You'll need those bums on seats once the movie's out. Schmooze and smile. I'll be watching them all, never fear."

Eris turned back to where Cole was cheering for her along with the other women. She slipped off her sunglasses and had to smile at Cole's happy face.

"Here's my leading lady." Cole held out a hand to pull Eris in close by her side. "Let's get these photos done quickly before airport security comes and kicks us all out."

"Where are you going, Cole?" someone asked as they all took turns having their photos taken with Cole and Eris.

"You'd better have read the books. First stop is London."

"I can't wait to see you two bring those characters to life. I hope you get to do the whole series of books."

"Get your friends to go see it with you and I'm sure Hollister and Emily will get their sequels." Eris thought they were finished, but there was one more woman who pushed in quite forcefully between her and Cole. The dark-haired woman leaned heavily into Cole. Eris wasn't surprised, Cole did cut quite the dashing figure and seemed to have some very ardent fans.

"I was devastated to hear you've left *Fortune's Rise*," the woman said.

Eris couldn't help but notice the muscle that tensed in Cole's jaw as she smiled one last time for the camera.

"It was time to move on. This movie offer was too good an opportunity to miss out on. And I get to work with Eris. It's a total win/win for me."

Eris knew she was blushing at the cheers that erupted from the other women. The woman with her arms still around Cole's waist didn't join in.

"Maria must have been devastated to lose you on the set," she said.

"Maria is thrilled I'm doing this movie. She's been very supportive. She's a marvelous friend."

Eris's keen sense of perception jangled at the lie everyone else took as truth.

"Will she see you in it?"

"I'll make sure she has tickets, along with the rest of the *Fortune's Rise* cast. I'll miss them all."

Eris found herself impressed by the masterful deflection Cole had employed.

"But Maria mostly, of course?" The woman's voice hardened as she pressed for the answer she so desperately wanted. "After all, you two were so wonderful on the screen together. You made a great couple."

Cole's smile wavered a fraction as she tried to move away from the fan. Eris knew Cole didn't need her help, but she stepped in anyway. She moved around the woman and linked an arm through Cole's and addressed the fans.

"Thank you so much, ladies, for making the start of our *A Pocket Full of Time* journey something we'll never forget. We need to go back to the waiting area now before our security guard comes after us. I really hope you'll go see the movie when it's released."

The women stood back, thanking them for their time, and Eris gently pulled Cole away from the persistent fan who clung on until the last minute.

Cole found her voice again. "Don't forget to check the official fan site for the movie, and follow us on Twitter. You'll get to see us trying our hands at time travel."

The women all enthusiastically promised they would. Eris unobtrusively tugged Cole away from the one woman who still didn't move on. Instead she stood staring directly at Cole.

"Oh, *I'll* be watching."

Eris turned back around, unsure she had heard right. The woman's words didn't sound as excited as the rest of the fans had. They'd sounded almost…*threatening*. All she saw though was the woman's back as she disappeared through the busy airport and soon vanished completely from Eris's sight.

"Did you know her?" Eris asked as they both took their seats back by George.

"No. She's just a fan. Believe me, with some of the fans of that show I'm just grateful she wasn't crying and making a scene. I have some diehard fans who haven't taken my leaving the show well." Cole handed her phone over to George and quickly pointed out which button she wanted him to press. Then she took her seat back beside Eris and draped her arm around her shoulder.

"Say 'We're gonna be movie stars'!" Cole grinned and Eris automatically smiled for the photo. "Mischa said to publicize the heck out of our journey with this movie. For our own memories of course but also to garner attention for a lesbian-produced project." Cole showed Eris the picture and then posted it to various sites. "Hey! Look at this! I put in *#APocketFullOfTime*, and a little pocket watch emoji appears beside it. That is so cool." She finished typing on her screen. "I want this to be a success. I've done so many half-assed bit parts. This is my chance to show an audience just what I'm really capable of."

Eris nodded. "I'd like to quit waitressing for a while. Even if my sister will be disappointed." She took a breath for a moment. "I just can't believe it's real. These last few months have been a whirlwind. Between signing all the contracts, reading the full script, meeting the cast, and being measured for a corset that mercifully is going to be forgiving…" Eris sighed. "It's going to be hard work, but I don't care because I'm so excited."

Cole's nod told Eris she was feeling exactly the same. It made Eris feel better to be sharing this with someone for whom the experience was going to be all new and shiny, too.

The boarding call for their plane sounded over the speakers. George left them at the gate with best wishes and a shy request for a selfie with them. Once settled in her seat in first class, Eris looked out the window and couldn't wait to be off the ground.

"I think you're going to have to teach me your happy dance." Cole leaned close to whisper in Eris's ear over the din of the aircraft's engine.

Eris had to fight not to close her eyes and lean in closer to the hot breath sending electricity over her skin. "Why?"

"I think I'm going to be very happy with this project. I can just feel it. And I could get used to this treatment." Cole settled into her seat beside Eris and sighed. "Are you a nervous flyer?"

"No. Why?"

"I was just going to offer to hold your hand if you got scared."

Eris risked a glance over at Cole, but she was digging in her carry-on for something to read. Eris firmly fixed her sights out the window again, but the reflection of Cole beside her left her unable to look at anything else. A thought struck her and she asked it before she could censor herself.

"Are *you* a nervous flyer, Cole?"

Cole looked up from her magazine. "I can be, if there's too much turbulence."

Eris held up her left hand. "Then consider this yours should the need arise."

Cole reached out for her hand and squeezed it. "I like you, Eris Whyte. I think we're going to have a great time on this movie together."

Eris loved the feel of her hand in Cole's. It felt oddly *right*. "I like you too, Cole Calder." She reluctantly released Cole's hand to get herself more settled in her seat. "I couldn't have wished for a better Hollister."

"And I couldn't have wished for a better Emily."

The smile Cole gave her before she picked up her magazine again made Eris's chest flutter with a thousand butterflies. She's just being kind, Eris thought. She knew better though. She felt like she could read Cole Calder like an open book. There was more than kindness in those blue eyes when Cole looked at her. Eris felt the same spark of instant attraction back. It was comforting being in Cole's presence. There was an ease between them. They just *clicked.* Eris felt like they had always known each other. For a moment, she wondered if they were going to have more in common with the characters they were to play than she expected.

Chapter Four

The set design of a Victorian London row of shops was so real Cole had to stop from pinching herself to make sure she hadn't really slipped through time. From the cobblestones and rough brick, to the deliberately muted color scheme, it was like looking at an old photograph. She knew she was walking down a street that was merely an elaborate facade yet it seemed real and would be home for the next month while they shot all their outside scenes. In her mind's eye she could see where CGI would add smoke rising from the old chimneys, darkening out the bright blue sky currently shining above them. It didn't make her surroundings any less real.

Eris gasped beside her. Her eyes were lit up like a child's at Christmas.

"Oh my God," Eris said as Aiden walked over to greet them, a massive smile on her face.

"I know, right? How cool is all this?" Aiden gestured around the studio lot at the buildings bustling with people adding the final touches to every shop, inside and out, to make them look lived in.

Eris was all but bouncing on her toes. "Where's *my* shop?"

Aiden gestured farther up the street. "Do you want to take a look around?"

Eris grabbed Aiden's arm and squeezed it in excitement. "God, yes! I want to see everything." She set off ahead of Aiden and Cole, picking one side of the road to discover first. Cole traded a smile with Aiden.

"You know, for someone who played a stern and serious agent in *Code Red,* Eris is the brightest, bubbliest soul I have ever met."

Aiden nodded. "She could be the love child of Dominique Provost-Chalkley and my Cassidy."

Cole laughed at that thought. It was oddly accurate, in both her looks and her actions. She could see Eris's friendliness out in full force as she stopped to share a word or two with the set dressers.

"There's nothing false about her at all," Cole said.

"No, that's why she was perfect for this character. Eris is pure sunshine, and she draws people to her with her warmth." Aiden nodded to where someone was letting Eris help place a few items just so in a window front. Eris was chatting merrily away, and everyone started to gravitate to her and engage with her. "Every time Hollister meets Emily, whatever the timeline, wherever the place, she has to fall in love with her all over again. To love *each* Emily with as much passion and devotion as the one she left behind. Look at her. It's plain to see why Hollister could do that without reserve."

"God, I hope I can do Hollister justice." Cole was overwhelmed with the pressure to get the character right. To be the Hollister Aiden had written and to be the Hollister the millions of readers expected to see.

Aiden patted her shoulder. "You're going to be fantastic. You forget, I saw you every time you auditioned. You blew those other actresses out of the water. The minute you read with Eris my characters materialized before me." She reached up to tug on a very short piece of Cole's hair. "And this seals the deal."

Cole self-consciously ran her hand over her newly shorn head. It was shorter still than the intermediate cut she'd had to announce the movie. "I haven't had hair this short in years. My agent wouldn't let me. She said I'd get typecast if I looked too gay."

"Well, you can't look gay enough for me in this project. Besides, it suits you more than the length you had to sport in your show. This looks more your style, to be honest."

Cole nodded. "It feels more me too. How sad is it that it takes a haircut for me to feel more authentically myself for the first time in years?"

"The girls in the makeup department were all swooning while you were having it cut. Always be yourself, Cole. You've got the talent to rise above worrying your hair isn't girly enough."

A noise up the street caught Cole's attention and she spotted Eris in an older man's arms. He was twirling her around like a child. "Looks like Eris found a friend."

"That's Andy. They worked together on *Code Red*," Aiden said. "He's been so excited to see her again. He told me she was the only one on the show that ever acknowledged the folks working behind the scenes. I like that in a person. Someone who realizes it's not just them that makes the magic happen."

Cole watched as Andy finally put Eris back on her feet and then gallantly held out an arm to escort her down the cobbled street to what would be Victorian Emily's home. Cole reached for her phone as Aiden did the same. They both laughed.

"You got Mischa's message that anything not too spoilery is a photo opportunity?" Aiden began snapping photos of Eris reverently touching the numbers hanging on the dark green door of the Brown's Jewelry shop. Eris spotted her and laughed, turning so Aiden could take more photos of her pointing at the door and then standing in front of the shop itself. Aiden finally put her phone down.

"Is there a significance to the shop being number twenty-one?" Cole asked, laughing as Eris struck a red carpet pose for her. A deliberate, over the shoulder, smoldering look that kindled a fire low in Cole's gut. Cole raised her phone and quickly snapped a few shots. She made sure she saved those photos just for herself.

"It's Cassidy's birthdate. Of course, I did it deliberately back then because I was enamored with the up-and-coming young actress just making her debut on the TV screens. Never in my wildest dreams did I imagine I'd get the chance to meet her and fall completely and utterly in love with her. Dreams do come true, Cole. I'm living mine with her."

"Can I ask if there's something more personal to the pocket watch other than as a time travel plot device? I've always been curious."

Aiden nodded. "I was adopted by two fantastic people, Trudy and Frank Woods. Trudy took me to the movies and opened up that whole world of fantasy for me. She was the first person in my young life who actually paid attention to me and what I was interested in. But it took time for me to be as comfortable around Frank. He was patient though and shared his hobby of watch mending with me. I loved the pocket watches best of all so it seemed only fitting that would be what Hollister used in her travels. Frank still tinkers with watches. He recommended the jewelers to us who supplied us with the watch Hollister has. That watch was my nod to him for all he did for me…and still does." Aiden didn't meet Cole's eyes. Her voice was gruff with emotion. "This movie will be dedicated to Trudy. I hope to God I can keep it together when I see that roll up on the screen. She'd have been so proud of this venture."

Cole gave Aiden a moment to get her composure back. She couldn't help but watch Eris who was now happily taking selfies with Andy and anyone else who wanted one. Cole sensed someone was watching her. She side-eyed Aiden who was looking back at her expectantly. *Busted.* Cole smiled ruefully. She wondered what it was about Aiden that made her want to open up and spill all her chaotic thoughts and feelings she had for her leading lady.

"She's…too good to be true," Cole muttered, watching the ease Eris had with everyone who came to her. She treated them like old friends. "I've never, in all my years of acting, been drawn to another actress. I've made a lot of friends, but…Eris feels like *more*. I've admired her work for years, she's so damn talented, but we never crossed paths until now."

"And now?"

"Now I'm overwhelmed by how genuinely sweet she is. And silly as hell, which is honestly adorable." She winced at how lovesick she sounded. "Fuck, this is so not how I wanted to start off my movie career. I won't mess up the movie, Aiden, but I have the feeling what I'm starting to feel for her will bleed out of me into Hollister."

Aide smiled. "Then use it. Honest emotion, raw and heartfelt, will only enhance your performance as lovers. And who knows, maybe the movie will grant you *your* happy ending. Give you your own Emily, perhaps."

Cole smiled at the thought.

"Just keep any shenanigans out of the eye of the press and public," Aiden said. "We don't need that kind of publicity."

Cole nodded. "Oh, I don't intend to cross any lines while filming, Aiden. I've heard too many tales about on set romances turning out to be a nightmare for all involved. No, I'm not bringing that drama to the set. Besides, look at her. I might not even be her type."

"Cole, with that haircut and your looks? You're every lesbian's type." Aiden grinned then added, "And Mischa's. Now come and stop your leading lady from stealing all the limelight. You're both in the spotlight with this project. Go meet your new family for the next month."

❖

On the first day of shooting joint scenes, Cole stood nervously running her hand through her hair and letting the soft bristles against her palm calm her. She was way too warm for comfort in the Victorian costume she wore for Hollister. It was deliberately cumbersome as it sat a little too big on her frame. She'd already filmed a scene where Hollister arrived in the 1890s to fall face first out of a wardrobe into a gentleman's bedroom, only to look out the window and be faced with a decidedly different time and place. Hollister had then swapped clothes to blend in, stealing from the wardrobe she'd arrived in. Cole had enjoyed pratfalling out of the wardrobe over many takes.

Cole's costume was a black formal frock coat, long and tailored to her height but purposely a size too big to disguise her female shape. She had a stiff white shirt coupled with a bowtie that, along with a vest, were the only bright colors in her costume. They were both a striking shade of sapphire. Mischa, flitting back and forth in the costume department while getting her own costume sorted, had said it brought out the color of her eyes. Aiden, who had been watching with a more measured eye had coughed what sounded like "flirt" into her fist. Cole's black trousers had suspenders attached. She loved the level of historical detail, but they drove her crazy as they were prone to slip. It was worse than fumbling to right a bra strap under all the layers. A comfortable pair of black boots were the one thing Cole didn't have to complain about. She picked up the black top hat that rested on a wall beside her and toyed with it. This she loved. It made her look dapper and she couldn't wait to tower over Eris even more with it on.

Eris had deliberately asked for them not to see each other in their full costumes until they filmed the "first meeting" scene. The request had surprised Cole, but she was more than happy to comply. She knew Eris had spoken with the director, and they had been working out together how to best frame the shot. Cole had been in awe of Eris's vision. If Eris didn't end up behind the camera at some point in her career she'd be surprised. She had an eye for detail, and the people Aiden had hired were more than willing to hear her out and answer her questions.

Cole couldn't wait to see how Eris was dressed and knew the element of surprise would work in both their favors when it played out on screen. Hollister had to recognize Emily. But this would be a different Emily than her love. Cole couldn't wait for Eris to see her fully dressed in her costume. She looked totally different from when Eris had first met her, and even more so since they'd been filming scenes separately. Today their characters would finally meet. Cole had to find Eris in the crowd of extras who were filling the street.

She already had butterflies in her stomach, big ones with wings the size of dragons. *What is wrong with me? We're just going to film a scene. Why am I nervous and sweaty and desperate to see her?*

A call went out to prepare for the first take and Cole quickly donned her hat and stepped onto the set. She bounced on her toes and ran through her lines one last time in her head. She searched over the heads of the extras trying to see if she could spot Eris already. She knew the pace she had to keep to meet up with Eris outside of Brown's Jewelry shop. The two of them had every step precisely choreographed. They just hadn't done it in costume.

Cole knew she'd find her. Like Hollister with her Emily, she'd just follow the beat of her heart.

Chapter Five

Cole strode through the street, dodging the crowd as they stood in the way to buy goods from the row of shops. Several horses and carts clattered past, but Cole's attention wasn't on any of them. She needed to find Eris, the shop was just ahead and—Cole came to an abrupt stop. She couldn't help herself. In that moment, she was Hollister knocked out of time, lost on an unfamiliar Victorian street, seeing the love of her life walking toward her. Cole hoped the hidden cameras in the shops had caught her stunned expression. It was all too real.

Eris smiled and greeted everyone as she passed them by. Her long maroon skirt fit tight at the waist, decorated with an ornate buckle. It flowed out fuller and fell to skim the tops of well-worn boots. She wore a shirtwaist, a starched white long sleeved shirt with a laced collar and a mass of ruffles down its front that befit the working woman Emily was. A small pocket watch dangled from a chain about her waist, and the silver casing shone in the light. The long length of Eris's hair was in an upswept but puffed out style and twisted into a bun at the top. She looked elegant and beautiful and seemed to fit seamlessly into the surroundings. She literally took Cole's breath away.

Cole spoke. "*Emily*."

Eris stopped and stared at her with a frown. "Do I know you, sir?"

Cole whipped off her top hat, bowing a little in respect. She ran her hand nervously along the brim of the hat.

"Forgive me. You just look so much like..." Cole paused deliberately, all the time aware of the cameras moving around them, but seeing only Eris. "Someone I know. Perhaps we met in another life?"

Eris eyed her suspiciously. "Do you have business with my father?" She gestured toward the shop that they both stood in front of.

"I..."

An extra deliberately bumped into Cole to knock her out of place. She spun away from Eris and the crowd was able to separate them.

"I have a pocket watch I fear may be in need of repair," Cole said as if suddenly conjuring up the excuse. "Your shop came highly recommended." She looked through the crowd, trying to catch Eris's eye.

"I'm pleased to hear that. My father has worked hard to build a steady business." Eris's look was still wary as she turned to enter the shop. At the door, she paused and looked back over her shoulder at Cole. "May I ask who sent you to us?"

"A friend of a friend." Cole shrugged and gripped her hat even tighter at the measured look Eris gave her. She smiled nervously.

Eris narrowed her eyes then shook her head as if dismissing Cole. "We open at ten. Good day to you, sir."

"Hollister," Cole shouted and purposely cringed at how eager she'd sounded.

Eris frowned. "Excuse me?"

Cole pushed her way through the people to stand before Eris once more. "My name, ma'am. I'm Hollister Graham."

"A pleasure to make your acquaintance, Mr. Graham. Now if you'll excuse me, I need to help my father open up his shop."

Cole nodded and stood for a moment staring at the door as it closed behind Eris. She waited in place as the door reopened and a cameraman took his position to begin filming her reaction close-up.

"*Emily*," she whispered. "She's *here*."

After a long beat, Cole turned to walk away, only to collide with a woman whose costume was way more extravagant than what Eris wore. It was brighter in color with large puffy sleeves. The corset was tighter, deliberately drawing attention to the woman's ample bust. Her hair was fashioned like Eris's but artfully teased out curls escaped their confines. Fine powder covered her face, and her cheeks were excessively rouged. Mischa smiled at Cole and deliberately lifted her skirt to a scandalous length to expose her ankles encased in fine stockings. It was a signal; this woman was *for sale*.

Cole just stared at her. Mischa reached out and gently ran her hand along Cole's jawline.

"So smooth," Mischa said. She let a fingertip rest on Cole's chin then tapped it. She leaned in to whisper. "I'd wager you could teach some of my *gentlemen* a thing or two about not chafing a lady's thighs."

That line had *not* been in the script. Cole's eyes widened as Mischa suggestively ran her tongue across her brightly painted lips. She caught the merriment in Mischa's eye and quickly put her hat back on to distract herself from wanting to laugh at Mischa's sly ad lib.

"Forgive me, madam, but I have to go..." Cole slipped out of Mischa's reach and hurried across the street, dodging between the carts toward the facade of a public house. She gave one last lingering look back toward the jewelry shop before heading inside to wait for the scene to end. The director shouted cut, and everyone started applauding. Cole let out a sigh of relief then went back to join the crew as they set up for the next scene.

Eris tried desperately not to envy the ease Cole's costume afforded her. She would freely admit that Cole looked incredibly handsome in the formal attire and that the top hat oddly suited her. The masculine costume brought out an androgyny to Cole that Eris found captivating. It made it easy for her to play Emily's growing interest in Hollister. She found herself starting to fantasize about peeling Cole out of her attire to get to the woman inside. She hoped the cameras weren't lingering too long on the desire she knew had to be shining from her eyes. It was an ache forming deep within her. Eris couldn't help but wonder whose yearning it really was now—Emily's, or her own.

An early lunch had been called for while they waited out a sudden downpour that wouldn't match up with a scene they'd filmed earlier. Eris chatted amiably with the craft service people who were serving her. In just a week of filming, they already knew exactly what her menu choices would be and always snuck her a richly iced cupcake on her tray. Eris was just thankful she didn't have to wear a real corset. She wore a less torturous one designed specifically for her slender shape. It gave her the silhouette that bespoke the era but left her able to eat without discomfort. She eyed the rich buttercream frosting whipped up to a point on her cake and whispered a heartfelt thank you to the costume department.

She made her way over to a table under a huge umbrella where Cole and Aiden sat. Aiden looked up from her tablet she'd been busy tapping on and addressed them both.

"We've set up an interview for you both with Donatella Childress from the lesbian TV/Movie review site Refraction. She's visiting various movie locations in Europe for the site so I asked if she had space to add us while she was in our neighborhood. She jumped at the chance. What I like about her is she's honest in her reviews and an entertaining interviewer." Aiden checked something on the screen. "She's scheduled to come in a week's time so we'll still be filming our outdoor shots and will have time to entertain her. We'll just tailor the shoot that day around her because we need the publicity, and we need our leads to generate it."

Eris nodded but she noticed Cole wasn't as enthusiastic. Cole gave Eris a sheepish smile.

"I'm not that great with interviews. I always worry they're going to get me to reveal some deep, dark secret even I didn't know I had."

Eris felt there was something else hidden behind her words but didn't call her on it.

"Are we being interviewed together or separately?" Eris asked Aiden.

"Together so she can see how well paired you two are."

Eris and Cole shared a grin at the compliment. Eris shrugged a shoulder at Cole.

"I'll play gatekeeper for you. I'll field any untoward questions you don't want to answer."

"You'd do that?" Cole looked surprised.

"I'm a master at it. I covered up for my big sister when she snuck out of the house so many times as a teen I should have studied to be a lawyer. Interviews are easy as long as you can anticipate what the interviewer *wants* to ask, what the audience wants to *know*, and how much *you* actually want to divulge."

She caught sight of Cole nervously chewing on her lip and wondered why the mention of an interview was making her so uneasy. She wracked her brain trying to think if she'd heard of any gossip surrounding Cole Calder, but nothing sprang to mind. Whatever was worrying Cole, Eris was determined to deflect it should the interviewer even dare to bring it up.

She just didn't know what it could possibly be.

Chapter Six

Eris woke with a start and hurried to check her alarm. It hadn't gone off, and she panicked she was going to be late to the set. Heart racing, her brain scrambled to remember what day it was. *Thursday.* She fell back against her pillow with a sigh. It was a rare day off from filming. She quickly snuggled back under the sheets and basked in the luxury.

She'd been surprised when they'd arrived in England to find they were staying at Mischa Ballantyne's spacious London abode. It was a big enough property to house Cole, Aiden, Mischa, and Eris with ease and privacy. Everyone had their own room and en suite and at no cost. Eris couldn't believe her luck. She'd expected to be living out of her suitcase in a hotel room.

She listened to the birds singing outside and just relaxed. She was too used to her early call schedule to be able to fall back to sleep though. The sound of someone else moving around roused her further. She guessed it was Cole because Aiden's room was on the other side of the building and Mischa was the last to get up but always the loudest about it. Eris would miss hearing show tunes belted out before the dawn chorus had a chance to start their singing.

She got out of bed to take a quick shower. She was looking forward to spending the day wearing something less restrictive than her Victorian costume. Once done, she left her hair to dry naturally and didn't bother applying any makeup. Eris dressed in her favorite faded jeans and a rainbow colored tie dye tee. She slipped on a pair of Nikes and headed downstairs with a spring in her step. There she found Cole perusing cereal boxes.

"I guess neither of us could take advantage of a lie-in today." Eris reached over to pick out a box of muesli and grabbed a bowl from the cupboard. She surreptitiously admired Cole in her tight black jeans and a black T-shirt bearing the *A Pocket Full of Time* pocket watch. It was a flattering fit. A frisson of desire sparked through Eris and she returned Cole's welcoming smile.

"I couldn't sleep. My body clock is programmed to be up and ready for us to head to the studio lot." Cole finally decided on corn flakes and poured a healthy portion into her bowl. She eyed the kitchen clock. "I'm surprised we're the only ones up."

"Well, we usually hear Mischa way before she gets to the kitchen."

Cole grinned. "I wonder what Disney tune she has in store for today? Her spirited "Circle of Life" rendition yesterday made Aiden spill her orange juice." She laughed. "I love watching those two together. Aiden just lets all of Mischa's outrageousness slide right off her."

"Aiden told me being with Cassidy helped her deal with that. Apparently, the flair for the dramatic is something both Cassidy and Mischa share. To be honest, I think it entertains Aiden more than anything. And you can't miss that she worships Cassidy. It's really sweet."

"I'm glad she's here with us. It's unusual to have the writer so hands-on with a project."

"I'm enjoying it too. Who better to ask a question to about your character's motivation than the author herself?" Eris gratefully received the cup of tea Cole handed her. She was enjoying having someone other than her sister know exactly how strong she liked her tea in the morning.

"So, what do you have planned for today?" Cole asked, sipping from her coffee cup.

"I'm heading out to Tunbridge Wells to visit the cemetery my nan and grandad are buried in. It's set in Frant Forest. It's such a beautiful place, filled with endless trees and greenery. It's the perfect resting site. I always like to go pay my respects when I'm here." She caught the interested look in Cole's eyes. "Are you busy or does the sound of hanging out in an English cemetery opened way back in 1873 appeal to your sense of history? I'll shout you dinner at a pub after and you can try the local beer."

"I'd love that. I was just going to lie around here like a slug and binge-watch TV. Seeing some English countryside would be fantastic. Are you sure I wouldn't be in your way? It's your day off, you might want a break from seeing my face."

"That face? Never." Eris delighted in the soft blush that bloomed across Cole's cheeks. "Though I'd much rather you meet my living relatives. They'd be way more interested in what we're doing here."

"Do your parents still live in England?"

"Yes, my mother and stepfather live in Kent. They're extremely disappointed that the cruise my sister paid for them to go on coincided with us filming over here. My mother would have begged to be on set to watch."

Cole looked disappointed. "That sucks."

"I'll make it up to her at the London premiere because we're going to be back in the States by the time they get home. You do still have an open invitation to my sister's restaurant, don't forget."

"I haven't forgotten." Cole got up to wash out her bowl and set it to drain. "Do we leave a note for Aiden and Mischa so they know where we are?"

"It wouldn't hurt." Eris joined Cole at the sink. They worked around each other with an unconscious ease. Cole set the coffee machine percolating for their housemates. She quickly wrote a note and propped it up against Mischa's coffee mug.

Eris gathered up her handbag while Cole shoved her wallet into a pocket. A set of car keys lay on the counter nearby. Eris checked they were for the car they had use of and followed Cole out of the house and into the garage. Eris took the driver's seat in the elegant Austin Martin Vantage. Mischa had told them it was her husband's baby. She watched with a smile as Cole settled in beside her. From the look on her face, Cole was unabashedly in love.

"If your motorcycle saw the heart eyes you have for this car it would get very jealous."

Cole laughed as she ran her hand over the leather interior. "It's a work of art. It deserves to be admired."

"As long as it gets us from A to B I don't care what it is." She started the engine and moaned. "Okay, that is a beautiful sound considering my car sounds like it's clearing its throat when I start it up."

"I'm driving us back," Cole said. "I want to experience this beauty with my own hands."

Eris's mouth dried at the sinfully sexy way Cole expressed herself while trailing a finger along the steering wheel so very close to where Eris's hand lay. She prayed that she wouldn't stall the car like a novice while trying to back it out onto the driveway.

Cole sat back in her seat and put on her aviator glasses. "I'm at your mercy. Take me wherever you want to go."

Eris's heart stuttered in her chest. She liked the sound of that way too much. Cole gave her a look over the rim of her glasses.

"Just don't get me too giddy on your British beer that I can't drive."

"I'll keep us out of trouble, I promise. This will be a nice, genteel, English escapade."

Cole snorted. "I've seen you in *Code Red*. You're no shy English rose."

Eris grinned at her and revved the engine. "Do you want to see what I learned at driver's ed for that show?" She deliberately opened the engine up again and hoped Mischa couldn't hear it roar. Cole nodded and held on tight as they peeled off the driveway and out onto the road.

❖

Aging tombstones, bearing the names of those long forgotten, shared a quiet space with more modern ornate headstones. All stood amid a multitude of green, yellow, and red leafed trees. Hills stretched for as far as Cole's eyes could see as she stood, shading her eyes against the bright sun. It was a strange oasis, the perfect resting place for so many departed souls. Cole wandered through the older stones while Eris tended to her grandparents' plot. She marveled at how many years had passed, but the markers for the dead had remained standing firm in their forest setting.

Eventually, she wandered back to where Eris was crouched before the black granite headstone bearing both grandparents' names. She'd picked a tasteful bouquet of tight budded pink roses and was fitting them into the posy bowl.

"Don't worry," Eris said, putting the finishing touches to the arrangement. "I'm not going to sit here and talk to them. They're not really here."

Cole helped Eris to her feet.

"I mean, their ashes are here, but I believe their souls are somewhere else. I sometimes feel them with me when I need my confidence boosted." Eris narrowed her eyes at Cole. "Do you think that's weird?"

Cole shook her head. "Not that you feel them, more that you need your confidence boosted."

Eris made a face. "You'd be surprised. It's easy to feel overwhelmed by a sense of inadequacy. My grandad helped me with some breathing techniques to calm my anxiety and just…" Eris closed her eyes and lifted her face to the sun. She took a deep breath in and then let it out. "Be in that moment, own it, and *use* it." She opened her eyes again and brushed her hand across the top of the headstone. "They were together sixty-five years. Grandad always said Nan was the first girl he saw that his heart pulled him toward. He knew immediately she was his soul mate and he vowed to never leave her side. Nan died first. Grandad lasted long enough to bury her here before he returned back to her side. It was the biggest grief I have ever felt, losing them both in so short a time. But he kept his promise to the end."

Cole swallowed hard at the emotion welling in her throat. She was upset that Eris had to lose such loving grandparents so close together. "Soul mates."

Eris smiled at her. "Do you believe in that, Cole? That instant tug toward someone you've never met before? Feeling like you've known them all your life? The ease of being together as if you've lived and loved in so many previous lifetimes?"

"I believe we're currently filming that kind of love."

"I'd like to think it's real. I definitely saw it in these two." She tapped the headstone gently. "It's not something I see happening in my life though. You have to give up so much of yourself and your hopes and dreams while another fulfills theirs instead. I'm not prepared to do that. I've worked too hard to get where I am in this business not to reach for the stars I've dreamed of touching."

"Why do you have to give your own dreams up?"

Eris shrugged. "Nan had to move all the way from Scotland to live in London with Grandad. She was studying to be a nurse, but they met, fell in love, got married, and she had my mom. She never got to be a nurse. She was the housewife while Grandad ran his own business." Eris ran her fingertip along the edge of the stone. "I watched Melanie do exactly the same. She was at college with aspirations to be a policewoman, but she met Georgio, who was over here on a student exchange, and they felt that same connection that Grandad would tell us stories about. So Melanie packed up and moved to the USA and became a chef. Both said it was because they needed to be with their soul mates. I can see the love these couples shared, but I'm not prepared to lose my dreams and ambitions to follow someone else's."

"What if your soul mate was the one willing to follow *your* dreams instead of their own?"

Eris considered this a moment. "In this business?" She shook her head. "My last romantic failure couldn't even cope with me filming on a night shoot. She told me quite bluntly no one would put up with how focused and shut off I can get when I'm working. So, no soul mate for me. It's skipping my generation of Whytes."

Cole stared at her. She'd felt an instant attraction to Eris even before she'd met her in real life. But being a fan of someone and finding her beautiful in a show didn't mean they were soul mates.

But now that we're together…

Cole knew one thing for certain. She loved being around Eris, on the set, having a meal together, vegging out in front of the TV at Mischa's with Eris pointing out who in the shows she went to drama school with. Did that pull toward her have extra meaning other than Cole found her endlessly interesting, a pure joy to be with, and downright desirable? She caught Eris staring at her and hastened to change the direction her thoughts were heading in.

"So, will you be buried here too?" Cole cringed at what came out of her mouth. "Okay, that sounded weirder and creepier than I intended."

Eris shrugged. "It's beautiful here, but I'd like to think I'll find my resting place by the side of my partner if I do ever settle down, wherever in the world she and I end up. I'm a romantic at heart, despite being married to my career." She kissed the tips of her fingers and pressed it to the gravestone. "How about we go find a pub now and order lunch. I'm starving."

"You promised me beer." Cole hesitated before following after her. She made sure Eris still had her back to her and quickly kissed the tips of her fingertips and touched the gravestone too. "Nice meeting you," she whispered. "Your granddaughter is amazing." She hurried back to Eris's side and listened attentively as Eris rattled off a list of beers her stepfather had emailed her for Cole to try.

Chapter Seven

Nerves jangling at the mere thought of the looming interview, Cole tried desperately not to mess up her lines or miss her cues. She was grateful that most of what they were filming were filler scenes. Scenes where she didn't need to remember reams of dialogue when all she really wanted to do was remain silent, slink off set, and hide. The nearer to time for the interview, the more jittery Cole became until Eris captured her fidgeting hands between her own and whispered for her to *breathe*.

A call came through that Donatella was on set and Eris slipped her arm through Cole's and tugged her close.

"We've got this," she said and, surprisingly, Cole believed her.

Donatella Childress was tall, dark-haired, and cut a striking figure as she waited beside Aiden. Her smile was genuine when she saw them, and Cole relaxed a fraction.

"It's fantastic to meet you both. I'm so excited about this movie. I've read all of Aiden's books, and this is by far my favorite series." She looked past them toward the set and grinned at Aiden. "Forgive me, but I'm going to be an utter fangirl for a moment. It's just how I pictured it in your story. It looks so real!"

"Our set designers have done a fantastic job," Aiden said. "It got very emotional for me that first day to see this street and how they'd built *exactly* what I'd imagined."

Eris stepped forward. "Do you have time for a tour?"

Donatella eagerly took Eris's proffered arm. "Yes, please. My God, it's like walking into the book."

Eris led the way, talking animatedly the whole time and making sure Donatella didn't miss a thing. Cole and Aiden trailed behind them. Cole noticed Aiden kept checking her watch with a smile.

"You look happy today, boss. Hmmm, I wonder why that could be." Cole knew perfectly well why Aiden was radiating joy.

"Cassidy is flying in as we speak. I've missed her so much." Aiden checked her watch again as if those few seconds made a huge difference. "She should be landing in about two hours. I have someone picking her up at the airport, then we'll all meet back at Mischa's where I'll prepare us a meal to welcome her 'home.'"

Cole was enjoying her stay at the Ballantyne residence. Aiden was an excellent cook, and Mischa had been a very entertaining host with a penchant for salacious gossip. With her filming finished and her break over, Mischa had returned to America two days prior and now Cassidy was on her way.

"Wouldn't you rather have the house to yourselves?" Cole asked.

"She's going to want to be fed because airplane food is, and I quote, 'mere chicken feed.' We'll have plenty of time after that to catch up, don't you worry. Apparently, that's one of the reasons why Mischa had me stay in a room on the far side of the house. It's for when Cassidy arrives." Aiden rolled her eyes at Mischa's mischievous planning. "Cassidy's excited to come spend time with you two. Mischa had such a great time with you both."

"It's a shame she couldn't have stayed to catch up with Cassidy."

"Believe me, sharing a house with those two is an experience. Mixing Mischa and Cassidy together can be like juggling with nitroglycerine sometimes. But Mischa has her family to go back to and Cassidy just finished her guest role on *Law & Order: SVU* so they'll catch up later. They talk all the time on the phone anyway. I'm well aware Mischa is Cassidy's work wife."

"I bet Cassidy's excited to come back to England."

"Yes, she is. Her home and work are in the States now, but she misses the crazy weather this country is renowned for and its quieter pace of life. Who knows, maybe we'll retire here when she tires of reading lines and I tire of writing them."

Cole scoffed quietly. "Somehow I can't see that happening, for either of you."

"True. I have so many stories left to tell. But seeing this one filmed?" Aiden's eyes shone. "Makes me so damn proud."

"I can't wait to film with Cassidy. I just hope she doesn't catch me unawares like Mischa did."

"I warned you; she's a scene stealer. Damn the woman for coming up with a better line than I did. Cassidy, however, is more professional. She won't change the line, but she'll spin it in such a way that you won't forget it. Now that we have Darrow/Hayes Productions I want to get her into more movies that will showcase her talent. She's brilliant as Karadine Kourt in *The Alchemidens*, but she has a vast range of talent beyond that show that needs utilizing. And that's not just a biased lover talking." Aiden grinned. "Though I *am* pretty biased."

Eris called Cole over to have her photo taken with her and Donatella in front of the jewelry shop. Talking with Aiden had steadied some of Cole's nerves, but later, walking back toward Aiden's trailer where the interview was to take place, she couldn't help but feel just a little apprehensive about what questions lay ahead.

❖

Donatella didn't film the interview, but her phone was recording everything they were saying. Cole was very conscious of it but was grateful that, so far, all the questions were about the movie. Eris had made sure that Cole answered what she wanted to before giving her own answers and it made for a very enjoyable, informal chat to publicize the movie.

"Eris, you're best known for *Code Red*. How difficult has it been switching from the high-tech, fast-paced, all guns blazing of DC to the cobbled streets of Victorian London?"

Eris patted at her dress. "Well, the costumes are hugely different for a start. I don't think my government agent would have lasted long trying to run in these skirts. It's been a nice change of pace and

I've never done period drama before so this has been an exciting role to take on."

"And, Cole, it was a shock to your fans when it was announced you'd be leaving *Fortune's Rise* after this season."

Cole tried not to stiffen and fought not to let her smile falter. "This movie was too good an opportunity to miss. I'll miss working on the show, but I felt it was time to move on."

Donatella stared at her. "There's a rumor…"

Cole cut her off smoothly. "You're way too professional to listen to rumors, Donatella." She watched Donatella hesitate for a moment, then reach over to turn off the recorder.

"You're probably aware that Maria Ramos's husband has been receiving threatening tweets…"

"I'd rather not comment." Cole saw Eris move a little closer to her, ready to spring into action.

"I don't need you to confirm or deny anything, Cole. I'm not publishing anything said now. It's all off the record and I promise you, I wouldn't gossip about things like *this*. The show garnered some very ardent fans for you and Maria. Refraction has been getting some nasty messages ourselves from those kinds of fans because we won't champion the rally to get you back in the show so that they can get their supposed 'endgame.'"

Cole winced. "I'm sorry you all got caught up in that. It was never going to happen. It wasn't the direction the show wanted to take."

"Oh, my bosses told them quite bluntly that since Chris and Nat had never been written or played as a canon couple on the show, then our stance was that the 'relationship' the fans were adamant to see should be best left to fan fiction and their own imaginations." Donatella sighed. "Just like your own bosses did when it became clear a certain part of the fandom was going to be very vocal about a ship that was never written to sail in the first place."

Cole sucked in a breath. "I bet that generated some hate on your site."

Donatella nodded. "Which is why I am warning you, off the record, about what I have seen. Some of the fans, that select few in every fandom, aren't happy that Chris and Nat weren't lesbians. They feel they were baited."

"You can't bait if the hook is empty," Cole said. "We were just two straight women who were neighbors who sometimes argued about stuff when we saw each other. Our scenes caused sparks, but we weren't a slow burn romance. On or *off* the screen."

Donatella nodded. "Fandom has changed over the years. People aren't just satisfied with the characters they get on the screen. They readily pair off anyone and everyone now, however ridiculous the pairing is, and demand that it gets airtime. But the hate we got on the site for not 'shipping' your characters was immense. I don't know if any of what happened concerning them is why you left the show and I certainly won't mention it in my post to add fuel to their fire. But I need to warn you, as an admirer of your work and your talent. Judging by the hate mail we got and what we are seeing on fan boards? You have some crazy fans who will go to any lengths to get their happy ending."

Eris leaned into Cole and placed her hand on her knee. Cole couldn't do anything more than just nod her thanks at Donatella.

Her message delivered, Donatella took a deep breath and reached over to turn the recorder back on. "Now, I have to know, have you gone off set in your costumes like the guys from the Marvel Universe do? And, if so, were the British public too polite to say anything to you?"

Chapter Eight

The atmosphere on the set was buoyant and playful, but Cole felt restless and on edge after the interview. The director was making sure everyone's spirits were high take after take as they ran through a scene filmed from multiple angles. At one point, Eris was put behind the camera and got to direct the scene. Cole loved how attentive Eris was to every suggestion, making sure everyone was in their positions and that the cameras were ready to roll.

The mood brightened even more when a car pulled up onto the lot and Cassidy Hayes stepped out. Aiden spotted her, let out an excited whoop, and ran across the lot to her. Cassidy left her driver looking somewhat bewildered as she took off at an impressive run in her high heels. Aiden skidded to a halt as Cassidy launched herself into her arms, wrapped her legs around Aiden's waist, and clung to her like a koala. She pressed urgent kisses all over Aiden's face until they shared a passionate kiss that made the entire movie crew stop to cheer and holler.

For a split second, Cole was envious of their connection. She hadn't experienced that kind of love where separation led to a joyous reunion, giddy smiles, and fervent kisses. Eris sidled up beside her.

"I guess absence really *does* make the heart grow fonder." She laughed as Aiden swung Cassidy around and reluctantly had to let her go before they both fell over in an embarrassed heap.

Cassidy kissed Aiden one more time, long and leisurely, then began to quickly wipe away any traces of lipstick smearing Aiden's face. Aiden just stood and smiled indulgently as Cassidy made sure they were both presentable to acknowledge the whole of the cast and crew watching them. She held up a hand and waved.

"Hi, everyone!" Cassidy wrapped her arm tightly around Aiden's waist. "Thanks for keeping Aiden distracted until I could get here." She spotted Cole and Eris nearby and gasped. "Oh my God, the photos Aiden has been sending me just don't do you two justice." She sauntered over to them, running an exacting gaze over their costumes. "Perfect, absolutely perfect." She ran a finger over the lapel of Cole's jacket and across a frill of lace on Eris's shirt then looked over her shoulder to Aiden. "The level of detail is magnificent. I'm so glad Mischa recommended the costume designer for us."

"Does Mischa know everyone?" Eris gathered Cassidy in for a welcoming hug.

"Yes. She says it's because she's got wicked connections everywhere in the business. I say it's because she's so nosy she knows anyone and everyone."

Cole laughed and got a hug of her own. "Welcome to the set we've been calling home."

"I'm expecting a tour of it all once you've finished filming for the day. I'll just go stand out of the way and watch you all go about your business while I canoodle with my fiancé." She held out a hand and Aiden took it, pulling her back into her side and releasing a heartfelt sigh. "Did you miss me, darling?"

"Every second of every hour of every day," Aiden's unabashedly adoring gaze gave weight to her words. Cassidy laid her head on Aiden's shoulder and hugged her close. She spared a look at Cole and Eris.

"Got to love a writer. They have such a way with words." She pressed a kiss into Aiden's neck and grinned as Aiden squirmed at the tickle.

"I thought you were going straight to the house from the airport?" Aiden said, not letting Cassidy out of her grasp.

"I couldn't wait that long to see you. Come help me get my luggage out of the car and into yours and then we can send the poor driver on his way. I may have talked his ear off all the way here about how marvelous my sweetheart is. You might need to tip him a little more for that inconvenience."

Cole loved how well Aiden and Cassidy seemed to fit together. She thought back to her visit to the cemetery and looked down at Eris. "Would you say those two are soul mates?"

Eris nodded. "Absolutely, in every sense of the word. You can see it, can't you? That almost spiritual connection that goes beyond attraction or lust?"

Cole nodded. She'd never had that feeling with a lover, one where they were more than shared conversations over some meal and good sex afterward. She'd always felt separate and self-contained, not bound to anyone by a mystical bond. She enjoyed the company, the intimacy, but she wasn't left devastated when they inevitably parted ways and she was single again. She joined Eris watching Aiden and Cassidy wrangle multiple suitcases from the trunk of the car.

"Funny how Aiden wrote about a couple whose souls bond through multiple lifetimes. She seems to have her very own Emily in Cassidy," Cole mused.

"Fate," Eris said simply.

"There is no fate but what we make," Cole intoned darkly then paused. "Wait, isn't that a *Terminator* line?"

"Close enough. You obviously didn't grow up binge-watching *Terminator 2* to not know the exact quote by heart." Eris made it sound like a crime.

"I've maybe seen it a few times."

"Linda Hamilton and all those delicious muscles." Eris sighed dreamily. "My sister wanted to be Julia Roberts whereas I wanted to be Sarah Connor and handle the big guns."

Cole followed Eris back on set where everyone was getting ready for another take. "You had some pretty big guns in *Code Red*."

Eris grinned at the memory. "I did. And I knew how to use them all too. The director said I just needed to know where to point, but I got someone to show me the correct way to use those beauties.

If you ever need a Laser Quest partner, I'm your gal. I can handle everything from a pistol to a rocket launcher."

"That's good to know." Cole couldn't get over what a constant surprise Eris was. "I might be in need of some protection from those crazy fans Donatella was talking about. I'll know who to call."

Eris immediately lost her spark. "Is it really as bad as Donatella makes out or is it just one or two fans amid thousands who can't differentiate real life from scripted?"

"Let's just say that posting this film all over Twitter and Instagram is the first social media interaction I've had in over a year and a half since the trouble started."

Eris looked like she was about to ask more, but the director called for them and conversation was at an end.

But that didn't stop Cole from worrying about it.

On the car ride back from the studio lot, Cassidy regaled them with anecdotes of her guest starring on *Law & Order: SVU* and how the camera didn't do enough justice to Mariska Hargitay's talent and beauty.

Once at the house, everyone took a suitcase or bag from the trunk of the car and carried them inside. Cassidy wheeled her suitcases down the hallway and Aiden helped her carry them up the stairs.

"Did you leave anything at home for when we return?"

Eris overheard Aiden's dry comment and the sound of Cassidy's laughter answering it. She and Cole quickly made a beeline for the kitchen. They raided the fridge for bottles of water and grabbed handfuls of fruit for a quick snack. It wasn't long before Aiden returned to the kitchen, her hair a little ruffled but with a happy smile plastered across her face. Cassidy trailed in behind her looking equally dazed.

"You two are *that* couple, aren't you?" Cole said, moving away from the counter she'd been leaning against when Aiden shooed her aside so she could start work.

"We are. Nauseatingly so," Cassidy said, reaching into a drawer for a corkscrew. She opened a cupboard to reveal a very well stocked wine rack and perused it with a serious intent. She selected a bottle and hugged it.

"Mischa got my favorite," she said, leaning against Aiden and kissing her cheek.

"Of course she did. She made sure everything you'd want would be here when you arrived."

"All I needed was you, my love," Cassidy said, kissing Aiden again then dancing off with the bottle. She picked up a large clean glass off the sink as she went. "But a bottle of Ogier's Chateauneuf-du-Pape, Bois de Pied Redal, Organic Red is a worthy second to your gorgeous self."

Eris laughed at Cassidy's playful nature. She was as irrepressible as Mischa but gentler somehow, maybe a touch sweeter. She watched Cassidy expertly open the bottle.

"Ladies, would you care for a glass?" Cassidy poured herself a generous amount.

Eris pushed a glass in Cassidy's direction indicating she just wanted a small amount. Cole hesitated.

"What kind of wine is it? It looks a little too fancy for my beer and pretzels palate."

"My dear Cole, this wine is cultivated by only natural means, no pesticides for these gorgeous grenache grapes." Cassidy took a sip from her glass. Her eyes closed as she savored it. "Black cherries, black currants, licorice, and herbs. We're talking a bold, full-bodied wine." She took another drink. "Mischa gifted me a case for Christmas, I was instantly a fan."

Aiden looked up from where she was chopping onions. "It's her happy wine and she's offering to share it with you. Don't pass up this once-in-a-lifetime offer because she will cradle that bottle like a child all evening."

"Hush, you." Cassidy waved her glass at Aiden. "I can share. I just don't choose to very often when it comes to the good stuff."

Eris took a sip and licked her lips after it. "Wow! My sister needs to serve this in her restaurant." She took another sip and let all the different flavors burst onto her tongue. "That is really nice."

Cole took a tentative sip. Eris bit her lip to stop her laughter at the grimace Cole tried to mask.

"Neanderthal." Cassidy rolled her eyes at her and took the glass from Cole's unresisting hand, not willing to waste a drop. "I'm sure you have a beer in the fridge you'd rather chug, Homer."

Aiden reached in the fridge for the final ingredients she needed and handed Cole a can. She laughed quietly at Cole's chastised look. "I only drink soda," she admitted, "so the wonderful world of wine escapes me too."

"Did Mischa order in enough Sprite for you?"

"She did. She knew the minute you set foot in here you'd demand wine and food. She prepared for all."

"I miss her." Cassidy raised her glass in a toast. "To Mischa, owner of many homes that she lets us abide in. God bless her, and God help all those in LA who she is terrorizing as we speak."

Eris raised her glass, Cole popped the ring of her Budweiser, and Aiden raised her knife.

Eris settled in at the kitchen table watching Aiden prepare their meal with quiet efficiency. Cassidy spent most of her time peering over Aiden's shoulder, nuzzling her, and stealing pieces of the cheese Aiden was grating. Aiden seemed more than used to her behavior and just kissed her at every opportunity.

"I missed you." Cassidy pouted pitifully as she leaned into Aiden's side while she stirred a rich tomato sauce.

"Me or my cooking?"

Cassidy scoffed. "Why both, of course. I got tired of having to order in or invite myself to eat with our friends. And once Mischa was over here with you, I fell into a deep depression."

Aiden held out a spoon of the sauce for Cassidy to taste test. She did so with a sinful moan of pleasure. "Poor baby." Aiden made a pouty face at her and received a gentle slap in return.

"She kept sending me photos of you, you know. Ones I don't think you were aware of. She did it so I wouldn't miss a day of seeing you, even if it was just a picture of you on set." Cassidy sighed. "It just made me miss you more. Our house just wasn't the same without you in your writing room typing away on your laptop."

"I missed you too."

"Do you think these two would notice if I ravished you on the kitchen table while we wait for the food to cook?" Cassidy's eyes sparkled with mischief.

Cole spluttered into her beer while Eris just grinned.

"We can just set the table around you two if we have to," Eris said, totally unfazed by Cassidy.

"I'm surprised you came out of the bedroom at all," Cole muttered, wiping beer off her chin.

"I've lived with Cassidy long enough to know that the way to her heart is through her stomach. Spaghetti Bolognese with an abundance of cheese on top is what she needs first after no doubt critiquing every meal on the plane journey here."

"The portions are paltry. I'm a growing woman, I need more than a dry bun and peanuts. Or greasy lasagna with sugar snap peas. And your cooking spoils me for anything else."

Aiden finally placed the spaghetti in a pan and stepped back from the stove. "You have fifteen minutes for the pasta to cook. Plenty of time for you to catch up on the gossip on set before you get ready for your cameo on it tomorrow."

Cassidy reached for the bottle and topped up her glass. "Mischa said she was certain two of the makeup women are having a secret affair."

Eris frowned as she tried to think who Cassidy meant. "Oh! Lucy and Alison?" She shook her head. "Those two have an on/off relationship. Mischa must have spied them on an 'on' moment when they were more flirtatious than bitching at each other."

Cassidy tutted. "Well, that's not enough. I need more than that." She eyed Eris and Cole deliberately. "What about you two?"

"*Us*?" Eris cursed how high her startled voice rose. Cole stared at her.

"Yes, you had your interviews today, didn't you? Did Donatella make you spill any salacious secrets? She tried that with me in an interview once, but I was the model of decorum."

Aiden sat beside her at the table and poured her soda into a glass. "Is that the interview when you admitted you'd gone skinny dipping in a castle's ornate fountain while filming the pilot for *The Alchemidens*?"

Cassidy's head whipped around at her. "You read that?"

"We've long established I'm one of your biggest fans. I read anything that came out connected to the show and you."

Cassidy ran her finger around the edge of her glass, trying to look coy. "It was all Mischa's fault. I certainly wouldn't have dared to do such a thing on my own."

Aiden gave Cassidy a pointed look. "Mischa says otherwise."

Cassidy huffed. "She's such a tattletale. Anyway, the security guards were perfect gentlemen and turned their backs on us while we scrambled out to slip back into our complementary bathrobes." She paused for a moment, obviously lost in the memory. "The castle had exemplary room service too."

"Thankfully, our set is devoid of a water feature," Aiden said.

"There's a very large bathtub upstairs." A sultry smile curved Cassidy's lips.

"We'll soak in it later to help you get rid of all the kinks from sitting so long on the flight." Aiden clasped Cassidy's hand in her own, the promise in her eyes making Cassidy's cheeks bloom.

Cassidy tore her eyes away reluctantly and turned her attention back to Eris and Cole. "So? How did your interview go?"

Eris had no clue what to say. The interview had been smooth sailing, but the revelation at its end had Eris's mind in a whirl. She looked at Cole, desperate for her to say something. She didn't want to be the only one knowing what message Donatella had left them with.

"It was wonderful," Cole said. "It should make for some great publicity, especially as we were able to give Donatella a quick tour of the set so she could see what we're doing here. And she's a fan of Aiden's books so that's a huge plus and should garner us extra kudos." She smiled at Eris. "As interviews go I'd say we came out well, wouldn't you?"

Eris stared at her and marveled at how calm Cole seemed. She didn't like it or truly understand it, but she respected her decision to stay silent.

"Yes, I think we answered everything genuinely too. We certainly didn't sound stiff and rehearsed."

"You two make a good team, on and off set." Aiden returned to the stove to stir the spaghetti. "You're a dream team."

Cole raised her beer. "I'll drink to that."

Eris joined in the toast. Finding fame on TV or in movies was what every actor strove for, but sometimes it came with a fearful price. Eris really hoped this thing with Cole was just one of those "fans being fans" moments and it would die down as Cole took on other roles and left *Fortune's Rise* behind her.

She looked at Aiden and Cassidy and couldn't stop herself from remembering what had happened to them. She knew they, of all people, would understand what Cole was experiencing. Been there, done that, she thought morosely as her mind fed her the details that had streamed all over the internet, telling of a stalker who had dogged Cassidy for years. It had started with a steady stream of fan mail from him where his initial admiration soon turned into abuse and threats. It continued throughout Cassidy's career. He was untraceable and unstoppable. Landing a starring role on *The Alchemidens* launched Cassidy firmly into the spotlight, which spurred her stalker to try a more terrifying tactic to get her attention. He broke into Cassidy's home, leaving her a chilling message. Cassidy fled to stay at a friend's house, one right next door to Aiden. Eris loved that Cassidy and Aiden had found each other, but the stalker wasn't planning on them getting the happy ending that, in his mind, should be *his*. His story ended at a packed convention hall where he'd intended to kill Cassidy in front of her fans to prove his love. He hadn't counted on Aiden, proving *her* love for Cassidy, taking the bullets meant for her instead.

"Eris?"

Cassidy sounded concerned and it pulled Eris back into the room. She smiled at everyone's concerned looks. "Sorry, I was just…wool gathering." Eris waved a hand dismissively.

"How frightfully British you sound," Cassidy purposely overplayed her own accent and made everyone laugh. She leaned over and filled Eris's wine glass. "Less thinking, more drinking. Now that's a motto I should have tattooed on my butt."

Aiden laughed. "Don't even think about it or Mischa will make it her life's work to get it done. I'll get it sewn on a cushion cover for you instead and save you the pain."

Cassidy beamed. "Isn't she a sweetheart? Goddesses were smiling on me the day they had her walk into my life."

Eris risked a look at Cole who was gazing right back at her. Eris raised her glass to her just a fraction and Cole tipped her beer can back.

She swore she could hear her own goddesses laughing at her.

Chapter Nine

Eris didn't know which hurt more—her feet from a day running up and down the cobbled street in her Victorian boots or her pride in having done her own stunts in previous roles and yet never hurting like this. She had been glad to get back to Mischa's house to take off her shoes, plant herself on the sofa in the living room, and wriggle her toes in the plush carpet.

"I'm going to have to ask the director if I can do a Peter Cushing if my feet don't stop complaining." Eris gratefully reached out for the cup of tea Cole brought her.

"A Peter Cushing?"

"His Star Wars boots pinched him so he wore his slippers on set except when they needed a full length shot," Eris explained, taking a sip from her cup and enjoying the tea that always tasted better when Cole made it for her. "Are you going to sit down?" Cole hovered beside her, looking indecisive and a little distracted.

"I'm looking for a cushion to prop your feet up on."

"I don't need one. Honestly, I'm just whining."

Cole sat down beside her on the sofa. "I'm surprised you didn't twist an ankle having to run in those boots of yours. I'm glad mine don't have those stupid heels that stick in the cobblestones."

"I should have worn a pair of thick socks to pad them a bit. I just didn't expect us to be spending most of the day running up and down."

"Yeah, it was definitely a cardiovascular kind of day. How you managed to run in those boots, in that crazy long skirt of yours and *still* keep your hair in place is beyond me. I had enough trouble keeping my hat on."

Eris laughed. She'd lost count of how many times the director had yelled "Cut!" because Cole's hat had fallen off as they'd run the length of the set. It had been a crazy day, one with endless retakes for mistakes, missed cues, hats falling off, and the leading ladies slipping on the cobblestones. By the end of it, Eris had been footsore but strangely euphoric.

"God, I had so much fun today," she mused. "It was manic, and maddening, and my feet hate me, but it's such a fantastic set. I don't think I've laughed so much in ages." She stretched her arms above her head, grateful to feel her spine pop in a few places and bring her relief. She flopped back against the cushions feeling boneless. "I love my job."

Cassidy wandered in carrying a platter of crackers, cheese, and fruit. She cradled a bottle of wine under her arm and had a large glass dangling upside down from between her fingers. "Supper will be delivered in about an hour and a half. Aiden has a few calls to make and then she will join us. Meanwhile, I have snacks to graze on if you are interested. Though, Eris, I'd recommend you go soak in the hot tub for an hour to ease your aches."

"There's a hot tub?" Cole's head snapped up.

Cassidy nodded, placing her goodies on the coffee table and starting to pick out the grapes and the various cheeses she wanted on her cracker. "It's next to the laundry room. It's totally private and even has a small fridge in there."

"A fridge?"

"My dear Cole, do you really see Mischa as the kind of girl to sit in a hot tub and contemplate life?" Cassidy chuckled. "It's stocked with drinks and chocolate. Avail yourselves." She popped a grape into her mouth and savored the taste. "And I do mean *selves*. There's a strict two-person rule on the tub, just in case someone falls asleep in it and ends up drowning. That's something we can't afford this early into the shoot. So, Cole, be a darling and share the tub with Eris, please." She continued perusing the cheeses. "You don't mind Cole joining you, do you, Eris?"

Cassidy's voice was innocent enough, but Eris's inner radar pinged. She caught a glimpse of something mischievous in Cassidy's eyes before she looked up and stared Eris right in the face.

"I don't mind at all," Eris said honestly, a touch suspicious of Cassidy's motives.

Cole let out a disappointed huff. "I didn't exactly bring hot tub attire."

Cassidy uncorked her wine bottle with a practiced hand. "Just wear your bra and your boxer briefs if you're not ready to skinny dip." She laughed at Cole's surprised look. "What? Did I guess correctly? Forgive me, but you don't strike me as a Victoria's Secrets lingerie kind of girl. At least, not when you ride that monster of a motorcycle. All that lace would chafe like a bitch." She poured herself a glass of deep red wine and sniffed at it appreciatively before taking a drink. "You'll see each other naked soon enough when we go back to the States and film your love scenes. Sure, they'll artistically drape the bed sheets about you, but you'll still be unclothed. Anyway, what's a little flesh amongst girls?"

Gay girls, Eris thought, trying to keep a calm demeanor when inside her head she was frantically fanning herself at the thought of seeing Cole close up in a hot tub in just her underwear. *Especially this gay girl with a massive crush growing for her leading lady who is just too beautiful for her to ignore.* She stood and tried not to moan as her feet immediately started complaining.

"I'll go get ready while I can still move."

Cassidy's attention focused back on the food before her. "Good. I switched the tub on for you before I came in here. I figured it would help. After today, you both need to just lie back and soak in the bubbles. Then, before you get too wrinkly, supper will be here. It's Chinese tonight." She let out a happy sigh. "I love noodles."

Eris had to smile at her. "Cassidy, how do you stay so trim for someone who can eat the way you do?"

"I have a very speedy metabolism. It drives Mischa insane!" Cassidy grinned then instantly sobered. "I always take time to remind her, though, how beautiful she is every day because she really *is*. She has some delicious curves I would kill for, and those curls. I'm so envious of her hair and she knows it." Cassidy fell silent. "I wish she'd been able to stay a little longer here. I absolutely dread *The Alchemidens* finishing because I'm so used to seeing my best friend every working day. Aiden has promised she'll find projects we can work on together as we're too good a team to break up. Aiden's words, not mine, but I wholeheartedly agree. Sometimes you find a working partner who you just *click* with immediately and it makes the job a joy."

Eris couldn't help but glance at Cole who was getting to her feet.

"I totally agree," Cole said, directing a smile in Eris's direction and gesturing for her to go ahead and leave Cassidy to her snacking. "We'll go have an hour soaking the day away."

"Perfect. Then we can all eat and relax for the evening." Cassidy waved them off. "Enjoy!"

Eris started up the steps. She sensed Cole was right behind her.

"I'm not going to fall," she said, amused that Cole was being so solicitous.

"Just keeping a watchful eye on you."

Eris looked over her shoulder and caught Cole swiftly raising her gaze away from the direction of Eris's butt. It made Eris's heart lighten and she would have had an extra spring in her step if her feet weren't making her feel more like an old woman.

"I'll just get changed." Eris pushed open her bedroom door but paused, watching Cole head to her room.

"I'll just..." Cole gestured to herself, "take these off and try not to be too self-conscious walking through the house in my skivvies. I'll grab us some water to drink unless you want to raid Mischa's hot tub fridge."

Eris shook her head. "Water will be fine. I'll just wait until supper comes before I eat."

Eris wandered into her room unbuttoning her shirt and taking off her jeans. She lifted the lid of her suitcase and pulled out a modest one-piece swimsuit. She hadn't bothered placing it in one of the drawers because she didn't have access to a pool staying at Mischa's home. The hot tub, however, would serve its purpose nicely. She stood naked in her room, holding up the cherry red one-piece, and thanking God she'd thought to shave the previous night. She heard Cole leave her room and go downstairs. Eris quickly slid into the swimsuit and checked herself out critically in the mirror. She wondered if Cole would like what she saw. If that spark Eris could see in Cole's eyes would flare and ignite, letting Eris know this *thing* between them wasn't just her wishful thinking. Cassidy was right though, they would be naked with each other soon enough. The thought of that set Eris's heart racing at a frantic pace.

Eris was disappointed that it would be just because of the script. Their nudity, their kissing, the pretense of desire, all of it would be part of a narrative to further the movie's plot. A few lines in the script, directed by an eye drawn to how it all *looked* but not *felt* for the two women in the bed.

At least, how I feel about it. I want her hands on me *and not just as Emily.*

Eris took one last look in the mirror, picked up a clean towel, and headed back downstairs to find the hidden room and Cole.

The hot tub room was an extension added on the back of the house. When wandering outside in the orchard and flower gardens, Cole hadn't paid it much attention, it blended so seamlessly onto the original building. She also wasn't the sort to open every door and explore around someone else's residence when they had been so gracious enough to invite her to stay.

Cole wandered into the room and whistled in appreciation. The large hot tub sat center stage in the middle of the floor. The walls of the room were clad with a pale wood effect that made it feel like she was in a spa. There was a large TV screen hung on one wall while the other walls had windows that let in an enormous amount of light and gave a fantastic view of the trees and their fruits. Cole loved it.

"Wow. When I move out of my apartment I have got to get me one of these."

"If I ever get to move out from above my sister's restaurant I'd love one too."

Cole spun around to find Eris leaning in the doorway, her eyes scouring the room in delight. Cole stood rooted to the spot as Eris breezed past her, checking everything out and touching every surface as she did so.

Cole couldn't tear her eyes off her. For someone far shorter than Cole, Eris had long legs that did not seem to quit. The swimsuit showed them off spectacularly and sparked an endless round of visions in Cole's head of having those legs wrapped around her waist or around her head. Almost dazed, Cole reached up to run a hand across her chin to make sure her tongue wasn't hanging out at the sight of Eris in a swimsuit that fit her like a glove. The cut of the suit revealed a generous amount of Eris's breasts. Cole balled her fists tight. All she wanted to do was trace that neckline and then have her tongue lick between the sweet line of Eris's cleavage. Eris turned around and Cole got a view of buttocks framed in the tight, bright red fabric. She knew if she didn't get in that tub soon her shorts would be wet for another reason. Never had the phrase "good things come in small packages" rang so true. Cole told herself to move toward the tub because if she didn't do what they were in there to do she would scoop Eris up and, noodles be damned, she'd make sure they never came out of her room all night.

God, I want her so bad. She's gorgeous, inside and out.

"Isn't this fantastic? I wish I had known about it sooner. I'd have been in here every night." Eris moved toward the step to get into the tub.

That finally galvanized Cole into moving. She hurried to Eris's side to offer a hand as Eris stepped up and settled herself to sit on the edge of the tub with her legs in the water. The moan of delight Eris let out made Cole's stomach clench in reaction. It was the most erotic sound she had ever heard.

"Oh, this water is sinful!" Eris slipped down into the tub and sighed, running her hands across the bubbling water. "I needed this." She looked over her shoulder at Cole. "Coming?"

If you make that noise again I will be, Cole thought. She gestured to herself in her black boy shorts and black bra. "I'm feeling a little dull and dreary after seeing you in that sweet little red number."

Eris laughed. "You're totally rocking the bad boi image in your black underwear and your shaved hair." She held out a hand. "Please, come join me. Your abs are very distracting. Who knew *Fortune's Rise* had a character with such rock hard abs hidden under those plain blouses?"

Cole blamed the reddening of her cheeks on the temperature in the room. She let Eris lead her into the tub. "Oh my God, how decadent is this?" Cole sat opposite her. She drank in the sight of Eris with her head back, eyes closed, luxuriating in the hot water. The paleness of her breasts was just visible above the white bubbling waters. Cole deliberately kept her distance. She wanted to kiss Eris senseless. The need was growing stronger now. Without thinking, she reached for Eris's foot and began to massage it under the water. Eris startled and Cole immediately stopped, chagrined that she had just acted on impulse.

"I'm sorry. I should have asked first. I used to have a roommate at college who was training to be a physiotherapist. She taught me the pressure points on the feet that brought relief. I thought maybe I could help you feel better."

"That would be great." Eris relaxed and wriggled her foot in Cole's still hand. "Please continue."

"I don't usually go around grabbing women's feet." Cole began pressing her thumbs into Eris's sole, gently at first then applying more pressure. "Sometimes, I forget that you and I haven't known each other for years. You just seem so *familiar*. Like you've always been a part of my world."

Eris nodded. "I know. It's weird but oddly comforting."

"I mean, I've watched everything you've done on TV so I have that familiarity with you as an actress. However, the *real* you? You as just Eris and not the characters you've played? I feel like I've known you forever." Cole shook her head. "It sounds crazy. Especially with the story we're filming."

"I like it though," Eris said, her voice soft and soothing.

Cole nodded. "Me too." She worked her way along Eris's toes, pressing into the soft pads, massaging along her arch and delighting in every moan that escaped Eris's mouth at her ministrations.

"You could do that all night," Eris sank farther in the tub, looking more relaxed than when she first stepped in.

"I offer my services to you any time. I don't like seeing you hurting when I can help."

"You're too good to be true."

"I'm nothing of the sort." Cole reached for Eris's other foot and started the same pattern of treatment. "I just know which area to massage to get the right results. Like this spot here," she pressed in, "this is for the spleen."

"You're possibly the first person to make themselves acquainted with that," Eris said with a grin.

"Here is for the liver, then here the kidney, stomach, and thyroid." Cole meticulously pressed out each one on Eris's foot. She purposely squeezed one of Eris's toes. "And this little piggie apparently had roast beef."

Eris laughed at her silliness. "You goofball!" She sat up a little and reached for her water bottle.

Cole went back to her serious massage. If this was the closest she could get to touching Eris, then she'd happily sit in this tub all night, get a cramp in her hands, and still make no complaint. Cole had never been one for a foot fetish, but even Eris's feet were cute. *God, I have it bad for her.*

After a while, Eris gently nudged her with a toe and told her to stop. "Come, sit by me. The sun is starting to set through the trees and it's too beautiful to miss."

Cole slid around the tub to sit beside Eris. She could feel Eris's side pressed against her own. She longed to run her hand along Eris's thigh, to feel the long, lean muscle that she had seen. She wanted to run her hand higher, to move the skimpy fabric aside and touch Eris. To make Eris pant against her neck as she explored her, wet and wanting. To press kisses across the tops of her breasts then pull the costume down and feast on her.

"Isn't it beautiful?" Eris's eyes were on the tree line as the sun sank in the sky, coloring it in streaks of pinks and oranges.

"The most beautiful sight I have ever seen," Cole said, her eyes only on Eris.

Eris turned at the tone of Cole's voice, and for a long moment, they gazed at each other. Eris leaned in just a fraction and Cole felt drawn toward her, helpless to her magnetic pull as she had been since the beginning.

A sharp double knock on the door made them both jump and sent water sloshing everywhere.

"Ladies, you have twenty minutes before our meal is delivered. Anyone not in the kitchen in a timely manner once the takeaway touches the tabletop only has herself to blame when Cassidy calls dibs on their food. Consider yourselves warned."

Cole laughed at Aiden's public announcement voice. Reluctantly, she pulled back a fraction, not missing how deep and dark Eris's eyes had gotten. "You go ahead. I'll turn this tub off and then Cassidy can show me what I need to do to clean it after we've eaten."

Eris nodded, unusually silent. She accepted Cole's help out of the tub. She dried herself off quickly then lingered a moment. She leaned over and kissed Cole on the cheek.

"Thank you for the massage. I feel great."

"Glad to have helped."

Eris left and Cole couldn't help but watch her go. She was mesmerized by the sway of Eris's hips. For too long, Cole had seen Eris in her Victorian clothes, all long skirts and tightly buttoned up shirts. Seeing her in nothing but a swimsuit, Eris's soft skin on show, only made Cole hunger for more. She was painfully aroused, and for a fleeting moment considered getting off in the hot tub, but time was against her. Aiden's warning was ringing in her head. She needed to eat before her share vanished onto someone else's plate. She would deal with her other problem later, in the privacy of her room. When she could fantasize about Eris slipping out of her swimsuit and inviting Cole to do more than massage her feet. With a groan, Cole hastened out of the tub, quickly dried off, and ran upstairs to take a much-needed cold shower.

Chapter Ten

After three weeks of doing mainly outdoor shots, Cole felt almost claustrophobic filming inside a real building. They were using a Victorian house that had once been the residence of a very wealthy family and their servants. Certain rooms were untouched by the passage of time, and the current owners of the house regularly rented it out for movies and period dramas. Cole knew Aiden had been thrilled they'd been allowed to film there. The exterior shots were already completed. Inside, the set decorators had just added a few embellishments to a room that already possessed a truly authentic Victorian England air.

The crew was wandering around a very elaborate sitting room adjusting the lighting one last time. A group of ladies in their finest costumes were chatting just like their characters were soon to be on film.

Cole and Eris were standing out in the hallway waiting on the call back in. Eris was perusing the framed photos on the walls that documented the building's passage through time. Cole was watching her, loving the expressions that flitted across Eris's face at what she was learning. They'd spent a great deal of time in each other's company, on and off the sets, and Cole was already dreading going back to America. They'd still be filming together every day, but the closeness she and Eris shared from living together was something Cole would desperately miss.

I don't want to go home.

"I'm going to end up needing glasses soon," Eris muttered, squinting at one photograph.

"You'll look cute in them." Cole cursed herself for not engaging her brain before using her tongue, but the smile Eris bestowed on her more than made up for her slip.

"Why, thank you, kind sir." Eris performed a quick bob of a curtsy and moved to another photograph. Cole noticed her smile stayed put.

Cassidy sauntered into the hallway looking extremely elegant in her Victorian clothing. The style was similar to what Eris wore, but the quality was visibly richer as befit her character Odelia Wright's higher status in society. The scene they were waiting to shoot was of Emily and Hollister delivering a repaired piece of jewelry to Odelia. She'd invite them in, and Hollister would find herself the center of attention, surrounded by rich women, all eying *him* as potential husband material. It was the turning point in the book.

Cassidy smiled as she joined them. "I love this story. Where else can I get to wear these gorgeous clothes, have my hair styled to within an inch of its life, and sow the seeds for our Emily to look a little closer at Hollister and finally see the woman behind the gentleman's clothes." She paused for a moment. "Actually, I'm surprised Mischa didn't fight me for this part."

"I think Mischa enjoyed playing a prostitute too much and getting to be the first woman to flirt with Cole on screen."

There was just the slightest edge to Eris's tone that sparked Cole's curiosity. She sounded almost...*jealous*? The wide-eyed, eyebrows raised look Cassidy directed at her didn't help either. Cole hated that she felt so hopeful. Time spent with Eris had made Cole's fangirl crush grow into something much more real. Cole *wanted* Eris. Not just the actress but the woman herself.

Eris moved away from the photo she'd been perusing. "Besides, Cassidy, it's only fair you should be the one to make Emily look deeper into the feelings she's fighting for Hollister. After all, had this been filmed earlier, *you'd* have been playing Emily. I have no doubt of that."

"It is kind of weird to realize I was the inspiration for Emily, way before Aiden and I ever met. I can't say I'm not disappointed that I can't be her in this movie but, unlike Mischa, I recognize when an actress might be a little too *mature* for a role. So instead I get to gently nudge Emily toward the love of her life." Cassidy grinned. "And help produce the movie. *And* sleep with the writer. I see no downside to this."

The director appeared in the doorway and called Cassidy away. Cassidy lingered a second more. "Before I forget. The pretty little redhead from the ladies circle would like to know if you are single and available, Cole."

Cole couldn't help herself. She looked over at Eris who seemed to be staring a hole through the picture she was near.

"I'm single but…not interested at this time, but please, thank her for asking. We leave for America soon and it wouldn't be fair to start something." Cole noticed the long exhale Eris released. She startled at the sharp pinch on her hand that Cassidy gave her. She opened her mouth to complain but shut it quickly when Cassidy nodded toward Eris with a stern look.

Cassidy gave her a "what are you waiting for" look, shook her head at her, and walked off muttering, "Useless lesbians."

Cole rubbed at her hand to ease the sting from Cassidy's nails. She noticed Eris still wouldn't look at her.

"I…er, I don't usually go out with women I work with. It can get so complicated if things go wrong."

Eris nodded. "I follow the same code of conduct. There's nothing worse than lovers who bring their quarrels to the set. Not that I've ever fallen for a costar before, so I've never had to worry."

Before. The word swam around Cole's brain setting off a fanfare and she cursed it for giving her hope. "I'm not saying I *wouldn't* ever date a costar though. Not if I found someone who likes me back."

Eris finally looked up at her and winked. "Likes you? What are you, nine years old and hoping the pretty girl at school *like* likes you?"

Cole playfully glared at her mocking. "Hey! I'm being serious here! If I found myself drawn to someone on set, one who made me laugh and think, and I just loved to be around? I'd rethink my position in a heartbeat."

"Jolie, the redhead, seems like a nice woman. I spoke to her in makeup."

Cole shook her head. "She's not my type."

"You haven't even spoken to her yet. You've spent all day with me."

Cole threw all caution to the wind. Life was too short and her heart was starting to ache for Eris. She had to know, one way or another, if she stood even a sliver of a chance to be her Hollister in real life. Cole stepped closer and kept her voice low from the prying ears of the crew.

"Eris, I've had a raging crush on you since you appeared in *Code Red*. I never dreamed I'd get the chance to work with you. Then I found what I'd felt before was nothing compared to the reality of being around you." She smiled as Eris's face softened into a shy smile. "Am I right in sensing you didn't appreciate Mischa flirting with Hollister when she was here?"

Eris's skin reddened visibly under her makeup. "It was part of the scene, but you know as well as I do she wasn't just flirting with the character."

"Mischa wanted an honest reaction from me for the take and she got it. She's way smarter than her deliberately cultivated diva persona. You know how shrewd and downright calculating she is. You've played poker with her. You were lucky Aiden talked her out of it being *strip* poker."

Eris sighed. "I know, it just…"

"What? *Emily* didn't like Hollister being flirted with?" Cole said as she watched Eris squirm. When Eris faced her, Cole was shaken by the naked desire visible in Eris's dark eyes.

"No, *I* didn't like *you* being flirted with. I can't seem to separate reality from fantasy at the moment. Especially as we're about to shoot a scene where all those women in there are going to be all over you. And I know it's Hollister and not you, but it still *is* you and I know it sounds crazy to feel something for one's costar so fast but I just…" She paused and let out a grumpy noise. "No, don't give me that devastating smile of yours and make this harder for me than it already is."

Cole tried so hard to stop her smile from growing even bigger, but it was a lost cause. She loved how honest Eris was. It was refreshing. *And damn, she just looks so pretty. I'm not wasting this opportunity to tell her I feel the same way too.*

"Eris, I want to kiss you and not just when I'm in Hollister's shoes." Cole loved the look of surprise on Eris's face. It made her look so sweet that Cole wanted to kiss her there and then, makeup be damned. *How long have we both been skirting around this attraction? Hiding behind Hollister and Emily like scared children?*

Eris reined herself in, her face suddenly deadly serious. "This is neither the time nor the place to discuss this," she said. "We're at *work*."

Cole laughed and swiftly covered her mouth to hold back the rest of her amusement while Eris stared at her. "I'm sorry, you sounded like Olivia Coleman doing the Queen in *The Favorite*. So commanding."

"God, you're goofy." Eris shook her head at her.

"Yeah, but now I'm decidedly giddy *and* goofy knowing you *like* like me too."

"It's wearing off fast."

"Nope, you can't take it back."

"I'm sure I can."

"No, you can't," Cole singsonged.

Cassidy popped her head around the doorframe. "Children, if you're quite finished? Go play outside. We're nearly ready for you."

Cole straightened up and reached for her hat. "The minute we're done for the day you're buying me a beer."

Eris scoffed at her. "And why should I buy you a drink?"

"Because when we tell our grandbabies about our first date it isn't going to be known as 'that time you took me to the cemetery.'"

Eris nearly tripped over the doorstep as she walked out. "*Grandbabies*?"

Cole grinned, enjoying knocking Eris off-kilter. "Of course. Tons of goofy grandbabies that we tell our story to while feeding them candy."

Eris ran her hand over her skirts, brushing them down needlessly. "I don't know about me buying you a drink. I think you're going to need to buy me three if we're talking grandbabies already."

Cole hoped the afternoon's filming would move swiftly. She wanted some serious time alone with Eris to see where this thing between them could lead. She opened her mouth to say something, but the director's voice boomed out from the building.

"Quiet on the set!"

Cole honestly felt sorry for the actresses who were going to feel the *real* heat of Emily's jealousy in the upcoming scene. She quickly ran through her lines in her head and prayed she wouldn't screw up because she wanted today's shoot over quickly.

There was a beer and a heartfelt discussion in her future, and she didn't want to waste time getting to either.

The booth they sat in was about as private as they were going to get out in public. The pub was busy with customers coming in for drinks and evening meals. It oddly worked in Eris's and Cole's favor. No one was looking for actresses dressed in jeans and sweatshirts, eating tikka masala and a shepherd's pie, all while they were busy getting their own orders sorted.

"I dread to think what Cassidy is going to get up to tonight when I told her we were going to eat out and come back later," Cole said, ripping off a hunk of poppadum and dipping it into her meal. She gathered up a mixture of rice and masala and took a healthy bite.

"Judging by the looks Aiden was giving Cassidy on the set today I think we know *exactly* what's going to happen with them left alone for a few hours." Eris took a sip from her beer and licked at the foam clinging to her upper lip. "I can't remember ever being in a relationship where everything was that fun for that long. My last girlfriend and I fizzled out like a damp squib. I don't think either of us even noticed until it was too late. Relationships are hard to maintain. I have enough trouble keeping my cacti alive."

"I haven't really done relationships. My longest was seven months, a personal record. But she decided that having her privacy invaded by my fans wasn't worth the hassle. She skipped out after she got increasingly nasty tweets about how she should leave me because I was Maria's. It was silly at first that people would do that kind of thing to someone they don't know. But it got steadily worse and she didn't dare answer back because, if she did, then it got downright ugly. She spent all her time blocking people sending her hate messages. Then the rumor started circulating that Maria was cheating on her husband with me and it got a million times worse. She knew it wasn't true, but having that constant barrage of hate and innuendo thrown in her face wore her down. I don't blame her for breaking up with me. If I could have walked away from it all I would have too."

"But it's still following you now." Eris couldn't believe how much of Cole's life the fans affected.

Cole nodded. "I know the fans are trying to get me back on the show. My manager keeps an eye on it all. She's seen the polls and the messages calling for me to come back. Apparently, my name has trended a few times on Twitter too, but it's all a waste of time. I'm not going back. I know many are genuine fans for whom Chris was their favorite character. But it's the others, the ones who won't let go of the fact Chris and Nat weren't a couple and damn well demand them to be as if they are owed it."

"What do you think started the rumors about you and Maria?"

"You know that some fans not only ship the characters but also the actors? Yeah, we got stuck with that too. I understand it with established couples, the whole Brangelina and Beniffer thing. But Maria and I were friends, good friends, but still only costars. We would never have been anything more than that. But certain fans wished we were and started up those fucking awful rumors and doctoring photos to make it look like we were together." Cole took a long drink from her glass. "Wanting something so bad doesn't just make it come true. If it did, I'd have a garage full of Harleys and be a few links higher on the Hollywood fame chain."

"I'm grateful not to have seen that side of fandom." Eris didn't think she could handle the stress that came with fans who deliberately undermined your private life so that they got what they wanted. Or at least, hoped to.

"It's not pretty, that's for sure." Cole took another bite from her meal. "This is gorgeous. I'll miss this food when we go back." She held out a forkful. "Here, try this."

It wasn't the first time Cole and Eris had shared food, but this time it seemed more intimate. Eris took the bite and savored the spices in the morsel. She licked her lips appreciatively. "That's nice. Almost as good as one of the masalas at my sister's restaurant. One of her chefs does amazing things with curries."

"Then when we return you'll have to invite me out on a date there so I can meet your family and sample their tikka masala at the same time." Cole looked delighted by that thought.

Eris smiled at her. "What, we haven't finished this date yet and you're already angling for a second? You're confident."

"I'm hoping for as many as I can get with you. I'm enjoying every minute I get to share with you, Eris. On set and off. I can't be the only one who wishes it to be more?"

"No, I've wanted that too from the moment I laid eyes on you, but I thought you were unattainable. Instead you've been plotting and planning for our grandchildren. I have to admit, for the free spirit you appear to be, that sounds awfully domesticated."

"We can be free-spirited together. And I like the idea of building a family. Not right now, of course, but maybe one day. If that isn't your dream though, we can just sit back and see what life brings us. I won't ever trample on your dreams, Eris, personally or professionally."

"Do you usually ask a girl out and immediately hit her with the 'kids and future' vision?"

Cole thought about it for a moment. "Nope, you're the first one I've ever seen that with. I mean," she leaned forward over the table conspiratorially, "it's not like we haven't already slept together."

Eris's brain scrambled to decipher what Cole meant. She tutted at her when the penny dropped. "We fell asleep on the sofa watching *The Great British Bake Off* together. That doesn't count!"

"We'd gravitated to each other though. You squished your face into my arm and cuddled in. I'm sure I still have the drool patch on my shirt to prove it. I kept it as a souvenir." She grinned at Eris's affronted huff. "Face it. You're the Lady to my Tramp. One piece of spaghetti between us and we're going to meet in the middle of it."

"You're equating us to cartoon dogs?"

"Hey, no dissin' Disney. I earned a nice little nest egg starting out in commercials promoting Disney World. They're somewhere on YouTube, sprinkled with comments about how young I looked and asking what in the hell I was wearing."

"Maybe I should start calling you *Goofy* for real," Eris said, enjoying their banter and just basking in the happy light shining from Cole's eyes. It hadn't been there a lot since the interview had taken place. Eris never wanted it to leave. She pushed her plate aside. "So, are we going to order dessert? I'm not ready to go back to the house yet. It will make this day end too fast. I can't believe we finished shooting today. Tomorrow we pack everything up and the day after we head back to the States. That four weeks has sped by. We're done here."

Cole reached across the table, her hand open, inviting. Eris rested her own in it. She marveled at how well they fit together.

Cole squeezed her fingers gently. "But *we're* just beginning."

Chapter Eleven

Cole felt like a teenager walking a date home. Instead of leaving Eris at the front door with a chaste kiss good night, Cole led them both through Mischa's unusually quiet house and upstairs to their rooms.

"I guess Aiden and Cassidy have turned in for the night," Eris said, swinging their joined hands gently between them. She leaned against the wall beside her door, not stepping any farther.

Cole was reluctant to leave. She lifted Eris's hand and held it in hers. Gently, she ran her fingertips over Eris's knuckles, across the life line on her palm, and along the length of her fingers. She couldn't stop a sigh from escaping.

"You look like you're trying to find a way to let me down gently," Eris said.

Cole tried to explain what was racing through her mind. "I'm not exactly problem free at the moment, what with all the gossip surrounding me. I'm worried that you being with me might bring that madness right to your doorstep, to bleed all over your career. Some fans don't care who they lash out at as long as it gets a reaction. One photograph of us as something other than our characters could drag you into a whole heap of aggression from the crazies. I wouldn't ever wish that on you."

"They're not stopping me from being with you. I'll tread carefully, but they're not chasing me off social media. I have my own fans I need to keep updated on my career." Eris squeezed

Cole's hand. "Forget the world outside. Right here, right now, what do *you* want?"

"*You*. But I wish we didn't have to worry about this. I wish this," Cole gestured between them, "could just be about *us*."

"But it is." Eris looked up and down the hallway. "There's no one else here. It's just you and me. No cameras, no prying eyes. No Mischa waving pom-poms to cheer us on. Just us."

Cole rested her head on Eris's shoulder. "I'm going to have to eat my words in front of Aiden."

"Why?"

"I kind of promised I wouldn't cross any lines by fraternizing with my beautiful costar while filming."

Eris laid her head against Cole's. "Aiden knows how you feel?"

Cole nodded against her. "I guess the heart eyes I was sporting were kind of hard to miss. I promised not to bring romantic drama to the set. I didn't dare dream I had a chance with you. I was just going to worship you from afar and make the most of every moment spent with you."

Eris's breath tickled at Cole's ear. Her lips were so close to Cole's skin she had to fight back a moan. "You made a promise to Aiden you wouldn't try to seduce me while we were filming?"

"Kind of?" Cole was kicking herself for mentioning it.

"Too late, Cole. You already did that without making any moves." Eris brushed her lips against Cole's ear and then gently nipped at her earlobe.

A hot burst of delight exploded from the bite straight down Cole's spine. It electrified her. She stifled a groan of pleasure into Eris's neck. Reluctantly, she shifted her head up so she could look directly into Eris's eyes. She was desperate to know that Eris shared what she felt. In that moment, Cole couldn't have moved had a hurricane hit. Transfixed by the intensity of Eris's gaze, Cole could *feel* the desire she saw within. It touched her with a lover's intent. A naked desire for *her* written clearly all over Eris's face.

"You made a promise. I can appreciate that." Eris's voice was soft with understanding.

Cole tried not to whine with disappointment. Eris's lips were so close. She just had to lean forward a fraction and she could reach them, taste them, and finally kiss her for real. Eris tapped at Cole's face, but Cole's attention lingered on the slow smile curving Eris's lips. She watched Eris form the words to set her free.

"You made a promise and that's on you. But, sweetheart," Eris tugged Cole's head down and smiled seductively, "*I* didn't promise a thing."

Eris kissed her and, for a split second, Cole almost didn't react. She was too busy savoring the feel of Eris's lips on her own. The softness and the barely restrained hunger as Eris unleashed her own desire. They had kissed before as Hollister and Emily. This wasn't the carefully choreographed kissing constantly interrupted by someone shouting "cut" and them having to begin again from a different camera angle. This time Cole could take her time to learn the shape of Eris's mouth under her own, savor the feeling of Eris in her arms, and run her hands over her clothing and seek out the soft skin beneath. She opened her mouth to let Eris's tongue run along her lips, tasting her. Every kiss they shared became more fervent, more desperate, pent up feelings breaking through the professional barriers they'd had to keep in place.

Cole brushed her hands down to Eris's hips and picked her up. Eris wrapped her legs around Cole's waist as Cole pinned her against the wall. Eye to eye now, she stared at Eris, lost in how beautiful she looked with her lips ravished and her eyes blown wide with lust.

"As good night kisses go this has to be the best one ever," Cole said, unable to stop taking one more kiss then another from Eris's sweet lips.

"I don't usually entertain lovers on the second date." Eris's hips rocked against Cole's stomach in a lazy rhythm that drove Cole insane. "But if you don't take me into that bedroom and finish what we've started out here, then I'm going to have to take matters into my own hands. *Literally*."

Cole moaned at the images that conjured in her head. "Save that for another time, please. I don't want to let you go tonight."

"Then don't. Take me to bed, Cole. I want to make love with you. Hollister and Emily will have their time soon enough. Tonight is ours."

❖

They tumbled through the doorway and managed to get it closed behind them while never breaking a kiss. Eris, desperate to feel Cole's skin on her own, loosened her legs' grip around Cole's waist and for a moment hung suspended only by Cole's strong arms. Cole seemed reluctant to let her go.

"You have to put me down at some point," Eris said, melting at Cole's lips tracing a lazy pattern down her nose and across her cheeks.

"I don't want to let you go." Cole's grasp tightened.

"I'm not going anywhere. I just want you out of those clothes and in my bed."

Cole reluctantly lowered Eris to her feet but didn't step back. Instead she reached out to tug Eris's sweatshirt up and over her head then divested herself of her own. Eris was suddenly nervous about how she looked. She was used to sporting a more toned figure after the physically demanding role she'd played in *Code Red*. Since leaving the show she'd been able to cut down on some of the rigorous exercise she'd needed to create a stronger physique. She had been required to soften her look for the movie because Victorian Emily sporting Eris's finely chiseled abs wouldn't exactly fit with her character. It had been a relief for Eris to relax her exercise regimen. She loved the softer shape her body now possessed. Judging by the look on Cole's face, she liked it too. She all but devoured Eris with her eyes.

Eris did her own perusing of Cole. Taller and broader than Eris, Cole cut a dashing figure. She obviously had her own exercise regimen judging by her defined abs that begged for Eris to run her tongue over them. Cole's breasts were much smaller than hers, a perfect complement to the sexy androgynous look Cole displayed. Eris unfastened her bra, watching Cole mirror her. After the frantic kissing they'd just engaged in, slowly undressing and just taking each other in was, Eris knew, the calm before the storm. Both tossed their bras aside. Eris was pleased that Cole swayed toward her, drawn like a magnet to her nakedness. Cole checked herself, clenching her fists for a moment and took a deep, measured breath in and let it out slowly.

"I just want to run my hands all over you," Cole said. "Followed swiftly by my tongue."

Eris felt her mouth dry up as she stared at Cole's dark pink nipples. She was desperate to run her own tongue over Cole. She was more beautiful than Eris could ever have imagined. She was done with the teasing. "I swear, if you don't get out of those jeans right now I'll rip them off you and you'll be wearing them as chaps."

Cole popped the buttons open and hastened to get out of them. Eris thought there was something oddly endearing watching Cole stumbling and fumbling to get her jeans off. Her boxer shorts were pushed down to join the pile at her ankles and Cole heel-toed her shoes off and yanked her socks off within seconds. Gloriously naked, Cole presented herself to Eris and waved a hand to hurry her up.

"Your turn. Don't leave me hanging here."

Eris didn't linger. The time for a coy striptease was long past. She made swift work of her remaining clothes and barely had time to look up before Cole had her back in her arms and was moaning into the crook of her neck.

"God, you feel so good." Cole nuzzled her lips against the sensitive skin that drove Eris wild.

Eris smoothed her hands over Cole's back, then she suddenly stopped.

"What's wrong?" Cole whispered, stilling her own hands and waiting for Eris to explain.

"Before we go any further, we have to be careful to leave no nail marks, no hickeys, or any incriminating bruises on each other. We have a love scene to film when we're back on set, and we'll never hear the last of it if there's anything on our skin that has to be covered up by makeup."

"So no love bites on your very delectable ass?" Cole deliberately squeezed Eris's buttocks.

"Not until after the filming of that scene, no."

"But after that?" Cole drawled softly before nibbling at the fleshy lobe of Eris's ear.

"After that, the sky's the limit."

Cole's eyes flashed with something almost sinful that stole Eris's breath away.

"Guess I'll have to find something else to do that won't leave any telltale marks." Cole deliberately ran the flat of her tongue around Eris's pulse point on her neck. Eris clung tighter to her, fearing she might swoon.

"Oh my God. How do you know exactly where to touch me?" Eris panted against Cole's chest.

"I don't know. I just do what feels right." Cole walked Eris back toward her bed and they crawled onto it.

Eris pushed Cole onto her back and lay on top of her. She began to slowly rub herself up and down Cole's body. She made sure their nipples brushed together as she rocked. "It's so much easier to reach all of you when you're flat on your back. I'll have to remember that." She kissed Cole's smiling lips. "Are you sure you want to do this?"

Cole's eyes widened incredulously. "Are you fucking kidding me?"

"Consent is sexy, Cole. Besides, this is a big step we're taking."

"You could have asked me before you started rubbing your sexy body all over mine. I want you, Eris. Not just for tonight but for as long as you'll have me."

"I like the sound of that. Costars to lovers though. History is never kind to us."

"Screw history. We'll rewrite it. In years to come everyone will say they wished they had a romance like those lesbians who took Hollywood by storm."

"Who knew you were such a romantic soul?"

"I know what I want and *who* I want." Cole ran her hand through Eris's hair, brushing it back from her face. "And I want *you.* I feel like I've waited my whole life for you."

Eris pressed a series of kisses along Cole's chest and around her heart. She moved steadily toward her goal and licked at Cole's straining nipple. Cole's reaction was electric.

"Fuck, I could come from you just doing that," she groaned, shifting restlessly under Eris's weight. Her hips bucked with every teasing touch Eris bestowed.

Eris captured the other nipple between her fingers, rolling the hard, taut nub between her finger and thumb. Cole began moving so much Eris shifted to straddle her to keep from sliding off. She moaned as her heated core touched Cole's abdominal muscles and the mix of hard muscle and soft skin left Eris weak. She moved and her clit rubbed against Cole's firm stomach. Eris deliberately pressed down harder and smeared her arousal across muscles that twitched and strained beneath her.

"Fuck, you're wet." Cole moved her hands to rest on Eris's hips to press her down harder. "Rub yourself over me. Get yourself off on me."

Eris did just that. She concentrated on the pleasure building inside her as Cole's hard flesh stimulated the head of her increasingly sensitive clit. She rocked back and forth, but her fingers never ceased rubbing and tugging at Cole's breasts. She cupped them, molding them in her hands, then flicked over the nipples causing Cole to cry out with pleasure. That only spurred on the speed of Eris's hips to press in harder, closer, scenting Cole to make her *hers*. She shuddered as the pleasure bloomed out and spread through her body. She could feel Cole holding her in place. She could feel the beat of Cole's heart beneath her palm as she ran her hands over her chest and learned every curve of Cole's breasts. She rocked harder and trailed her fingers down Cole's stomach to feel the straining muscles beneath her.

"Can you come like that?" Cole asked, her fingers straying from Eris's hips and smoothing out along her thighs.

"Not usually, but it just feels so good." Eris's head fell back and a gasp escaped when she felt Cole's fingers slide between their bodies. The slightly roughened skin on her fingertips slipped in between Eris's legs and lay flat so that Eris was rubbing all over her left hand. Cole's fingers moved to Eris's lips and swollen softness before she laid her right hand close and maneuvered a finger directly over Eris's straining clit.

"Oh." Eris shuddered as the added stimulus pressed more firmly against her and she jerked as a bolt of pleasure shot through her veins. She rocked faster, desperate to reach for all the pleasure she could gather. In a swift move, Cole entered Eris. One finger slid straight inside and Eris's walls clamped down on it, holding her in place until Cole could move and begin to stroke within her.

Oh God, don't let me be loud, Eris begged as she felt everything inside her concentrate on the firm finger hitting all the right stimuli while the constant pressure of Cole's finger drawing her clit from its hood was driving her equally insane.

"You are so beautiful like this," Cole said. "I can't wait to taste you."

Eris almost whited out at the thought of Cole between her legs. She began to shake uncontrollably as pressure grew and grew until she couldn't hold it back anymore and she climaxed. She hoped that Cassidy and Aiden were far enough away not to hear her all but scream Cole's name out as she came long and hard. Her body took every ounce of pleasure it could get and swiftly began building toward a second orgasm before she'd even managed to finish riding out the first. Stunned by it, Eris clung to Cole's strong arms and fucked herself harder on Cole's finger, chasing the high each stroke promised. She came again with a squeal and fell onto Cole in a quivering mass. She tucked her head under Cole's chin while her body spasmed and shook and her desire soaked her thighs and Cole's hands.

"Wow," Cole whispered. "That was fucking amazing!" She kissed Eris's head and gently removed her hand from Eris's now overly stimulated clit. Eris jerked as it grazed the tip and sent another shiver of ecstasy through her center.

"*You're* amazing." Eris tried to get some breath back into her lungs. "I have never had a multiple orgasm in my life."

"Really?"

"No, never. It was always hard enough to reach a first, let alone try to squeeze another one out." Eris snuggled into Cole's chest and sighed languorously. "What do you do to me?"

"Anything your heart desires." Cole began to chuckle and Eris lifted her head up slowly.

"What?"

"Any fantasies I had about you? You just blew them all out of the water." Cole hugged her close with her free arm. "Damn, I wish I'd brought my strap-on with me."

Eris felt her face flame. Cole tried to look at her, but Eris deliberately hid her face.

"What? You've used one before, haven't you?"

Eris cringed. "Kind of. I'm beginning to think I dated the wrong kind of girls because they always expected me to use it."

"Then it's a good thing I'm here to spice up your sex life." Cole held her close. "Damn, we're going to have so much fun."

"Will you show me what you like?" Eris lifted her head again and caught Cole's smile.

"I *like* you. You can do whatever you want with me."

Eris raised an eyebrow at Cole's totally sincere face.

"*Anything*?"

"I'm adventurous. I'll try anything once. And you strike me as the kind of woman who'll rock my world."

Eris shifted and reluctantly slid off Cole's finger. She grunted at the loss and then grinned as Cole flexed her hand, captivated by Eris's wetness dripping from her fingers. Eris sat back up and rubbed her hands on Cole's belly while Cole stuck a finger in her mouth and sucked on it. Eris just stared, feeling arousal start to grow inside her again so soon after it had been sated.

"Oh yeah, I'm going down on you every chance I get," Cole said, running her tongue along another finger and grinning at Eris's gasp. "You taste better than any fancy wine Cassidy could uncork."

Eris ran her fingers through the soft patch of neatly trimmed hair that framed Cole's sex. Never taking her eyes off Cole's sensuous display, she inched down to rest between Cole's legs. Cole was beautiful. Eris deliberately ran a finger through Cole's own arousal and brought it to her lips. Cole stopped what she was doing to watch her intently as her tongue swirled around her finger and removed every drop. Eris shifted again to lie on the bed, pushing Cole's legs wider and positioning herself between them. Eris ran her tongue deliberately through Cole's abundant wetness. She sucked gently on the ruffled edges of her lips and then teased at Cole's clit with the tip of her tongue. Then she grabbed for a pillow, placed it under Cole's hips, and settled in. Without preamble, Eris entered her with her tongue. She dimly heard Cole's exclamation because Cole's thighs immediately tightened around her head, holding her close, keeping her exactly where needed. Eris managed to reach up and tease at Cole's breast. She tugged at the nipple and smiled into Cole's flesh as a fresh wave of wetness burst onto her tongue. She could hear Cole urging her on as she fought to keep her body still so Eris could touch her wherever she wished. Eris reveled in Cole's scent; it was heady and intoxicating. She pressed her tongue in farther then replaced it with two fingers that slid in deep. Cole let out a rumbling moan, spreading her legs wider so that Eris could get the right angle to fuck her.

Eris watched Cole beneath her as she gasped and moaned at Eris giving her pleasure, taking her higher and then mercilessly pushing her toward the edge. Cole was vocal and Eris loved it.

"Harder. I'll come all over you. That's it, right there. Oh God, you've got the lips of an angel and I thank God you're going to be mine." Cole strained, her back bowing off the bed as Eris sucked her clit into her mouth and deliberately hummed. "Oh fuck!" Hips bucking wildly, Cole let out a strangled whine and then convulsed into an orgasm that had Eris quickly replacing her mouth with her hand to rub at Cole's clit to keep the pleasure going until she could take no more. Cole finally fell to the bed with a thump and lay sprawled there. Her breathing was erratic under Eris's palm. Cole could barely lift her hand to beckon Eris back up the bed to her.

Eris threw the pillow aside and crawled up to cuddle into Cole's side, laying a leg across her possessively and holding on to a breast.

"Where the hell have you been all my life?" Cole muttered, rubbing her face in Eris's hair and kissing on her head.

"Waiting until the right moment, apparently."

"Well, this is it. Our moment, leading to many more moments because I am never letting you go." Cole was silent for a moment then asked, "Do you think there's a chance *we're* soul mates?"

"Do *you*?" Eris had felt it from the moment she had set eyes on Cole. There was a pull unlike any other she had ever felt. She was intrigued to see if Cole had had the same feeling.

"Yeah, I do. Because even if I never had sex with you again, I'd still always want to be by your side."

"That's sweet, but we're having sex again as soon as you've recovered." Eris ran her palm under the swell of Cole's breast, more for comfort than to arouse. She couldn't touch her enough and she'd always been a breast gal.

"I swear I can't feel my legs."

Eris pinched her there and Cole gave her a playful glare as she jumped.

"So, do you?" Cole asked, drawing Eris closer to cuddle her.

"Do I what?"

"Think we're soul mates?" Cole's voice trailed off as she got sleepy.

Eris raised up to kiss Cole. "I don't know, sweetheart. I've fought so long not to want that in my world." She couldn't ignore her feelings any longer though. "But I think maybe we could be. It's something we can explore together."

"I'd find you in every lifetime, Eris, just like Hollister. I promise. I'll always be there for you."

"And I for you." She watched a silly smile curve Cole's lips.

"I *like* like you, Eris Whyte. We're gonna have so much sex, and I'm gonna meet your sister, and I'm gonna take you for a ride on my bike and have you feel those vibrations rock your clit off… and we're gonna be great together."

"Take a nap, Goofy." Eris kissed her eyelids sweetly and laid her head back down on Cole's chest. She listened to the steady beat of Cole's heart under her ear and let it lull her to sleep.

CHAPTER TWELVE

"Never have I ever...drunk real liquor on a set and gotten drunk off my face."

Cole stared at Eris. "You did that?"

Eris nodded. "I was supposed to be drinking ginger ale. But I got very drunk *very* fast over the course of the retakes. Some guys on set thought it would be funny to get sixteen-year-old me drunk, so they spiked my drinks. When the director found out who did it he fired them on the spot. It was a huge health and safety violation as well as an assault. It caused them an extra day of filming waiting for me to sober up. Apparently though, I was a friendly drunk so that's one thing to be grateful for. That and me not puking all over the set."

"Well, I've never been drunk on set so you owe me a kiss." Cole tapped at her lips and smiled when Eris did as bid. "I like this game. I get kisses." They were resting from a second round of intense lovemaking. The sun was barely touching the horizon and they were greeting the new day wrapped in each other's arms. "My turn. Let's see. Never have I ever...dated a costar before." They both kissed on that.

"That's kind of cheating as we both know that one." Eris tickled at Cole's belly button and made her squirm. "Never have I ever... slept with anyone before at least three or four dates and a less than discreet grilling from my sister."

Cole grimaced. "No kiss from me, I'm afraid. I had a few one-night stands as a youth when I first came out. But they were so unfulfilling I never bothered to continue with that trend. And as I started to get recognized it wasn't worth risking my reputation with some woman selling her story to the tabloids." That line of self-respect had saved her from many a disastrous hookup with someone just out to catch a celebrity in their net.

"No kiss from me either. You, my dear, broke that 'never' last night in spectacular fashion." Eris stretched out lazily beside her, looking so delightfully smug Cole couldn't resist her.

Cole shifted closer. "Oh, I think we both deserve a kiss for that."

They kissed for longer than the game kisses had traded for. Cole couldn't get enough of Eris's soft lips beneath her own. The feel of her naked skin against Cole's own was a heady delight, and Cole didn't want the kiss to end or their time spent lazing in bed to be over. When they finally came up for air, they both flopped back on their pillows, grinning.

Eris sobered first. "I can't believe we have to pack up today. I've gotten so used to living here in Mischa's house. It's going to be weird going back to the States to my place above the restaurant. *And* seeing clear skies again."

"Do we have time to go pay your grandparents one last visit?"

Eris looked torn. "I don't think so. Not with packing and then going to the set for the wrap party Aiden has planned for the British cast and crew." She shifted to rest her head on Cole's shoulder and traced a lazy pattern along Cole's abs with her finger. "Maybe we can come back when all the filming is over?"

"Perhaps I can meet your mom and stepdad then?" Cole knew she sounded hopeful. She couldn't help it. The moment they met Cole felt their connection just click into place. She couldn't explain it. She was just grateful that, whatever the universe had in store for her, it intended Eris to be at her side.

"I'd love that," Eris said. She sighed. "God, we're going to have to be so careful not to let anyone guess we're more than just costars now."

"True, but we can be professional on set and get the job done and then go home together and burn up the sheets!"

Eris laughed. "You're incorrigible." She gasped as Cole's hands began wandering again. "And insatiable!"

"I'm making up for all the times Hollister got to kiss you and I wanted it to be me."

"Hollister is very handsome and sexy in her top hat and dapper suit. But you, Cole, *you* are all I want." She ran her hand over Cole's cropped hair. "I hope you never have to go back to Chris's hairstyle. This shorter look suits you so much better."

"I don't intend on ever going back to Chris's character or anything like her. I like this new look." She ruffled at her hair. "Though wearing it a little longer might be something to aspire to once this role is complete. Something a little less severe."

Eris smiled, her gaze wandering over Cole's face. "God, you're so beautiful."

Uncharacteristically bashful all of a sudden, Cole kissed her as thanks. "And you are utterly breathtaking. Do you think your sister has need of another waitress? Because I think I'm going to be spending a lot of time in that restaurant."

"I'll find a much better use for you, don't you worry." Eris grinned and cupped Cole's face in her hands. "How fast can you pack your suitcases?"

"Real fast if we help each other. Many hands make light work, after all."

"Then I suggest we use this time wisely. The sun's just rising, the day is beginning, we have a party to go to and play nice at. Then we have to leave this marvelous haven to head for the airport hotel ready to fly out. It's a busy day ahead."

Cole pouted. "We're in separate rooms there. I'm not liking that idea at all."

"Remember my role in *Code Red*?"

Cole nodded. She knew that series inside and out.

"Thanks to that show, I excel in performing covert operations that result in serious *undercover* work." She gave Cole a saucy wink.

"That's a real fancy way of saying you'll sneak into my room and get in bed with me, right?"

"You're not the only one who doesn't want to spend any more nights alone."

❖

Eris had playfully pushed Cole out of her room after a shared shower threatened to get steamier than the bathroom was getting and Eris's need for a cup of tea proved overwhelming. She walked into the kitchen and found Cassidy hovering over the coffee maker, oblivious to everything but the hissing sound of the machine as it brewed her drink. As unobtrusively as possible, Eris put the kettle on and watched Cassidy snatch up her cup from the machine the second it finished filling.

"Oh my God." Cassidy groaned sinfully after she'd taken a drink. "Nothing beats that first sip of coffee in a morning."

"Nothing? *Really*?" Cole asked as she walked in. She slipped her own cup in the machine and leaned back against the counter. She winked at Eris behind Cassidy's back.

Aiden walked in with her iPad. She kissed Cassidy and grimaced at her coffee-flavored lips. "I'll never understand how you can drink that stuff." She helped herself to the carton of orange juice from the fridge and poured a glass. "Eris, Cole, how was your meal out last night?"

Eris poured her tea and took a seat at the table. "It was beautiful. Thank you, Cassidy, for recommending the place. It got really busy, but we weren't kept waiting for our food. And the apple crumble was to die for."

Aiden nodded. "And how was Cole's meal?"

Cole gave Aiden a puzzled look. "It was great?"

"No, I'm asking *Eris* about your meal."

Eris wondered what Aiden was getting at. "It was a tikka masala. Why?"

Aiden held up her tablet so everyone could see. The lurid headline stood out big and bold across the screen.

Sharing food...and maybe something more?

Cole groaned, but Eris just stared at Aiden and shrugged. "She shared a bite of her meal with me to try it. It was delicious."

"I never saw anyone in there," Cole muttered. "And I was looking."

"Whereas I was just enjoying a meal in good company. You know how those sites love to grab people's attention with what-ifs. It's clickbait. We were just eating a meal."

Aiden grinned at her, clearly not angry. "They gave a lengthy report on us filming here and what the movie is about, and a nod to my book too, so it's some very nice free publicity." She looked at the screen. "You two look great, by the way. Photos taken in haste in restaurants aren't usually as good as this one."

Eris could see Aiden wasn't mad they'd garnered a headline on an entertainment site that made the *National Enquirer* look highbrow. "I'm just thankful they didn't catch me dripping custard from my crumble down my chin."

"Is there anything else you'd like to tell us?" Aiden nonchalantly sipped her orange juice.

"Like what?" Eris countered, keeping her expression deliberately neutral and not daring to look at Cole who had tensed.

Aiden laughed at her. "No wonder your sister never got grounded for sneaking out. You're very good." She took another drink from her glass. "You know, there's another reason why Mischa put us in rooms so far apart."

"It was so you two could have privacy when Cassidy arrived." Eris wondered where Aiden was going with this line of conversation.

"Yes, but Mischa saw something with you two that made her make sure you had privacy too."

Eris couldn't stop her jaw from dropping. Cole's silence showed she was surprised too. Cassidy just laughed at them.

"Oh, all-seeing, all-knowing Mischa is never wrong in the affairs of the heart. Besides, I happened to see Cole sneaking out of your bedroom this morning wrapped in a towel. I'm guessing she wasn't just helping you be environmentally conscious and conserving water." She took her seat beside Aiden and reached for the iPad. "This photo is out there now, put your own spin on it. Use it to your advantage."

Eris took her phone from her pocket and looked up the site. She made sure to get the name of the photographer and then copied the photo. She opened up her Twitter account, tagged in the *A Pocket Full of Time* account, and began typing.

Last day of filming here. Celebrating with @ColeCalder over an excellent tikka masala @CaptainJacksRestaurant. Excellent service, go try the crumble! Thank you, London. #APocketFullOfTime photo by @AFCribbins

Eris posted her piece and heard everyone's phone ding as they received a notification of a post on the official site.

Aiden nodded. "That's perfect. That should diffuse their headline and have that photo under our control now, spinning our narrative."

"We'll be more careful," Cole said, worry clouding her tone.

"You're entitled to your private life, Cole. This is a perfectly innocent picture. You're in a restaurant, you're eating. You're not standing on the bar half naked, dancing to LeAnn Rimes, and pouring beer for the masses."

Eris grinned. "We were going to do that later, but I've seen Cole's dancing."

"Hey!" Cole grumbled.

"You know what I said." Aiden looked over her shoulder at Cole. "Just be circumspect on set. We've been careful with our choices in cast and crew, but some still like the excitement of leaking things to the press. It's the nature of the business you're in. Publicity is publicity, good or bad." She gave them both a smile. "But I'm happy for you both. You make a striking couple and one hell of a team. But I'm not using your budding romance to sell the movie. That's your private life, so guard it well. Hollister and Emily will have their own story to tell separate from yours."

Eris knew she was blushing. Cole's own smile was abashed. Their first time acknowledged as a couple. They both jumped when Cassidy clapped her hands.

"So! We have a party to attend to bid our UK cast and crew farewell and thank them for all the footage. Then back here to grab up all our many suitcases." She cut Aiden a wicked side-eye at her snort. "My apologies, all *my* suitcases and Aiden's pitiful few, then pile into a taxi and head to the airport. One last night here in the land of our birth," she nodded to Eris, "and then home to America to hole up inside the studio for the next few months. The indoor sets are completed, our crew is ready. Oh, and Mischa has promised a welcome home party to end all parties…"

"Oh God," Aiden muttered. "I swear she throws a party at the drop of a hat."

"Hush, she's planning our wedding so we know it's going to be spectacular."

Eris found Aiden's face most entertaining. It was both resigned and joyful at that news. A strange contradiction she often wore in the presence of Mischa.

Cassidy leaned across the table to pat at Eris's hand. "She's thinking of getting these cupcakes made. The icing is all pink frills and swirls like labia, complete with a small edible pearl set at the top. Mischa says she's going to tell everyone to just lick right up the middle…" She mimed exactly what she meant.

Aiden choked so hard on her orange juice she had to have Cole pound her on her back to help her to breathe. She mopped at her mouth with a napkin and stared at an unrepentant Cassidy.

"Please tell me you're joking."

Cassidy played coy. "You said I could have anything I wished for. Mischa took that and ran with it."

"Oh my God." Aiden hid her face in her hands. "Isn't it enough she's your maid of honor and already planning a bachelorette night to end all bachelorette nights?"

"She's more experienced in throwing a party than I'll ever be. She wants us to have the best and she knows the best caterers." Cassidy switched her attention to Cole and Eris. "Ladies, you'll be getting your invitations. We can't not invite our leading ladies from our first ever blockbuster movie."

"From your lips to God's ears." Aiden's muffled voice came from behind her hands.

Eris shared a look with Cole. "That would be lovely, wouldn't it?"

Cole nodded. "Absolutely. Besides, cupcakes are my favorite." Her wicked grin made even Aiden laugh.

Chapter Thirteen

Brooke Harman stared at the headline on her laptop screen until it burned itself on her retinas and became all she could see.

Sharing food...and maybe something more?

She studied every inch of the photograph. She saved it to her downloads and brought it up separately so she could enlarge key areas and look more closely at the expressions on Cole's and Eris's faces. On the surface, the photo looked innocent enough. But Cole was Maria's, and everything inside of Brooke was screaming at her to throw her laptop on the floor and smash the screen to bits. She wanted to obliterate that incriminating photo, shatter it to a million pieces, and destroy the evidence that Cole had apparently moved on.

She brought up her Twitter feed and prepared to dash off a nasty tweet on Eris's page just to stir up trouble. She noticed another Morter fan had beaten her to it. Brooke was set to add her fuel to the fire when she caught sight of the numerous and lengthy comments the first post had received. Eris's fans had swooped in en masse and were standing up for her. They warned this person off, telling her not to bring delusional shipping wars onto Eris's Twitter feed. Whoever ran Eris's site had put out a message that there would be zero tolerance for bullying, either of the actress or of her fans. It was a bold move stating any hate was to be immediately blocked and the author reported. Brooke backed away. That was a fight she'd start another day. She switched instead to the Morter site, her safe haven.

There was a stream of unhappy tweets from people blocked from Eris's page for complaining about her and Cole being "together." Brooke sat back a little in her chair and considered her next move.

She typed up a quick tweet calling for the Morter fans to not watch the last episode where Cole left the show. Immediately, the general response to that idea was a resounding no. Everyone wanted to see Chris leave to believe it was really happening. They were holding out hope for a scene between her and Nat. Maybe a kiss, some were praying for a declaration of love, anything that would reveal that the show's producers had finally realized this was the show's best couple and were giving the fans what they wanted in Cole's final scenes. All hoped for Chris and Nat's relationship to be finally recognized and that there'd be an indication that Cole might return at a later date.

Brooke fervently wanted every scenario they dreamed up too but knew they were clutching at straws. She began devising her own plans. Cole had left, that much was obvious. And Cole and Eris socializing outside of them filming together was not what Brooke wanted to see.

"You know you're Maria's." Brooke brought the dining photo back up and stared at Cole. "I didn't spend months planting false rumors of you two having an affair for you to waste it on this new girl. She's not Maria. That idiot husband of hers wavers every time a rumor appears in his emails. He's so easy to get to. He never even changed his private email address from the one listed on his company website."

Brooke brought up Photoshop and painstakingly began to alter the dining photo to her own ends. She cut Eris out of the photo, taking delight in removing her head and replacing it with a photo of Maria instead. Piece by piece, she changed the coloring on Maria's skin to match the tone set in the photograph. Adding shadow and shadings, changing angles and expressions, Brooke finally leaned back in her chair and cast a critical eye on what she had rendered. The photo composition looked unchanged, except now Maria Ramos sat opposite Cole Calder. She was smiling at her, ready to take the morsel Cole was offering her as they enjoyed their clandestine date.

Brooke saved the file then opened up one of her secondary email accounts. She had at least eleven aliases online, all untraceable back to her. She'd spent hours arguing with herself on chat boards, easily manipulating the fans into believing other viewers were seeing something more in Cole's and Maria's performances. That every line they shared was dripping with subtext, their eyes and body language conveying more than what the scene had told them to play. That the obvious attraction the characters were trying to hide on the show had spilled over into their real lives and it was only a matter of time before Maria left her husband and moved in with Cole. They were *endgame*, pure and simple.

Brooke sent the photo without a message straight to Rico Ramos's inbox. Maybe if he walked out then Cole could walk right in to comfort Maria and take his place. Brooke would take whatever it took to bring them together to fulfil her fantasy of these two women.

Cole's last episode was airing soon. Brooke knew it would kill her to watch it. Cole was deliberately walking away from the show. Away from Chris and Nat. And Maria.

And, unforgivably, from *Brooke*.

"I need to do something more." Brooke walked over to the wall covered in photos and autographs and artwork of her favorite couple. "What do I have to do to get you to see what I see you share?" She absently picked up her phone as the notifications tone rang out.

Cole was back in the States. Posted online was a photo of Cole, accompanied by Eris, Aiden, and Cassidy, all walking through the airport.

Welcome home, Brooke thought, smiling at the photograph of Cole pushing her luggage cart through the crowded passenger lounge.

And back to Maria, where you belong.

Rendered helpless by her sister's crushing hug, Eris had no choice but to drop her suitcases and wrap her arms around her. She'd barely stepped a foot inside the back door of the restaurant before she'd been deafened by an excited squeal and her sister descending on her.

"Oh, I've missed you so much!" Melanie swayed them both from side to side playfully. "Tell me everything! I want to know all the things you left out of your emails and our calls."

"I will, as soon as you let me breathe." Eris laughed at her sister's sulky pout as she reluctantly let go and eased back a little. "Thank you, now let me say hi to my nephew or niece." Eris bent down a little to talk to the obvious baby bump Melanie sported. "Hi, baby! Auntie Eris is back and I brought you a British bear from Hamleys."

Melanie ran a hand across her stomach. "Baby's moving." Eris put her hand out and Melanie guided it to follow the flutters and bumps against her belly. "This kid knows your voice."

"They know I'm going to be the cool aunt." Eris smiled at the movement she could feel. "I missed this. I swear you've gotten bigger in just the few weeks I've been away."

"And I'm only going to get bigger. Enough of the bump. I want to hear what it was like going home to shoot on your first movie set." She reached to pick up a suitcase, but Eris smacked her hand away.

"Don't you even dare," Eris warned her and gathered her suitcases back up.

"I missed you, but your nagging…not so much."

Eris ignored her and started up the stairs to the apartment above the restaurant. She left her bags outside her bedroom door and set about making them a cup of tea. Melanie settled in a chair at the table, watching her putter about.

"I can't believe Mom and Dad missed seeing you. Damn, that was lousy timing. Last I heard from them, Mom was sampling every inappropriately named cocktail drink and Dad was only just finding his sea legs."

"Poor Dad." Eris sympathized with him. Time spent on the water wasn't one of her favorite pastimes either.

"I'm glad you got to go to the cemetery."

"I only managed the one trip. We were on a tight schedule and the typical British weather didn't help. Rain kept forcing us to hold off filming, otherwise continuity would have been shot to hell."

"I miss the erratic rainfalls," Melanie said mournfully.

"Me too, until it started getting annoying when I was stuck standing around under an umbrella in my period costume that didn't appreciate getting sodden. It was heavy enough."

"You look so beautiful in it though." Melanie took the mug Eris handed her and began to liberally sweeten it with honey. "You've had some fantastic roles, but this one seems to just *fit* you."

"So far it's been my favorite shoot. I'm looking forward to seeing the sets they have waiting for us. Aiden is so excited about them. She's so enthusiastic about her story on the big screen. I want to do my best for her. To make my portrayal of Emily be exactly what Aiden envisioned when she wrote her."

"It's unusual having the writer on board so much though, isn't it?"

Eris sat down opposite her and carefully measured out her own honey into her mug. "Yes, but this company is new and going about things in a totally different way than I've seen before. It was a less rigid production, but no less managed. It wasn't like that indie movie I did when half the time the director didn't turn up because he was too stoned to stand. I like how Darrow/Hayes Productions works. It's very female orientated, and that brings a whole different vibe to the set as well. I'm having the most fantastic time. And it was wonderful being back home for a while where it was decidedly cooler." Eris quickly got up from her seat. "Before I forget. You need to stick these in the fridge before they melt into one big lump. I nearly had heat stroke stepping off the plane. Talk about going from one extreme to another." She pulled out a large bag from her carry-on bag and laid it on the table before Melanie as if it were treasure.

Melanie tipped the bag over and dumped a pile of chocolate all over the table. "Oh my God! The motherlode of Cadbury's and Mars!" She picked through the assorted bars and bags. She held up a big bag of Curly Wurlys. "My favorites!" She chortled like a mad woman then gathered all the other bags of that particular brand and put them to one side. "No one is touching those or I'll release the baby-making hormones on them." She began separating all the other candy into the fridge. "Georgio can have one of his Flakes tonight. I'll make him a sundae and sprinkle one on top. He'll think we're back in college." She peered over her shoulder at Eris. "Thank you. I miss our chocolate."

"I brought myself a big supply of jelly babies, and an extra couple of bags for Kerry who delivers your fruit and veg. She's a *Doctor Who* fan so she'll get a kick out of them."

Melanie sat back down and opened a Curly Wurly. She dipped the thin chocolate covered toffee bar into her tea, waited for a moment, then sucked on the melted treat. "Tell me all about you and this cast you were with and all the gossip about Cassidy Hayes and Mischa Ballantyne. I can't believe you got to stay at Mischa's house."

"I couldn't either. I was expecting to be living out of my suitcase in a hotel. Her house was wonderful, as you saw from the photos I sent. And it had a hot tub!"

"Did you get to use it?"

Eris put on her most innocent face and nodded while trying to hide behind her mug.

Melanie squinted at her. "Don't give me that look. It works on Mom and Dad, but I know better. Give!"

"What? There's nothing!" Eris deliberately teased her sister, knowing it would drive her crazy until Eris gave in. What were little sisters for other than to annoy their older siblings, Eris thought, enjoying watching Melanie trying to read her face.

"Okay, let me try this another way. Did you get to use the hot tub with anyone *else*?"

Eris was impressed. Her sister was catching on fast. She gave her an enigmatic smile. "Maybe."

"God, you can be annoying," Melanie muttered, dunking her bar into her drink. "Spill the beans, or I'll withhold the tiramisu I have downstairs with your name on it."

Eris laughed. "You play dirty, big sister. Okay, I shared it with Cole after we'd both had a strenuous day of running up and down the cobbled streets of merry ol' England in shoes not graced with memory foam inserts."

"You shared a hot tub with your love interest from the movie?"

"I did."

"The same love interest you took to the cemetery with you?"

"She loved the views. You know Americans and their love of history. That place teems with it."

"You realize this is why your love life is MIA. A walk in a cemetery isn't exactly the same as a romantic walk in the moonlight."

Eris couldn't help but feel smug. "Still got me the girl though."

Melanie nearly choked on her chocolate. "You're fucking kidding me, right?"

"Hey, impressionable little ears being formed." Eris pointed at Melanie's bump.

"The baby is blissed out on chocolate, I'm sure." Melanie waved at her dismissively. "You and Cole Calder? Oh my God!"

Eris was laughing at her shock until she spotted tears begin to run down Melanie's face. Eris rushed to her and knelt beside her. "Are you okay?"

Melanie slapped her on the shoulder. "I'm happy for you. These are happy tears. These are 'oh my God, my sister got a woman who is totally drop-dead gorgeous' tears."

"Yes, she is. Inside and out."

"You never said anything in your emails."

"That's because it's just a day or so since we decided to stop ignoring what was staring us right in the face."

Melanie grabbed Eris's face in her hands and cooed. "Ohhh, a budding romance! All bright and new and shiny. That's so sweet!" Her tone darkened dramatically. "You need to bring her home."

Eris sighed. "She doesn't need your shovel talk."

"I need to know she's good enough for my baby sister."

"She's very good *to* your baby sister," Eris said, still feeling the comfort from Cole's arms around her. Mischa had arranged a car for them at the airport and they'd dropped Cole off first. Their kiss good-bye had been lingering, their parting a physical ache that Eris could still feel.

"I haven't seen you look like this before." Melanie gave Eris a swift kiss to her forehead while she was still beside her.

"Like what?"

"Happy. There's a light in your eyes that you haven't had when you've told me about your other girlfriends."

Eris agreed. Whatever was between her and Cole was so different from anything she'd ever experienced before. "She's not like any other woman I've met. And before you ask, it's got nothing to do with the fact we're playing lovers in the movie. I've been in proximity to many women on a set and never once been drawn to one like I have been to Cole."

"I know you, Eris. You don't blur the lines between character and actress. When can I meet her?"

Eris bit at her lip, wondering if this was all too soon but knowing that Cole was eager to meet Melanie too. "Can I book a table for five sometime this week? We have a few days off before shooting starts again, and I'd love to invite Mischa, Cassidy, Aiden, and Cole to a meal here. Do you have a nice, quiet, out of the way table where we could entertain my producers and my lover?"

Melanie grinned. "I'll make room and will endeavor to blow their taste buds to bits with what we serve. Wow." Melanie's eyes sparkled. "Four amazingly talented actresses, and a writer of renown, at a table in my restaurant. Georgio is going to be excited and proud to serve you all. Don't worry, sweetie, I'll make sure you won't be on show for your meal. There'll be no paparazzi sneaking shots of you sharing food with your sweetheart this time. I'll keep you from prying eyes."

Eris hugged her as best she could around the bump. "Thank you."

"Now, tell me how you went from acting beside Cole to finding your soul mate."

Eris pulled back. "I never said anything about that."

Melanie smiled. "You didn't need to say anything. Your eyes are saying it all. I know that look. It's the same look I've seen in the mirror countless times since I met Georgio. I've waited a long time to see it shining from your face. Granddad always said it was like a light shining out from your eyes."

"It's too soon to really know," Eris hedged, even though in her heart she knew exactly how deeply she felt.

Melanie shrugged. "When you know, you know. So, put the kettle on again. I'm not due back in the kitchen until the evening rush. Come tell me all about this woman who looks," she placed her hands over her bump as if covering little ears, "fucking amazing in her suit and top hat. I can see the attraction. She's quite the stunner."

"She's all that and more. How much do you want to know?"

"Every salacious detail." Melanie settled herself in her chair.

"I had my first ever multiple orgasm with her."

"Goddamn lesbians," Melanie grumbled with more than a hint of jealously in her voice.

Eris just grinned and tried not to skip around the kitchen like a giddy child. "Let me tell you the tale of two women and a romance that you could only write about."

Chapter Fourteen

The atmosphere around the table was exuberant. Cole was unable to recall previous nights out where the food had been as delicious or the company quite so entertaining. Eris had invited Cole, Aiden, Cassidy, and Mischa to her sister's restaurant. They had a private room all to themselves where they were relaxing and chatting freely.

Eris had been regaling them with behind-the-scenes tales on *Code Red*. Cole had been fascinated to hear Eris's experiences on it but equally distracted by Eris's touch. Eris's left hand lay on Cole's thigh, and when she got excited she'd squeeze Cole a little tighter. Cole was loath to move. She loved the possessiveness of Eris's hand on her. Cole slipped her own hand under the table and rested it on top of Eris's, keeping her there, needing to feel her too.

Opposite them, Mischa sat deliberately between Cassidy and Aiden, soaking up the attention she received from them both. It was plain to see Mischa was thrilled to have her friends back on home soil. Mischa was effervescent as always as she kept the conversation flowing with her endless curiosity about Eris's and Cole's previous roles, interspersed with her teasing of Cassidy, and topped off by her own brand of salacious gossip. Cole had given up trying to drink after nearly choking on her beer at one particular sexually graphic anecdote. Instead she watched as Mischa delved into another round of gossip, seated between her best friends like a mischievous child. She clearly enjoyed making Cassidy laugh along with her and have Aiden roll her eyes at their antics.

"So I told her, 'Darling, you don't have to keep telling me how many women propositioned you in the bathrooms at the Oscar ceremony. Granted, I'm impressed you still manage to pull young women considering your *advancing* age…'"

Cassidy sucked in a sharp breath while Aiden grimaced comically at the cutting words, all deliberately delivered in Mischa's undeniable charming manner.

"It does, however, say more about the kind of people you attract," Mischa continued, "where their pick-up line of 'do you come here often' is uttered amid the smell of disinfectant. It doesn't exactly drip of romance, does it?"

Cassidy laughed. "And what did she say to that?"

"Well, she tried to frown at me, but she's had so much work done to her face that only one eyebrow managed to move. It looked like a drunken caterpillar trying to inch its way down her wrinkle free, wax-like, face." Mischa picked up her glass and took a sip. "I'm never getting plastic surgery. I'm going to grow old disgracefully. My face will have character and my laughter lines will have the last laugh as I get to play feisty old ladies while the nipped and tucked get splashed all over the *National Enquirer* when another procedure is botched."

Mischa sighed as she finished her story and leaned into Cassidy. "God, I missed you two," she said for the umpteenth time. "I wish I could have stayed in London with you both." She looked across the table at Eris and Cole. "I missed you two as well. I can't believe you waited until I left before you started f—"

"Mischa!" Aiden said, cutting off whatever word was going to spill from Mischa's lips.

"What?" Mischa looked innocently around at them all. "I was going to say 'fraternizing,' but whatever your dirty mind thought I was going to say works just as well too." She raised her glass toward Eris and Cole. "Cheers to you both as you embark on the joys of an on-set romance. May you break the trend and live happily ever after like these two beside me. At least I got to see their blossoming romance from the onset. I'd like to think I helped it along."

Cassidy snorted. "Darling, you flirted shamelessly with Aiden from the start."

"I'd read all her books before you even knew her name." Mischa laid her head on Aiden's shoulder. "You're still my favorite author."

Aiden smiled and thanked her while continuing with her meal as if these two women fighting over her was a regular thing.

Mischa suddenly sat up. "Talking of toilets. Cass, remember that convention in Chicago that one time? That's the worst thing about convention halls, you don't always get a separate bathroom from the masses. And there's nothing worse than a fan who gets off on the fact that they can run to their little friends and announce, 'I heard Mischa Ballantyne peeing!'" Mischa shuddered dramatically. "Some fans seem to think that it's okay to talk to you over the top of the stall while you have your underwear down around your ankles and are in mid flow."

"Oh my God," Cassidy groaned. "I remember that one."

"Thankfully, my crazy-assed fan left the door open to her stall as she scrambled up on the toilet seat to converse with me. Sweet Cassidy came to my rescue and yanked her down, hauled her out of the bathroom, and dragged her off to security." Mischa buzzed a kiss on Cassidy's cheek. "Swear to God, you saved me from the worst selfie opportunity ever."

"Some fans are just plain crazy," Cole said, thinking of what some of her own had done. She tried to push those thoughts firmly out of her head.

Aiden and Cassidy shared a poignant look. "No argument from us there."

Cole felt awful. "Oh fuck, Aiden. I'm so sorry, I never even thought…" Cole didn't know what to say. She gave Eris a pleading look to rescue the situation and her.

Cassidy reached over to pat Cole's arm in comfort. "It's okay, Cole. It's been, what, nearly three years since Bernett stepped out of his stalking shadows and tried to kill us. We've dealt with the consequences that came from what he did to us, both physically and mentally. We sat through a lot of therapy and learned to leave him in the past while we moved forward. Neither of us will lose the scars he left us with, Aiden especially." Cassidy reached across

Mischa to take Aiden's hand. Mischa rested her own on top of them, uncharacteristically silent for once. "But the business Aiden and I are in means we're never going to get away from fans and their sometimes impossible expectations of us. We chose to stay in the business and not let him frighten us off from our life's works."

Aiden looked up from her meal. "Anyone who puts themselves out there, as a musician, an actress, even a writer, leaves themselves open to people who love their work but don't always have a healthy reaction to it. Or the person behind it. In my opinion, it's gotten worse with the introduction of the internet which grants us all greater access to whatever we wish for. I'm not knocking social media, though. That would be redundant. It lets us show our product, it gathers fans to us, it generates interest in what we do, and we need that to sell our work. But the negative side is that some people then think they own a piece of *us*. Both Cassidy and I have had to learn the hard way that not all fans just want to enjoy what you put out into the world. They think because they see Cassidy on TV and online that she is there *personally* for them, at *all* hours, *every* day. Just a click of a button away on a message board, in an email, or a direct message online with whatever problem they need to solve at that moment. We understand so many people out there are lonely. But you can't place your only reason for being here on the shoulders of a celebrity who doesn't really know you exist. You're a voice among the many…which is why some, who can't cope with that, decide to make themselves *seen*."

Cassidy nodded. "And if you get to know your fans, then that can become a balancing act. There are the normal ones who love to meet and greet with you, get a photo, maybe an autograph, and support you in everything you do. Then there are the ones who follow you to your hotel room, sit in the bar and watch you drink, follow you everywhere, all the time trying to ingratiate themselves into your life. They'll try anything and everything to get themselves *close* to you, to befriend you. To be there for you in their mind alone."

"That happened to our friend Sheryl, didn't it?" Mischa said. "She was on tour singing, had quite the career going, and had a group of girls who followed her devotedly. They all had sad stories of how their parents/brother/friends were so mean, and how it was Sheryl's music that had saved them. Sheryl listened to them talk for hours after her concerts and tried to help as best she could. But she's not their mother, or their sister, or their family. They took her kindness and it made her *theirs*. They started chasing other fans off with their bullying tactics. They became totally possessive of Sheryl's attention. She lost her career over it because you can't get famous with only five fans at the stage. Their spiteful actions wrecked her dreams." Mischa stood up. "And on that note, if you'll excuse me, I need to use the little girls' room."

Cassidy watched her leave. "Mischa was faithfully by my side throughout the stalking, and she was there when Aiden was shot. She witnessed a side to fandom she'd never had to face before. But no two performers' experiences are ever the same. She's been our rock."

"She came and cheered me on through my physiotherapy sessions. Admittedly, she was also chatting with half the patients in the room and flirting with my very handsome, according to her, PT instructor. Her inimitable style of support stopped me from wallowing in self-pity. She kept Cassidy together when she blamed herself for me being shot." Aiden shifted seats and pulled Cassidy close to her. "I wouldn't hesitate for a second to stand in front of Cassidy again. I'd do everything in my power to keep her safe. And I did. And we're here, we're safe, and he's dead." The finality in Aiden's tone was chilling for someone usually so laid-back. Cassidy crowded in closer to her as if seeking comfort from the shadow that had stalked her.

"Did they ever find out what his trigger was? What made him tip from fan to fanatic?" Eris asked.

"Oh, they found a million little reasons why he thought he and I should be together," Cassidy said. "We'd met years before on a set and I'd spoken to him in passing. That was all it needed. It all made sense in the imaginary world he lived in where we were destined to be a couple. He was delusional and I starred in his twisted little fantasies until it wasn't enough anymore and he came for me."

"Some people don't need a reason. They have a fixed plan in their head of what you should be in their lives. What you want to do with your life means nothing to them because you should be doing only what *they* want. Play only the roles *they* want you to play. Like their tweet when they post on your page demanding your attention." Aiden looked directly at Cole. "I know you have some overzealous fans calling for you to return to *Fortune's Rise.*"

Mischa wandered back into the room, took Aiden's seat, and began to eat off Aiden's plate. "Donatella warned us of the noise they're making. And their ways and means of going about being your most devoted fans."

"I wish she hadn't. I have my manager dealing with it." Cole shifted in her seat, angry that what she'd tried to keep quiet was becoming common knowledge.

"The rumors concerning you and Maria reached my circle of confidants months ago." Mischa used her fork to reach over and take a piece of meat from Cole's plate. "I knew they weren't true. Everyone just laughed it off. I mean, sending doctored photos to the husband was so amateurish, it had to be a fan with an axe to grind. And his reaction really didn't do him any favors. He gave them the satisfaction they'd been after. Posting 'look at me and my wife, we're so happy' photos every other day was so desperate of him. Proclaiming their love and happy marriage on Instagram was also overkill. I don't know why Maria agreed to it. She looked so damn miserable in every photo he posted."

Cassidy agreed. "They looked like the *American Gothic* painting, all sour faces and stoic attitudes."

Cole was mortified. "Does *everyone* know what he accused me of?"

"Enough do. He drinks with actors, word gets around like wildfire in Tinsel Town. Ignore him. He's what my dear friend Cassidy would call a wanker. No one believed him. Your reputation is a stellar one, Cole. It's sad, because you were the one that lost out in the end." Mischa waved the piece of meat at Cole. "Your girlfriend at the time? A nice girl by all accounts, but not the right woman for you." She took a bite off her fork then waved it in Eris's direction. "I don't see this one being quite so easily intimidated by idiot fans who spread lies for the childish pipe dream of getting you and Maria together."

Cole felt herself deflate in defeat. "I didn't want anyone to know. It was humiliating. It all sounds so fucking crazy what they've done. I never imagined that fans of the show could try to deliberately wreck the marriage of my costar and be the cause of a split in my personal life. All because they want to *ship* us together. And we're not even both *gay*. It infuriates me and I can't stop any of it."

"Donatella only told us because she fears these fans might try to sabotage the movie to win you back. After all, it's not like the petulant whining of so-called adults didn't end up hurting the female *Ghostbusters* movie, or that *Star Wars* can't even cast a female lead now without there being a disturbance in the Force," Aiden said, clearly fuming.

"Carrie Fisher would bitch slap them all. The original movie hinged on her character," Cassidy said.

"We know bad publicity can damage a production," Mischa said. "Unless it's *Captain Marvel* where Brie Larson got a billion dollars' worth of middle fingers to stick up at the whiny man babies. Alas, we're not Brie Larson. We're a small company just finding our feet in the movie business. We need to keep an eye on any group that might stop people from seeing your performances light up the screen."

"I'm sorry I didn't say anything. I was hoping it would just die down and go away and no one would hear of it." Cole felt the comfort of Eris's hand on her leg again. It steadied her.

"Oh, my dear sweet child," Cassidy drawled, teasing her gently. "This is Hollywood. There are no secrets here."

Melanie chose that moment to walk into the room carrying a tray laden with desserts. It broke the tense and uneasy atmosphere around the table. "I trust you're all enjoying your meals?"

Distracted by the sweet treats, Cassidy began clearing a large space in front of her. "You might as well reserve this room for us indefinitely. I can guarantee we'll be back to work our way through your menu."

Mischa waved Melanie over. "You and I need to talk. A little birdie tells me you cater for weddings, and I happen to know a couple tying the knot who have left me in charge of the big decisions."

Aiden gave Eris and Cole a look. "I was preparing to just cook a meal for our friends after we signed our papers, but Cassidy's having none of that. She wants something a little more grandiose to celebrate the day. And what Cassidy wants, she gets." Aiden gave Cassidy an adoring look and Cassidy snuggled into her, equally smitten. "I do have the perfect suit picked out for the day though." Aiden leaned over the table conspiratorially, making sure Mischa's attention was elsewhere. "I'll be wearing a Superman tee underneath my shirt so Cassidy can rip it open *Lois & Clark* style for the official wedding pictures. That was my one concession."

Cassidy clapped her hands together in glee. "It's going to be a blast! I do love my Aiden's geeky side."

Cole sat back and watched the atmosphere in the room shift from somber to excited again. She wanted these people on her side. She needed these kinds of friends that were loyal and true. She felt Eris squeeze her hand again and welcomed her warmth as she leaned in to rest her head on Cole's shoulder.

"It's going to be all right, Cole. We'll get through this together," Eris whispered in her ear.

If this is what a soul mate feels like, then I want it. I want her. I want Eris by my side for whatever our future holds.

"And I'd like to thank all the fans from the bottom of my heart for all your support of us and the show. We wouldn't be here if it wasn't for you guys. I love you all! I'll see you at the meet and greets this weekend, and I hope you'll join Cole and me on our first solo panel together. It's so exciting! You'd better have your questions ready about Chris and Nat. Especially the one you're all desperate to know! 'Will they, won't they?'"

Brooke smiled at the video she was watching on her phone. She loved the way Maria teased the audience, she looked so happy to be center stage talking to the *Fortune's Rise* fans. Cole stood beside her, happily letting Maria do all the talking. Brooke buzzed the convention footage forward. She had been there and had videoed every second she could of Maria and Cole on stage. She'd sneakily managed to capture footage at the private meet and greet sessions, and even got some photos of them signing autographs. It had been a fun weekend. Brooke paused the video at her favorite moment. The moment that vindicated her shipping these two women. Shipping both their characters, and them personally.

Maria and Cole were laughing on stage as Maria answered the inevitable question of whether their characters would ever become romantically involved in the show. The audience had screamed when Cole had handed the microphone over to Maria.

"Sure, put me on the spot," Maria joked. "Okay, okay." She tried to quiet the boisterous audience so she could answer. "I can see why you ship Chris and Nat. They do strike sexy sparks off each other, don't they?" The audience erupted again with cheers and whistles. "I can see it. I get it. I mean, come on, just look at her." She pointed at Cole. "Would anyone seriously pass up the chance to be with a woman as gorgeous as Cole?"

It took a while for the audience to calm down again as they hollered and whooped. Brooke loved how red Cole turned and looked embarrassed by all the attention. Maria just laughed at her. She slipped an arm around Cole's waist which only set the audience off more. The woman who'd asked the question had to shout into the microphone to ask again. "*Will* the show ever give us you two as a couple?"

The audience cheered, and Maria and Cole just laughed at their exuberance. Maria looked at Cole and deliberately pointed the microphone at her. Cole shrugged and then leaned forward to answer.

"I don't honestly know. For now they're just antagonistic neighbors."

The audience groaned, clearly dissatisfied.

Cole shrugged again, carefully measuring her words. "I guess all I can say is, never say never."

Brooke rewound the clip a fraction and played it again.

"Never say never."

She rewound it again.

"Never say never."

"Never say never," Brooke whispered. She looked up from the screen and stared directly into a window at Andino's restaurant. From where she'd parked her car she could see into the back dining room area. She'd managed to catch glimpses of Eris and Cole all evening, along with their guests. Brooke checked her watch. The restaurant would close soon. She'd followed Cole on her motorcycle to the restaurant hours ago. The distinctive motorcycle wasn't hard to miss, and Brooke had long since worked out what part of town Cole lived in and had even narrowed it down to an apartment block.

She just hadn't been able to find the exact apartment number yet.

Not for want of trying, Brooke thought. She'd even resorted to flirting with an old man she'd seen exiting the building in the hopes he'd invite her in and she could go snooping around the floors. He hadn't been very helpful other than eyeing her up and down and asking her how much she charged by the hour before getting into his car. Later that night, Brooke had slashed his tires and scratched out *prick* on every free surface. It had taken her so long to wreck his tires that she had toyed with the idea of searching the apartment block for him and stabbing him instead. A small voice of reason pulled her back from attempting it. However, it didn't stop the thought from resurfacing multiple times as she stabbed at his tires and ripped them apart.

Brooke watched the window. She wondered what they were talking about. Would Cole be talking about her fans bombarding the *Fortune's Rise* Twitter account, calling for her to come back to the show? Brooke had instigated a stream of polls from her different accounts, all designed around favorite characters wanted back on TV shows. She'd stayed up all night setting off voting bots so that Cole's win was uncontested, tagging the show with the results. She checked multiple sites for any leaks from the set concerning Maria and how she was taking the split. She'd scrolled through endless streams of conversations, leaving nasty comments on any who inevitably posted for fans to "move on."

"We'll show them all when we get our Morter endgame," Brooke muttered. For now she had to put up with Cole hanging around her new cast and crew while she finished the movie.

She sat up straighter at a flurry of movement from the back room. She waited, barely breathing, her eyes trained on the exit that led to the parking lot. Brooke had deliberately parked in a less lit area. She intended to follow Cole home, just to try to talk to her. To make her realize that she needed to be back with Maria on their show.

Cassidy and Aiden bid everyone good night with hugs. Mischa did something that had Cassidy pulling her away while everyone laughed. Eris and Cole waved them off as they left in Mischa's car. Brooke lifted her phone and hoped she wasn't shaking too much to get a shot of Cole leaving the restaurant. She snapped a few shots, her mind occupied with framing the shot just right to show it really was Cole. Her phone screen was darker than she would have liked, but she had to make do. Then she realized what she was seeing. Cole had pulled Eris into her arms and was kissing her slowly and passionately. Brooke's phone slipped from her fingers to drop with a thud on the floor of her car. Bile rose in her throat and anger followed swift in its wake. She balled her fists tighter and tighter the longer the kissing continued. She couldn't tear her eyes away from what she was seeing. It was hot and arousing, but Cole was kissing the *wrong* woman.

Eris ran her hand up and down Cole's back. She tucked a hand into the back pocket of Cole's jeans, cupping a butt cheek.

Brooke bit back a scream. She sank her teeth into her tongue to stop herself from yelling at them and releasing her pain at Cole's betrayal.

Cole pressed kisses along Eris's face before taking her lips again as if she was starving for their touch. Brooke felt the sting of pain as her nails broke through the skin on her palms. She welcomed it. She ignored the blood that began to run onto her flesh and dripped onto her skirt. She was numb to it all but the sight of Cole cheating on Maria.

Eventually, Cole put her helmet on. Eris leaned in for one last kiss and then stood back while Cole started her motorcycle and finally drove away.

Eris remained at the back door of the restaurant for a moment longer. She turned and called someone's name. A heavily pregnant woman joined her. Brooke could just about make out their conversation.

"You need to get that light fixed over there," Eris said, pointing in Brooke's direction. "It's not safe. That car underneath it is in shadow."

"Funny, it was working last night," the other woman said. "I'll get one of the guys to take a look in the morning."

Brooke waited for them to go back inside before she pulled out of the lot. She'd missed her chance to follow Cole but was too angry now to go after her and confront her on her infidelity.

She's ruining everything, Brooke mourned. She took her hand off the steering wheel and reached over to throw her makeshift slingshot into the glove compartment for the next time she needed a dark spot to spy from. It landed against her gun. Brooke slammed the compartment shut, then deliberately gripped the steering wheel tightly. There was a part of her that got off on the pain from her lacerated hands and the fact she was smearing blood all over the steering wheel.

Sacrifices had to be made to bring true loves back together. Cole's dalliance with Eris wouldn't last. She'd go running back to Maria as soon as she finished the movie. Eris was just a distraction.

Maria needed to rein Cole in. Brooke was more than willing to help her, whatever it took.

Chapter Fifteen

Eris was used to waking up to the familiar sounds of the restaurant below preparing for the day ahead. Here it was quiet, except for the soft hum from the ceiling fan that stirred a cool breeze. It was a gentle blessing on her warm skin. Eris deliberately kept her eyes closed, letting her senses reach out to touch her new surroundings. A soft sheet covered her nakedness. She stretched a little and smiled at the ache of muscles well exercised the night before. She sniffed a little at the air and easily caught the mingled scents of herself and Cole. The combination was heady, soothing and sensual, wild and sexy. Eris ran her tongue across her lips and could still faintly taste Cole. She remembered their lovemaking. It was soft and gentle to start, before switching to hard and desperate, until they both collapsed on the bed spent. They'd lain tangled in each other's arms, sweaty, smelling of sex, and grinning.

Eris looked over at Cole fast asleep beside her. She looked delectable. The sheet was low across her chest, exposing her breasts. Eris ached to kiss them again, but she was loath to wake Cole up just yet. Instead she drank her fill of just gazing at her. The short hair brought out Cole's strong features, and Eris ran her fingers across the soft bristles. She loved the feel of it. The style suited Cole so much more than the softer, more feminine cut she'd worn for her previous role.

"I could get used to this," Cole mumbled, turning her head on her pillow toward Eris's touch. She smiled sleepily as Eris ran her fingers through the cropped hair. "If you keep that up I'm likely to fall back to sleep."

Eris deliberately removed her hand and laughed at Cole's exaggerated pout. Eris couldn't resist. She lifted herself up and kissed Cole's pouty lip.

"There's better things we could be doing than sleeping away our day off."

Cole shifted on her side, pushing Eris onto her back so Cole could snuggle in closer. She nuzzled her face into Eris's neck and made her giggle. "Such as?"

"Well, I kind of have an idea I'd like to run by you."

Cole lifted her head and searched Eris's face. "Is that what has you awake way before we needed to greet the day?"

"My love, it's nearly midday. Sooner or later, we have to surface for food and coffee."

Cole lay back on the sheets and stretched like a big lazy cat. "I'm still sleepy. Someone kept me awake all night with her insatiable appetites."

Eris loved how satisfied Cole looked, spread naked on the bed, just begging for Eris to start all over again. She was tempted to put her idea on hold while she took all that Cole had to tempt her with. "You weren't complaining last night."

"My mouth was too busy elsewhere and I had my own appetites to feed." Cole's tone was smug and she stretched again then cracked open an eye at Eris. "So, come on. What has that beautiful brain of yours been working away on while mine was turned to mush?"

Eris hesitated, but one look at Cole's serious face gave her the impetus to speak. "I'm wondering if our director would let me choreograph the love scene we shoot next week."

Cole looked intrigued. "You do remember it's a PG-13 rating, right? We can't get up to half the stuff we did to each other last night." She trailed a hand over Eris's shoulder, down her arm, and cupped her breast. "And we did a lot of *stuff*."

Cole's thumb rubbing across Eris's nipple nearly derailed all thought from her head. Eris grabbed her hand and stilled it, enjoying the swiftness Cole had in bringing her body to life. "Let me get this out before I willingly give myself to you again."

Cole's grin was wicked. "Oh, I like the sound of that." She made a show of removing her hand from Eris's flesh and lay back against her pillow. She folded both hands under her head, keeping them away from touching.

Eris took a deep breath to quiet the need rushing through her veins. Cole laid out before her, unashamedly naked, was more than enough to scramble her thoughts. She tried to form words before she lost it all and just gave in to the sensual pull of Cole's body.

"I can see the scene perfectly in my head, Cole. I can't explain it. I know where to position the cameras and what lighting will keep our nudity in shadow but show enough for it to be real. I can see exactly how Hollister and Emily make love for that first time." Eris chewed on her bottom lip nervously. "I know they have ideas for how the scene should be, but I think we can do better than that. I want to give our audience the thrill of that first time Aiden wrote about, give the lesbian audience a love scene they can immerse themselves in, all while being respectful to the audience and the family friendly rating."

"Fuck respect. I want us showing red hot girl-on-girl passion in this movie." Cole pulled Eris down onto her. "Show me."

"Excuse me?"

"Show me your love scene, right here, right now, in my bed. Show me what you want us to do. Show me what Hollister and Emily share that first time." She reached up to plant a kiss on Eris's neck. Her tongue licked a little at a sensitive spot, making Eris shiver. She drew back to catch Eris's gaze. "You know I'm excellent at following direction."

Eris laughed at Cole's devilish grin and the sly wink she gave her. "You trust me with this scene?"

"With my life and heart too."

Eris's smile wavered at the seriousness in Cole's voice. She stared at Cole, reading her face, and saw only honesty and love. They hadn't spoken of that yet, but it was there, biding its time, waiting for the right moment. But Eris knew love was there. It had been from the start. Fate had brought them together, she had no doubt of that now. Her heart began to beat double time at the promise laid bare before her.

"I want everyone to see that moment when Hollister gives her love to Emily, knowing this is her soul mate, her one and only. That she has recognized her and will always recognize her."

"And willingly hands over her heart," Cole whispered,

"Exactly."

"We've already filmed the outdoor scene where Hollister walks Emily back home. Once inside they'll see Emily's father fast asleep by the fire and know he won't stir all night. Hollister goes to leave, but Emily takes her hand. By now she knows Hollister is a woman and this is where Emily makes her choice. Love over propriety. To take a woman to her bed would be considered shameful…"

"But there's nothing shameful about their love." Eris could see the scene so vividly in her mind's eye. Emily's bedroom, an old wooden bed, sheets worn and shabby but clean and neatly pressed. Nothing like the bed Eris was sharing now, with the soft sheets rumpled from their night of passion. "She leads Hollister to her room. Locks the door behind them. She's shaking but she doesn't know if it's from nerves or need. She takes off her hat, starts to undress slowly. She casts furtive looks at Hollister, desperate to know that she's doing the right thing."

Cole nodded, adding, "Hollister removes her hat and coat and, piece by piece, removes the clothing that lets her hide as a man in this time and revealing the woman she is."

Eris could see Cole was right there with her in the scene. This was going to be everything she'd hoped for and more. Hollister and Emily were in the room with them and their love affair was about to start.

"I want to remove your tie, to take part in Hollister's undressing. And I want Emily to touch you, a hand on your shirt perhaps when you remove it to reveal the binding underneath. She needs to help you and understand you as you peel those layers off. These clothes are how you survive. Removing them is dangerous, but she brings you her love and the promise she won't betray your trust." Eris ran her hand across Cole's chest. "Then I want the audience to see the same time as she does that you are very much a woman beneath the men's clothes."

"I've never done a nude scene before," Cole said.

"And you won't now." Eris ran her fingertips across Cole's breasts. "We can shoot just low enough to show the top of your breasts but nothing lower." She bent her head to press a soft kiss on each of Cole's nipples. "These are not for show."

Cole nodded. "Show me what you want, how you see this whole scene play out."

"You need to be above me to start," Eris said, lying down and helping Cole rise above her. "Your body will shield mine at first. Your hands will cover my breasts or your head lowered, giving the illusion of you sucking on me. The way I see it, our touches need to flow together like a sensuous dance where the audience will think they're seeing more than what they really are. They'll be watching us rising and reaching for each other and never notice that we are never truly nude before the camera."

Cole stretched above her, their legs intertwined and their faces close. "Just promise me one thing."

"What?"

"Don't do that thing with your tongue that has me spilling like a teenager because that would be the outtake to end all blooper reels."

Eris laughed at Cole's playfulness and nodded solemnly at her. "I promise to keep that strictly between us. Nothing of us appears on the screen. This is Hollister and Emily's scene." She reached out to run her hand over Cole's hair. "So let's show Emily what it's like to love a woman, Hollister."

"It would be my pleasure, ma'am."

Cole had never seen Eris as nervous as she was now. She was wringing her hands constantly under the table. Cole surreptitiously reached over to cover them, stilling Eris's agitation. They sat at a large table in the Darrow/Hayes offices. Aiden sat beside Cole. She was leaning back casually in her chair, but Cole knew Aiden was all business when it came to this movie. The movie's director, Olivia Todd, sat opposite, with the second unit director, Cynthia Steel, beside her. Both women made the sets a joy to work on. Eris had asked for a meeting and wanted Cole there because the scene Eris wanted to discuss involved her too. More honestly, Eris had told Cole she needed her there for moral support. Eris didn't really need it though. Cole knew Eris was confident in her ability to play the scene however the writers deemed fit. But Eris had a different idea, and Cole hoped they would all hear her out and not just dismiss her outright. They were professionals and all wanted the movie to succeed. Eris had proved herself over and over on the set. She had some innate sixth sense about what made a scene play better. Cole had witnessed it many times in their own scenes together. Eris just *knew* how to get the most from the lines and bring it all to life.

"Eris, the floor is all yours," Aiden said.

Eris took a deep, cleansing breath to center herself. For a moment, Cole fancied that she could see Eris's grandparents, one at each shoulder, telling Eris she could do this and urging her on. Cole removed her hands and Eris brought her own to the tabletop. She pressed her palms into the wood as if to steady herself. Then, in a calm voice and with an authoritative air, Eris walked them all through the movie's love scene. The love scene that she and Cole had been practicing every night for a week until they knew it by heart and gave it life off the screen.

Mesmerized by Eris's extensive knowledge of the technical aspects of their work, Cole sat almost bursting with pride as Eris not only set out the scene but also the layout of the room for the cameras and lighting. Cole had worked on enough sets to have a rudimentary idea of where to place a camera, but Eris was using terms Cole had never heard of. She snuck a look at Aiden who wore an enigmatic smile on her face as she watched Eris's presentation and nodded slowly to herself. Cole hoped that was a good sign.

When Eris finished describing the scene, both directors started asking her questions. Aiden leaned into Cole.

"I can't see Eris being an actress for much longer if those two have their way." She nodded toward them all chatting animatedly. The directors were using items off the table as markers as to where the cameras would be set around a plate of cookies doubling as

Emily's bed. "I think the Director's Guild will try to snap her up as soon as they can after word gets around about how talented she is." Aiden pointed toward the two directors in the room. "Those two are tops in their field. They know Eris is not telling them how to do their job. They recognize that she sees the movie through the same eyes they do. God, I was so blessed to have her try out for this role. She's got such a future ahead of her. And, damn, Mischa was right. We need to sign her up on our projects before some other production company snatches her away." Aiden grinned at Cole. "She'll be directing you one day in a blockbuster, mark my words."

Cole watched Eris with a new understanding. Eris's expressive hands became the camera as she described a shot that brought the lens straight to their position on the bed. An intimate shot, the one that would show their faces as passion rose and their hearts were exposed. Cole loved the sound of that scene. She'd read Aiden's book. She knew how that scene had played out in print. It was raw and passionate and poignant. Eris's view of it brought it to life. Cole felt a shiver of excitement race through her body. She couldn't wait to film the scene now. It would always be *Eris's* scene. It would always be something she created for *them*.

"Now we just have to get the costume department to fit you both with nude suits so we don't get a nipple slip and lose our rating," Olivia said.

Cole laughed and the sound drew Eris's gaze to her. Cole hoped Eris could see how proud she was of her. The slight blush that colored Eris's cheeks made Cole wonder if Eris really was a mind reader.

"So I guess we get this scene done and then we can move on to the angst." Aiden reached for a can of soda and popped the tab. "Poor Hollister, she finds the love of her life in another time and people just can't let them be happy."

"I guess there always has to be something to make an audience fear for them. It makes the happy ending all the more sweet."

Aiden rubbed at her chest reflectively. For a moment, her mind seemed to be somewhere else entirely. Cole realized that Aiden's hand was resting over where she'd taken a bullet meant for Cassidy.

Cole wanted desperately to comfort her but wasn't exactly sure what she could do. She remained silent until Aiden's eyes cleared from where her mind had strayed to and what she'd seen there.

"I'm a sucker for happy endings," Aiden said, her voice quiet but strong.

Aiden looked over at Eris again as she and the directors were now writing up notes as to how the love scene would play. One of them dragged over a whiteboard and began drawing out storyboards in quick succession. They tacked cards on the board, and it was soon filled with directions, descriptions, and rudimentary drawings of Eris and Cole in their roles. The storyboards showed everything exactly how Eris had envisioned it.

Eris was in the thick of it all, creating and crafting the scene that would be the center point of the whole movie. The scene when Hollister recognizes that this was her Emily now, in this time, in this place, in this *moment*. She had no way back to the lover she'd lost in time. But *here* and *now*, this was her Emily and she didn't have to face this new life alone.

"I'm all for the happy ever after too," Cole said, seeing her own future laid before her with Eris center stage in it.

Chapter Sixteen

The set for Emily's bedroom was bustling with people laying down tracks for the camera to follow. The camera would be on a circular track around the bed, catching every angle and nuance of Eris's and Cole's performances. Cole knew they'd shoot the more extreme close-ups afterward, but this would capture the love scene from beginning to end. Awed by how Eris wanted the scene framed, Cole had practiced it enough times to know exactly where the camera would be at each given beat to the scene. It was going to look amazing.

She looked over where Eris was chatting with someone. She seemed so calm. Meanwhile, Cole was sweating under her many layers of clothing with both nerves and a strange excitement.

Please don't let me screw this up. She's working so damn hard getting this scene to have a truly intimate look.

Cole couldn't hide her smile as Eris came sauntering back over toward her. Emily's costume was as formal as usual. When the director yelled "action" Cole would help peel it off, layer by layer. Eris had painstakingly schooled Cole on the correct way to let down her long hair from its fashionable weave without tangling it or getting her hands stuck. Removing Hollister's suit would be so much easier, yet she would be the one ultimately revealing the most. The binding wrapped around Cole's chest was uncomfortable, but she knew it was necessary for the story. She wouldn't be sorry to have Eris unwrap her from its constrictive hold.

Eris tugged at Cole's jacket lapel. "Why do you look so spooked?"

Cole was disgruntled. She thought she'd been doing so well keeping her nerves under wraps. "Can I keep nothing from you?"

"Apparently not. Are you nervous about the scene? You know there's only going to be the director and the camera operators in the room with us. Just three other people. And it's a closed set. Not even Aiden will step foot in here."

"I bet they had to warn Mischa not to come watch."

"I wouldn't be surprised. I've already sworn the women who'll be watching us to secrecy not to reveal how very sexy you are when you're naked."

Cole huffed at her. "At least I won't be completely naked on the screen."

Eris leaned in closer. "It will all be artfully filmed but will look so real. We can do this. It's going to be the talk of the movie."

Cole jumped when the director suddenly shouted, "Clear the set." The crew left, leaving just three women behind to capture the scene with Cole and Eris.

The director sat in her seat on the camera dolly and stuck her eye up to the camera lens. Cole and Eris took their positions by the door. Cole was shaking. She couldn't stop the faint shiver that ran through her entire being.

"I'm more nervous about Hollister and Emily sleeping together than I was when you and I had our first time," Cole whispered.

Eris reached up and cupped Cole's cheek. "Channel it. Use it. Give Hollister that vulnerability. This is her Emily but *not*. This is her first time with *this* woman, even though Hollister knows in her heart of hearts this is her soul mate. This is Emily's first time with a lover. Make it memorable for her. Love *her*."

"I do." Cole couldn't help the deeper meaning in her answer. Eris smiled at her. "I mean, Hollister does."

Eris's smile just broadened. "Then, Hollister Graham, come show her just how much." She stepped back and found her mark at the door. "We're ready when you are."

The director nodded and everyone prepared themselves for the scene. "Action."

Eris closed the door behind them and stepped away from Cole. She reached up to remove her hat then began nervously fussing with her hair. Cole stopped her.

"May I?" At Eris's nod, Cole began to gently remove the pins that held Eris's hair in place. She placed them on the tall dresser and then ran her fingers through Eris's long hair, setting it free from its confines.

"I like your hair like this." Cole tucked a strand behind Eris's ear.

"It's not exactly suitable for work," Eris said, ducking her head shyly.

"You're not at work now." Cole shrugged out of her large overcoat and laid it over a chair. Her suit jacket followed. "Are you sure you want to do this?"

Eris nodded and began to remove her blouse, revealing the corset beneath. She unfastened her skirt, letting the material drop to the floor. Petticoats followed. She stood dressed only in her corset and boots.

Cole looked stunned for a moment at the picture she made. She caught the glint in Eris's eye that was *all* Eris. "The boots have to go, sadly," Cole ad-libbed and Eris smiled, bending down to untie the laces that ran the length of the tall boots. Cole all but ripped off her waistcoat, tugged off her bowtie, and fought her way out of the suspenders. She pulled her shirt free of her pants. She removed pants and boots in one go, leaving her in a shirt that fell to mid-thigh.

Eris turned her back on Cole and presented her with the laces that kept her corset in place. Cole knew they could edit most of the undressing to make it run tighter, faster, so she took her time releasing each length until the corset remained on only by Eris holding it to her. She turned her back to the camera and let the corset drop. Cole ran her hand reverently down Eris's neck and across her shoulder.

"You are so beautiful. You always are."

Eris reached to unfasten Cole's shirt, but Cole's hand stilled hers. "Last chance for you to stop where this is heading. Where *we* are heading."

"I want you, Hollister. The *real* you."

Cole dropped her hands and Eris moved a little to the side to ensure the camera could watch over her shoulder as she undid Cole's shirt and revealed the binding beneath. She unwrapped it carefully then dropped the binding to the floor. Under it, Cole was wearing pasties to cover her nipples, but the camera was only going to film the top of her breasts in order to reveal Hollister's true gender but hide Cole's modesty.

"You are more than I ever dreamed of." Eris pressed herself into Cole's body and drew her head down for a kiss. Their kiss was soft and gentle, exploring the newness of each other's lips. Eris pulled away to rest her head against Cole's chest.

"And you are *all* I have ever dreamed of." Cole rested her cheek atop Eris's head and closed her eyes.

"And cut! That was excellent, ladies." The director had them move her dolly back to its starting position for the next scene. "You set us quite the challenge, Eris. Let's see if we can get this next scene all in one take, shall we?"

Eris grinned up at Cole. "Come on, Hollister. Let's show Aiden's readers what they could only have imagined." She led Cole to the bed and they scrambled in under the sheets. They waited patiently while one of the women skillfully draped them so that just enough flesh was visible. Both Cole and Eris wore flesh colored thongs to keep the illusion of nakedness.

Eris shivered beneath Cole. "Oooh, these sheets are cold!" She whispered in Cole's ear. "I much prefer your silk ones under me when you're on top."

Cole began to say something but jumped as a mixture of rosewater and glycerin was sprayed onto her back to simulate sweat. "Geez! We never factored fake sweat into the mix when we rehearsed this."

Eris laughed, lifting her chin to get her chest sprayed on.

Cole settled into position while the director finished her last-minute checks. She smiled down at Eris beneath her. "Think the Wachowski siblings will appreciate your homage to their sexy love scene from *Bound*?"

"That scene was expertly filmed. Hollister and Emily deserve the same treatment."

"Only with less nipples on show and no below the waist touching."

"True, but what exquisite nipples Gina Gershon showed." Eris sighed then squealed as Cole pinched her side. "Hey! No fair! I can't retaliate without coming untucked before my time."

"Quiet on the set and in the bed!" the director called, grinning at them from over her camera lens. "We're ready when you are. Eris, would you like to call the shots here?"

A clapperboard snapped, marking the start of filming. Eris stared into Cole's eyes, winked at her, then called out with an authoritative air, "And, *action*!"

The minute the credits began to roll on the latest episode of *Fortune's Rise*, Brooke grabbed her tablet and brought up her Skype app. She waited impatiently for Ava to answer. As soon as Ava's face appeared on screen, Brooke launched into her list of grievances.

"They were barely in tonight's episode." Brooke reached for her second tablet and began scrolling through the fan boards to see what the other Morter fans thought of the lack of their favorite characters.

"It was George and Frances' story tonight. They needed to complete their story arc so they could move on. That story line was dragging on way too long." Ava rested her chin on her hands and stared into the camera. "I like how they did it though. Those two are a cute couple."

"Chris and Nat are better and deserved more screen time."

"They were in the trailer for next week's episode."

"But they weren't shown together." Brooke was growing angrier by the minute. "They're just baiting us now."

"Brooke, we have this same discussion every week. Chris and Nat aren't together in the show so they won't show them as if they were in any publicity. It would be false advertising. They're not lesbians in the show nor are they a couple."

Ava's long-suffering sigh sounded through their connection and only incensed Brooke more.

"The damned show knows we want it though."

Ava laughed. "They'd be hard-pressed not to seeing as we hijack every post they tweet out, asking for Morter to be made canon." Ava looked away from the screen and at the phone in her hand. "You know as well as I do they won't change their show just because we would like to see Chris and Nat as lovers."

"*Person of Interest* did it. They recognized their leading ladies had chemistry and that the audience shipped them."

"Yes, but they also killed a lesbian off, and that's not how we want to keep seeing our representation end. I understand why they did it, I got that it was supposedly necessary to end that character's journey for her to 'evolve,' but it was still another name added to the Bury Your Gays list." Ava flicked through her phone's screens. "And not even canon characters are safe. Maggie Sawyer, Kate Kane, both screwed over by a company led by a gay man. Face it, Brooke. If we get a canon couple the chances of it done well are few and far between. Not every show is as lucky as *Wynonna Earp*." Distracted for a moment, Ava was silent. "Oh my God."

Brooke didn't look up from her tablet. "What?"

"Someone is trying to stir up a romance between Cole and Eris while they're filming together. They're saying this photo, taken at a distance and where you can barely make out two people, is them. How lame is that?"

Brooke's eyes narrowed and she lifted her head to stare at Ava. Ava wasn't looking at her, instead she was laughing at her phone.

"For one thing, it could be any couple kissing. You can't make out their faces at all. The lighting of the photo is terrible. It's obviously nighttime. Did they not think to have a flash on?"

"Maybe they didn't want to draw attention to themselves while Cole and Eris were sucking face." Brooke's voice was sharp. She tried to soften it, to not let her anger show, but Ava's amusement was wearing on Brooke's last nerve where Cole's blatant infidelity was concerned.

"Well, it's no paparazzi shot, that's for sure. And if it is them, good luck to them. They'd make a gorgeous couple."

Brooke slammed her tablet on the table. "Cole should be with Maria," she ground out.

Ava's head popped up. "You know that's never going to happen. I thought you'd resigned yourself to that fact ages ago?"

"*They'd* make a gorgeous couple."

Ava nodded. "Yes, they would. But Maria is married and straight and Cole is gay and not interested in her. It ain't gonna happen."

"In my world it would," Brooke grumbled, picking up her tablet again and scrolling through the long list of fan comments all bemoaning the fact their favorite characters didn't get even five minutes of screen time in that night's episode.

Ava put her phone down and watched Brooke quietly. Brooke could feel her eyes on her.

"What's the point of us sitting here being passive when they are all but writing our characters out of the show?"

Ava sighed. "Cole *is* leaving, but tonight wasn't about her or her character. The show is an ensemble cast. Everyone has a story to be told."

"I want Chris and Nat's story."

"And I'd be there watching that too. But Cole's already left and moved on to a movie role. We only have a few episodes left with her in. Chris and Nat aren't going to suddenly ride off into the sunset together."

"I'm not sure how I'm going to cope with her leaving," Brooke said honestly. She didn't have a clue how she was going to react. These were her characters, her women. Her world revolved around their meager story on the show, bolstered by the fan art and fan fiction the fans made to celebrate their favorite couple, giving them the stories they deserved.

"We'll go shopping before it and make sure you get in a ton of wine to drown your sorrows. Just like we did with Maggie, and Lexa, and Dana, and Root, and…" Ava waved a hand as she rattled off all the names of strong lesbian characters lost from their shows.

"You're not helping." Brooke refused to look up at her. Ava was the only friend she had left. Brooke's phone dinged as a message arrived. She opened it and found the grainy photo she had taken of Cole and Eris at the restaurant. She glared at Ava's laughing face. "Why are you sending me this?"

"To make you smile. Look at the tweet. Look how earnest this person is telling us that this is Cole with a woman. She's single, for crying out loud. Jeez, get a life, loser. There's nothing worse than a fan stalking their favorites and posting about their private lives as if we have a right to know every little detail. There has to be a line drawn somewhere."

Brooke looked at the photo and could see every detail that Ava was dismissing. She recalled all too clearly the passionate kisses exchanged, the way Eris's hand was touching Cole's butt, the way Cole held Eris so close that nothing could have gotten between them.

"Cole deserves some happiness. She lost her girlfriend because some stupid fans took it upon themselves to fabricate lies about her and Maria to break them up. You heard the same rumors I did about that happening. That's a step too far in fandom. We can follow them blindly on the shows, but we should never *ever* interfere with their private lives. We're grown women, for fuck's sake. Do we really have to lower ourselves to schoolyard tactics or *Mean Girl* tweets to prove we love an actress more than anyone else loves her? These actresses are *not* our property."

Brooke had heard enough of Ava's comments. She deliberately tapped a button on her tablet and her phone began to ring. "Oh, that's my mother calling. I'll have to catch up with you later, Ava,"

Ava smiled, not realizing Brooke was lying. "Oh, okay. Have a great night and I'll speak to you tomorrow."

Brooke ended the call and stared blankly at the screen for a long time. A red mist seeped into her vision. Brooke was seconds away from throwing the tablet across the room just for the satisfaction of watching it shatter to pieces and Ava with it. Ava was gone, but her words lingered in the air, burning their way into Brooke's brain. Each word a pointed condemnation of all Brooke believed in.

She took another look at the photo she'd posted anonymously from one of her accounts. Not every post beneath it felt like Ava did. Some were happy for Cole. Others accused them of trying to generate publicity for the upcoming movie. Some, like Brooke, bemoaned the fact that it should be Maria she was with and wondered what Maria would say if she found out. Brooke had deliberately tagged Maria in her post. There was still no reaction to the photo from her.

Maybe I'll have to find another way to bring this to her attention, Brooke thought. She smiled as an idea took root and pushed everything else out of her head.

I've met her before. We spoke for ages at the convention where I got to tell her how much Nat means to me.

She looked up at a photo hanging on her wall. It was of her and Maria, taken at a *Fortune's Rise* convention. Maria had her arm around Brooke and was smiling so brightly for the camera.

She'll remember me. After all, I'm her biggest fan.

Chapter Seventeen

The restaurant's kitchen held an eerily silent air when devoid of activity. Eris checked her watch. It was only 3:30 a.m. Eris figured she had enough time to have a very early breakfast, a quick cup of coffee to fortify her, and half an hour of peace and quiet before she left for the studio for an early call. She grabbed a pack of bagels and set two to toast while she programmed the coffee maker for an expresso to wake her up. She startled as Melanie waddled into the room, looking disheveled and in desperate need of more sleep.

"Bloody hell, Mel! Give a girl a heart attack!" Eris clutched dramatically at her chest. "Why aren't you in bed? The restaurant doesn't start for another couple of hours yet."

"Your niece or nephew is currently performing a River Dance, with every piece of nifty footwork concentrated solely on my bladder." Melanie grimaced as another pain struck. "I gave up trying to sleep as Michael Flatley here was being the Lord of the Dance and making me think I needed to pee every five minutes." She lowered herself gingerly into a chair at a table and rested her head in her hands.

"Can I make you anything?" Eris removed her bagels from the toaster and began to liberally spread peanut butter on them.

"Why on earth are you up this early? And why are you ruining perfectly good bagels with disgusting chunky peanut butter?"

"I have an early call, remember? I told you last night. And I need the energy boost."

Melanie's brow crinkled for a second as she tried to remember and then she nodded. "I remember now. Blame the baby-making hormones. My brain is like porridge." She waited for Eris to take a seat beside her and stole a bagel off her plate. She took a huge bite and returned it.

Eris glared at her. "You can't coast on baby hormone excuses forever. Take that bagel. I don't want it now." She shoved her plate over to Melanie who took the rest of the bagel and separated the two halves. She began to lick at the peanut butter. Eris made a face at her actions.

"For God's sake!" She got up again and opened the fridge to grab a carton of milk. She poured a glass full and passed it to Melanie before tidying back up and sitting down again.

So much for a moment of peace and quiet before she had to be on set.

Melanie reached into her dressing gown pocket and pulled out her phone. She began scrolling down the screen, unmindful of her peanut buttered fingers. She was quiet for a moment and Eris savored it. She knew it wouldn't last.

"Oh-ho," Melanie said, squinting at the screen, twisting it this way and that as she tried to get a better view. She made a disgruntled noise. "Guess we know now why the light bulb in the parking lot was smashed to smithereens." She handed the phone over to Eris.

Eris wiped her hands off on a napkin and sighed. She made a show of having to clean off the screen of her sister's phone. "You are such a pig. What are you showing me? It had better not be puppies because you cry way too long and hard over those videos." She stared at the screen. "Okay, what the hell is this I'm supposed to be seeing?"

Melanie jabbed a sticky finger at the screen, causing Eris to pull the phone away from her with a look of censure. "Well, that's definitely the rear of our restaurant at night, with what looks to be two people in the light cast from inside. And I think that lump is a motorcycle. To be honest, it's a really crappy photo."

Eris looked again. Her eyes widened. "Shit! Is that me and Cole?"

Melanie leaned back in her chair, snagging up Eris's napkin to clean her fingers off. "Her fans seem to think so and your fans are beginning to pay attention to them."

Eris checked the Twitter account that hosted the photo and had revealed who the shadowy figures in an embrace were. "What are you doing on a dedicated Cole Calder site?"

"You were tagged in it so I followed it back to the source. I keep an eye on what's said and reported on where you are concerned anyway. What kind of big sister would I be if I wasn't looking out for you?"

"Please tell me you don't antagonize the fans." Eris knew her sister all too well. A glass of wine too many and the Twitterverse was an open playground for Melanie to wade in and give her opinion on anything and all. Admittedly, she was off wine due to being pregnant, but Eris knew that didn't stop her from making her opinions known when the mood struck.

"Hell no. I don't engage them at all. Some of them bitches be crazy!" Melanie took a long drink from her glass. "I'm just fascinated by what your fans are saying. Though, believe me, I could have lived a long time never knowing that some people were sharing their sexual fantasies of you online for all to see." She shuddered. "Way too much kinky shit for this straight housewife."

Eris grimaced. She knew all too well what floated around the internet sites concerning her or her characters. It was a strange by-product of her gaining some semblance of fame. It wasn't something she could control or monitor. She just didn't like having mocked up nude shots handed to her by ones who thought she'd be thrilled to sign their fan art. Erotic fan fiction sent to her business email address with the "best bits" highlighted was another of the things that made her cringe and wish for a more respectful following.

"Yeah, all that takes some getting used to. Though, it being anonymous online is so much better than meeting a fan face-to-face where he feels the need to tell me that if I'd let him 'straighten' me out I would probably get better roles."

Melanie's face darkened like thunder. "You're kidding me?"

"It was at the last con I did, the one you came with me to? If I'd told you what he'd said you'd have had him hanging by his testicles from one of the ceiling fans in the hotel's lobby. He was a major dick. My manager dealt with him swiftly."

"Good, because if I'd have heard that…"

Eris shook her head. "No, you can't react to this kind of thing unless it's clearly dangerous. If I show any kind of anger they'll label me a bitch and my reputation will suffer. Fans are fickle, they can move on from one show to the next in a heartbeat. It's like if you call a fandom out for something, you need to be damn sure you know *all* your facts before you speak out. Fans can set a rival fandom up as easy as anything and have you blame the innocent party. They cry wolf about their victimization when they are the bullies. And nothing is worse than a family member acting high and mighty on Twitter, calling out fans, supposedly on their famous sibling's behalf. No one likes a hanger-on, someone who tries to boost their own notoriety at the expense of another's fame."

"I wouldn't do that," Melanie said.

"I know you wouldn't. But you need to be more careful now online. I'm going to be in a movie. That opens me up to even more scrutiny." She looked at the photo again. "This is a terrible photo, taken at night from a distance with no flash. It could be anyone, to be honest, but I know it's us."

"It looks like you have your hand in her jeans pocket," Melanie said.

"She has a great ass." Eris couldn't stop grinning. "I mean a *really* great—"

Melanie stopped her. "You might want to be a little more careful out in the real world off set. Someone got in here and took this photo. I promised you all that night you'd be safe from the patrons of the restaurant, that you'd have privacy." She pointed at the phone. "That's an invasion of your privacy and I had zero control over it. I don't like that."

"You run a business, Mel. I can't expect you to confiscate cell phones at the door so no one can snap a pic of me or my friends if we happen to be dining here. You already have security cameras everywhere."

"Do you think we still have whoever this was on tape?"

"Can you go back that far? This was a week or so ago."

"I'll check into it. I want you and Cole safe to do whatever it is you want to do together. I want her to be able to stay here for the night without worrying some idiot with a phone is going to take a picture of her as she does the walk of shame out of here, still dressed in the previous night's clothes."

Eris took one last look at the photo before handing the phone back to Melanie. "This is going to be the kind of publicity we've been trying *not* to attract for the movie."

"You can't help that you fell for each other. It would be cruel to have you wait until the movie wraps. You two are perfect for each other."

"I know, I feel it, but..."

Melanie gave Eris an incredulous look. "But what? The only buts in this conversation should be the one your hand in her back pocket was copping a feel of!"

Eris shook her head at her. "You don't understand."

"Explain it to me then. Tell me why you're so frightened she might be your one and only. You know what Grandad used to say, 'Every old sock...'"

"'...meets an old shoe,'" Eris finished dutifully. She could hear her grandad's voice loud and clear in her head, repeating his favorite phrase. "Yes, his soul mate mantra is still ingrained on my very soul. But I'm not like you, Mel. I don't want to give up my life's dreams to follow someone else's." Eris reached over to squeeze Melanie's hand. "I love Georgio, and I love our lives here together, but you had a dream of your own before him and you pushed it all aside. Nan did the same. She left Scotland for England and left everything she'd known behind."

"Nan left an abusive ass of a father behind who was determined to keep her at home to look after him indefinitely. She didn't leave anything good behind. Everything she wanted was in the life ahead of her with Grandad."

Eris considered this new information. "I don't remember hearing about her father."

"Because it had no place in their lives and you were too young to hear that kind of thing when I overheard the adults talking about it. She and Grandad lived the hearts and flowers life they dreamed of. You know how devoted to each other they were. They *literally* couldn't live without each other."

Eris couldn't argue with that. "But then there's you. You wanted to be a police officer and you gave it all up and moved halfway across the world."

"Yes, and you moved to be with me when you followed your own career. It's not like I fell off the face of the planet and left you forever."

"No, it's not about that. You gave up *everything* you'd wanted to be."

"That's because I never knew I had it in me to be a chef and run my own restaurant with the man I love."

"You always wanted to be in the police. It was your dream." Eris couldn't get past that fact.

Melanie shook her head at her. "But a new dream came and took its place. Look at what I'd have missed out on if I'd ignored the opportunity that Georgio blessed me with." She ran her hand over her stomach. "Don't ever think I lost out by changing my path in life. In fact, I gained everything I'd ever wanted. A job I love, a home, family." Melanie narrowed her gaze a little at Eris, making her squirm under her scrutiny. "I always thought you just had serious control issues. No wonder you never wished for a soul mate if you thought we sacrificed ourselves to get one. Is that what you're really afraid of, though? Because I know and love you, little sister, and I'm wondering if it's not what you'd have to lose of yourself if Cole is your soul mate but rather, what you'd stand to *gain*?"

Eris felt her chest tighten as her fears fought to spill out. "I'd be lying if I said what happened between Mom and our father didn't scar me for life. Because of him I have the need for my own protection ingrained so deep that I can read pretty much everyone's intentions before they voice them. Cole is such an open book to me, with every page filled with so many promises. I'm frightened I could lose so much of myself where Cole is concerned. I thought I didn't have time for a lover, but she's everything I could have dreamed of. She's become my world in such a short amount of time. I can't imagine my life without her now and that thought *terrifies* me."

"She's so attentive, and she looks at you as if you hung the moon and stars." Melanie hiccupped a little then began to cry. "It's just everything I've wanted for you," she wailed.

Eris hugged Melanie to her. "I know, I know." She tried to hush her before Georgio came down to see what all the noise was about.

"I'm just...just...so...happy for you," Melanie gasped between sobs.

Eris had to laugh. "God, Melanie. You're such a mess."

"And I'm fat," Melanie cried even louder.

Eris caught sight of the time on the kitchen clock. "Melanie, you know I love you and our discussion has been enlightening, but I really have to leave now to be on set in time."

"That's okay. Go be with your girlfriend and show the production how perfect you are together." Melanie buried her head in Eris's waist and sobbed even louder.

Eris saw something move out of the corner of her eye and was relieved that Georgio had come down to help extricate her from a very clingy and overwrought Melanie. She eased herself away as best she could out of Melanie's grip. Georgio, dressed only in his sleep shorts and with a serious case of bed head, took her place and murmured reassurances to Melanie.

"Come on, baby, you need to sleep," he said, all but cradling Melanie in his arms as he gathered her up out of the chair.

"Someone took a picture from our parking lot of Eris and Cole kissing and plastered it all over the internet," Melanie cried.

Georgio scowled and braced himself to fight.

Eris put a warning hand up. "No, I do not need two of you going off on this right before I need to go to work. We'll check the cameras when I get back just in case something shows up on there. It was probably just an opportunist who spied their chance to take a shot of us. It's not clear though, so don't worry. *Either* of you." Eris snatched up her bag and her coffee flask and pressed quick kisses to Melanie's and Georgio's cheeks. "I'll be home late tonight."

"I'll expect a call if you're not coming home at all," Melanie shouted after her.

"I'll phone you, *Mom*!"

"See that you do!" Georgio shouted too. "We worry!"

"God help both of you if that kid of yours inherits Melanie's teenage antics," Eris muttered to herself as she hurried out the back door to her car. With the key in the lock, Eris paused for a moment to look over at the light that had been broken. She vaguely remembered a dark colored car parked underneath it, but she couldn't recall seeing anyone inside that night. Her whole world had centered on Cole and their kisses good night. To think someone had watched them and taken a photograph was infuriating and downright creepy.

Eris wasn't sure if she wanted to mention it to Cole. She had enough invasions of privacy from fans without a grainy photograph added into the mix. It was probably nothing. Eris hoped it would just be scurrilous gossip for one day before something else would take its place.

Her conversation with Melanie had given Eris something else to think about. Was she so frightened of change that she could deliberately sabotage herself and her future with Cole? That revelation was way too deep for her to delve into now. She needed to put everything running around in her head to one side and just concentrate on getting to the studio on time. It was something she had to address though because the longer she and Cole were together, the deeper Eris fell in love.

Aiden's office door was open, but Cole still knocked on it before walking in. Eris sat in front of Aiden's desk and Cole joined her, giving her a puzzled look. Cole was curious as to why both she and Eris had been called to Aiden's office so early in the day.

"Why do I feel like I've been called to the principal's office?" she said, grinning at Eris and wishing her good morning with a gentle kiss to her cheek.

Eris reached for Cole's hand. Aiden was equally somber as she sat behind her desk. Cole looked at them both and started to get worried.

"Oh my God, who died?" Cole said, only half joking. The atmosphere in the room was odd and it made Cole uncomfortable.

"Have you seen your Twitter feed this morning?" Eris said.

Cole shook her head. "I barely check that thing anymore. I stopped when all I ever saw was a long stream of calls for me to go back to *Fortune's Rise*, all posted by the same ten people's accounts."

Eris handed her own phone to her. "This is what we woke up to this morning."

Cole looked down at the phone. The picture there didn't offer much in an explanation. "Is this one of those puzzles where you have to cross your eyes to see the hidden picture?"

"Look closer." Eris took the phone back, enlarged a specific area of the picture, and then handed it back to Cole.

Cole still couldn't really make out what she was supposed to be seeing. She was beginning to wonder if she was going to need glasses soon in her future when she read the accompanying message that had posted with the photo.

@ColeCalder @ErisWhyte #Andinos More than just acting? @MariaRamos

Cole looked more closely at the photo. "This is the parking lot of your sister's restaurant." She shook her head. The weight of the world settled itself on her shoulders once more and she could feel her back bowing under the pressure. "It was nearly midnight. Who the fuck was sitting in a parking lot at midnight taking photos of us?"

"You know people have their phones glued to their hands nowadays. Every picture is postable on some media or another. Someone spied their opportunity and got a photo of us."

"You can't honestly tell it's either of you from the quality of the photo and the fact Cole is pretty much covering you with her height advantage." Aiden had the photo up on her ever-present tablet. "But whoever took it recognized you both because they tagged you personally."

"And Maria." Cole clenched her teeth so hard her jaw screamed at the pain. She wanted to yell her head off at yet another intrusion into her private life. She and Eris had only just started seeing each other and already someone was capturing them in a personal moment. She was sick of it. What did she have to do to have them leave her alone? "How many fucking times do I have to be screwed by these damned crazy fans?" She dimly felt Eris squeeze her hand and that one touch reached through her anger and pain. Cole stared at her blindly, needing her help to pull her free from this misery.

"I'm here, Cole. I'm not going anywhere," Eris said, her promise firm on her face.

Cole nodded and, with one last look at the photo, handed Eris her phone back before she threw it across the room in annoyance.

"How do you want to handle this?" Aiden put her tablet on the table and addressed them both.

"Wouldn't just ignoring it be the best course of action?" Eris shrugged. "I really don't have a lot of experience in this kind of thing."

Cole let out a harsh bark of laughter. "Unfortunately, I have enough experience in this kind of thing for the both of us."

"Eris, your fans are a different kind from Aiden's. Of your fans who commented on this post, most were cheering you on and wishing you well. The rest were calling the poster out for being a stalker and a massive loser."

"It's got to be one of the *Fortune's Rise* crazy stans seeing as they tagged Maria in it. I left the show to stop this kind of shit from happening. I just can't escape it."

"So how do you want to handle this?" Aiden asked again. "Cole, you're the one it affects the most. You have the fan problem so what usually works for you? Do you ignore them, delete them, or block them? Do you want me to put out a statement denying it's you two or do you want to use this?"

"Use it how?" Eris moved closer to Cole, obviously sensing Cole was spiraling down into a deep, dark place.

"Well, you two might want to keep your fledging romance far from prying eyes for now, but Hollister and Emily could send out a pointed message to the photographer. Let's use this to our advantage like we did the last time someone snapped you unawares. Take the power back."

Cole wanted to hear what she had in mind. She knew Aiden, as well as Darrow/Hayes Productions, only had her best interests at heart. She also knew Aiden had lived through worse than what Cole was experiencing. She trusted her.

"Show us what you want us to do," Cole said. Eris nodded her agreement.

❖

Brooke had Ava on a video chat as they spoke over breakfast before both had to leave for work.

"God, I'm so not in the mood for work today. I wonder if they'd believe me if I phoned in sick." Ava took a sip from her coffee cup while her other hand was busy scrolling away on her phone. "Oh my God! Did you see what the *A Pocket Full of Time* official site posted as a clap back to that crappy photo that was put online last night?"

"Yes, I've seen it," Brooke said calmly.

Ava squealed and held up her phone to the camera for Brooke to see anyway. On her screen was Cole dressed as Hollister, but minus her usual heavy coat. Instead it was a more relaxed view of Cole in her herringbone patterned trousers, her suspenders firmly in place over a white shirt, and her back toward the camera. Eris was resplendent in her full Emily costume. They had the angle of the grainy photo to a T although this time both women were looking directly at the camera. Eris had her hand deliberately tucked into the tight rear pocket on Cole's trousers. Ava pulled her phone back and read the tweet out loud.

#APocketFullOfTime Picture this! We're hosting a Q&A session live online Wednesday 24th. Come chat with Cole and Eris, director Olivia Todd, and producer Aiden Darrow.

Ava burst out laughing. "I love it! They didn't acknowledge the paparazzi photo, instead they made a joke out of it." She looked at the photo and sighed happily. "God, they look amazing together.

Look how handsome Cole is. I can't wait to see this movie with her as Hollister. I didn't think I could crush out any more on Cole Calder, but seeing her with this magnificent masculine look just makes me get all hot and flustered." She fanned herself playfully and caught sight of her watch. "Oh damn. I have to get going to work whether I like it or not." She peered through the video at Brooke. "Are we still on for tonight? You bring your laptop over and we'll catch up on *Stumptown*? I'll cook us Chinese."

Brooke shook her head. "I can't. My laptop stopped working. I'll have to take a rain check for now until I can get it fixed."

Brooke looked over to where her laptop lay shattered on the floor. The dent in the wall showed the impact of where it had hit. Now it lay in pieces on the tiled floor, keyboard keys littered everywhere. The screen had a deep crack right through the middle. The remaining glass was a spider web of tiny fractures. Somehow, the laptop still worked. The screen was stuck on the photo of Cole and Eris playing to the camera and publicly calling out Brooke for her photo.

Ava's annoying voice brought Brooke's attention back to the screen.

"Brooke? *Brooke?* What happened to your laptop?"

Brooke gave Ava a sad smile and shrugged. "It crashed."

Chapter Eighteen

Brooke scrutinized Maria Ramos's early morning routine for over two weeks before she finally spied her chance to act. Every morning at 7:30 a.m., as regular as clockwork, Maria's husband, Rico, would step out of the house, get into his ridiculously large car, and rev the high-powered engine so that everyone in the street knew a big man was preparing to leave. Brooke had rolled her eyes at him driving a car that was such a blatant macho symbol. It was obviously one that was overcompensating for his lack of size elsewhere.

Maria had no set routine. That annoyed Brooke to no end. There were the obvious "called to set early" mornings and then there were times where, as soon as Rico left, within minutes, Maria was bustling around her car and taking off too. Brooke had been desperate to follow her to see if she was going to Cole. She couldn't without being late for her job though. Her boss had refused to grant her time off. Brooke had taken to sleeping in her car, waiting for an opportunity to confront Maria about Cole's infidelity.

This morning was it. Brooke had watched Rico roar off down the street, and soon Maria was out on her driveway seeing to her own car. Rico's leaving and Maria's imminent departure meant the little ornate gates to the property were wide open. Brooke took that as an invitation. She got out of her car, scanning the neighborhood as she hurried across the road, and headed toward Maria's house. Brooke was grateful that, for all her fame, Maria hadn't moved to a high security housing complex. She lived in an easily accessible house on a street where anyone could just walk up to her and have a chat.

That's all Brooke wanted to do. Just have a chat about her and Cole, Cole's leaving ruining everything, and the stupidity of the show not giving Brooke what she wanted. Just a fan talking to her favorite actress. Just a concerned Morter fan wanting her world put back to rights with Chris and Nat together as they should be.

She'll remember me, Brooke thought, checking again that no one was watching her as she slipped easily onto the driveway and approached Maria's car. The back door was wide open, and Brooke hesitated for a moment before slipping inside to wait.

Might as well make myself comfortable, she thought. She slid into the car and settled in. The noise next to her didn't register at first. She turned and found a young child, strapped in his car seat, staring at her. He waved his teddy bear at her then promptly dropped it. He stared at her expectantly. Brooke just stared back.

What the fuck is this thing doing in Maria's car?

The boy began struggling in his seat, squirming to get free so he could reach his bear. Brooke just watched him. She didn't move to pick up his bear. Instead she watched him twist and fight against his restraints until he was red in the face. Tears of frustration welled up in his eyes and his face crumpled. He let out a wailing cry and began sobbing.

Brooke still didn't move. His pitiful noises of distress failed to move her. It was the volume he was generating that made her own simmering anger start to boil.

"Shut the fuck up, runt," she growled at the child, only making him cry even louder.

"*Mateo*?"

The little boy's screaming intensified, and he began calling for his mother. "Mama!"

Brooke let out a disgruntled huff. Damn it. She'd forgotten that Maria had a brat. That wasn't part of Maria's world she paid attention to. In her world it was bad enough Maria was married to a man. Brooke had deliberately ignored the fact they had bred and produced this noisy brat.

Maria ran to the car carrying a brightly colored child's bag with a cuddly giraffe's head sticking out. She skidded to a halt at the sight of Brooke in the back seat too.

"What are you doing to him?" Maria said. "And what are you doing in my car?"

At the sight of Maria, Brooke smiled. "Oh, I am so happy to see you again. You look great. But then you always do." Maria gave her such a strange look that Brooke stopped smiling and let her irritation show. "We met at the last convention you did? I had my photo taken with you and Cole so many times. Surely you remember me? I'm your biggest fan." Brooke watched a myriad of emotions run across Maria's expressive face. Confusion, anger, fear. It was fear that settled on her features at the sound of Mateo's sobs.

"Please, get out of the car so I can get to my son."

Brooke waved a dismissive hand at the still crying boy. She raised her voice to talk over his screams for his mother. "He'll soon shut up. My mother used to say if you left a child long enough they'd soon run out of steam."

"He needs me. He's just a baby," Maria said, her voice pleading. "Just let me get him, please."

Brooke waved her away. "You can have him in a minute. He's not important here. But I do need to talk with you about what is happening on your show. I *need* to talk to you about Cole cheating on you with that new woman. And I want to know what you're going to do about it because she's spoiling everything." Brooke's voice rose until she was competing with Mateo's screams. Her anger began to rise at him interrupting her moment. "Mateo? Shut the fuck up! I am trying to have a conversation with your mother, and we do not need you making such a fuss. Do you not know that children should be seen and not heard?" She leaned over the child and screamed in his face. His eyes were huge as she terrified him. For a moment, he looked like he'd forgotten how to breathe.

Maria dropped the bag and grabbed for Brooke, furiously yanking her out of the car. "Get out! Get out!" she yelled at the top of her lungs. "HELP! Somebody help me!"

Brooke barely managed to keep herself from falling face first on the driveway. Maria roughly pushed her aside and leaned inside the car, trying desperately to console her son.

Brooke straightened her clothes so she didn't look disheveled. "Excuse me, but I hadn't finished talking." Brooke pulled Maria out by the collar of her blouse and slammed her back against the hood of the car. Maria cried out as the impact of her hip caused the metal to buckle.

Up close, Brooke could see how pretty Maria's eyes were. The fear in them only attracted Brooke more. "You have to fix what Cole is doing. She needs to be back on the show. *I* need for you two to be back together. You're a leading lady on *Fortune's Rise*, for fuck's sake. Use your influence to get Chris and Nat as a couple. The show knows that's what the audience really wants."

"Get the hell off my driveway," Maria said. "You're delusional. Chris and Nat don't exist in reality. They're just characters on a TV show. How dare you show up here and threaten my child over your stupid fandom." Maria pushed Brooke away from her and screamed at the top of her lungs. "Someone! Call the police! Help!"

Brooke heard the sounds of neighbors starting to pay attention to the noise. Doors started opening along the street and voices called out to Maria. Brooke knew she needed to go before someone investigated further.

"I will get what I want," she said as she backpedaled down the driveway. "And I want my Morter endgame. I'll stop at nothing to get it."

"You stay away from me and my family," Maria said, shifting to protect the open car door where her son was still crying inside. "You keep away from me. Help! Get the police!" She fumbled in her jeans for her phone and began calling for help herself.

"By the way, loved you in this week's episode." She saw the disbelief on Maria's face turn to fury and Brooke ran. She managed to run back to her car without anyone stopping her. Her heart was racing, and fear spiked at the distant wail of a police siren. Brooke started her engine and raced out of the neighborhood. She spared one last look back at Maria's house and groaned when she spied the surveillance camera that had no doubt captured her altercation with Maria on her driveway. She slammed her hands on her steering wheel. She needed to do something. She picked up her phone and began to dial.

Brooke didn't give Ava the chance to knock on her door. She wrenched it open, reached out, and dragged Ava inside. While Ava was blustering at her rough treatment, Brooke closed the door again and locked it behind her.

"What the fuck, Brooke?" Ava tried to straighten her crumpled blouse. "You can't just grab a girl and yank her into your house like she's a sack of potatoes." Ava looked up and startled. "Oh my God! What have you done?"

Brooke self-consciously ran her hand through what was left of her hair. Usually, it fell past her shoulders, but Brooke had hacked it off as best she could with a pair of kitchen scissors.

"Did you bring the hair dye?" Brooke ignored Ava's questions. She didn't have time for them. She needed her hair styled and her color changed, and she needed it done *now*.

"Why are you wearing your contacts? You hate them. That's why you got glasses. What's going on, Brooke?" Ava set down her shopping bag carefully, as if she was afraid she'd spook Brooke with any sudden moves.

Brooke snatched up the scissors and all but threatened Ava with them. "I need you to cut my hair and help me dye it. That's why you're here."

Ava shrank back at Brooke's vehemence. She reached out to take the scissors away from her. "I've brought my own scissors. When you said you wanted a haircut, I didn't expect you to have started already." Ava put the large scissors down and stepped closer to Brooke, eying the damage she'd done. "What on earth made you just cut all your hair off?"

"I wanted a change."

Ava scoffed. "Well, you look like you came out worse in a fight with a potato peeler." Ava ran her hand through the mess left of

Brooke's hair. "So, you want me to dye it a dark ash blond? I guess we blondes do have more fun."

"I need you to quit asking why and just help me." Brooke sat on a chair and waved Ava over. "Just cut it shorter and style it. I want to look different. Totally different."

Ava shrugged and began gathering what she needed out of her bag. "I was supposed to sleep in today. I had the day off from cutting and styling people's hair. Probably just as well you chose today for whatever midlife crisis you're going through."

"I'm twenty-six. I'm nowhere near a midlife anything yet." Brooke draped a towel around her neck.

"Why aren't you at work?"

"I phoned in sick. Told the boss I had menstrual cramps. That always freaks him out."

Ava tapped Brooke on her shoulder and motioned for her to get up. "I need hot water, Brooke. I'm not cutting that mess dry."

Brooke sighed and went to run some water in the sink. Both their phones started to ding. Brooke froze in place while Ava began to scroll through her messages.

"Oh my God," Ava said, her eyes glued to the small screen. "Oh, my fucking God!" She held up the phone at Brooke. "Someone tried to kidnap Maria Ramos's son. Oh my God." Ava stared back at the screen, frantically scrolling through all the news. "It happened this morning, barely an hour ago. Someone got onto her property, got into her car, and tried to kidnap her son. It says here Maria managed to scream for help and the kidnapper ran off. What a lowlife. You're pond scum if you try to steal a kid. They're saying it was a woman too. How could she do such a thing?"

Brooke turned the water off with an angry twist. "Maybe they weren't actually after the kid. Maybe they just wanted to talk to Maria."

"By getting *into* her car? Who gets into a celebrity's car just to say 'Hi! Love your work!' Damn stupid stalkers, that's who." Ava's anger was palpable. "They give the rest of us a bad name. Fans can worship their favorite stars without following them to their hotel rooms, or getting into their cars, or breaking into their homes. They have a right to privacy as much as we do. And you sure as hell don't try to take their child."

"I DIDN'T!" Brooke screamed. The words echoed around the kitchen while Ava was stunned into silence. Brooke gripped onto the edge of the sink, all but willing the steel to bend beneath her.

Ava's hand dropped as she finally ignored her phone. Her voice barely broke a whisper. "Oh, Brooke. What did you do?"

"I didn't touch the child, I promise. I just wanted to talk to Maria, see if maybe she'd help us get Cole back on the show. So I drove down to where she lives. I thought I'd catch her before she set out for the studio."

"You know her address?"

"Someone posted it online ages ago. No one lives in anonymity anymore. There's always someone who lets slip who their famous neighbor is."

"If you just went to ask her for help then how did you end up in the car?"

"The door was open so I figured I'd just wait for her."

"*In* the car as opposed to *on* the sidewalk like a normal person would?"

Brooke turned away from the sink and glared at Ava. "I wanted to talk to her. I figured she'd be more comfortable if we sat."

"In *her* car. With her *son* in it." Ava shook her head. "Brooke, can't you hear yourself? You sound *crazy*."

"I didn't realize there was a child in the car until I got in the back seat and saw him there, fastened in his seat. I forgot she had a kid."

"He's barely two years old. He's the reason the whole 'talking over the fence' thing started for Nat and Chris. They had to hide her baby bump so they had their scenes with the fence between them to hide it. You know this, Brooke."

"I'm not interested in her real life, Ava. I'm only interested in Nat and Chris. I want them back together." Brooke grabbed at her hair, tightening her fists into it. "I can't not have them in my life. They are my reason for living."

"They're characters in a show. They're not real."

"They're real to *me* and I'll move heaven and earth to get Cole back on that show so that Nat and Chris can have their endgame. Their happy ever after. I'm *owed* that."

"Did she recognize you from the conventions we've been to? You had all those pictures taken with them last year."

"I don't think so. I'm just another face among all her other fans to her. But I can't risk it. I ran as soon as she started screaming for the police. So please, will you help me dye my hair and cut it properly into a new style? Maybe changing my appearance will stop the police from banging on my door over a meet and greet that got a little out of hand. I swear to you, I didn't go after the child. I don't want her damn kid, I just wanted to talk to *her*."

"Couldn't you have just sent her a letter to the studio? Hit her up on her Instagram? You didn't need to go to her house, Brooke." She sighed. "How about we get in touch with the police and tell them this was all one big misunderstanding?"

"NO!" Brooke said, gritting her teeth to hold back her anger at Ava. "I'm not going to the police. They're not going to believe me over the word of an actress. They'll think I'm insane."

Ava made a face at her. "Well, let's face it, it's not exactly normal behavior to go confront your favorite TV star for something out of their control. She doesn't write the show, Brooke. She just plays the part they give her. It's not her fault her character isn't with Cole's. It's not in the show's storyline."

"Yeah, well, I'm not going back to talk with Maria again because it's obvious she doesn't care for her character at all." Brooke deliberately changed her tone and smiled sheepishly at Ava. "I kind of screwed up, didn't I?"

Ava shook her head at her. "You think so? Oh God, Brooke. You've just crossed a line most of us fans won't even think about sticking a toe by."

"I just want Chris and Nat together soooo bad," Brooke whined, pretending to be embarrassed and penitent. "You won't tell anyone, will you? That it was me that went to Maria and caused this mess?"

"Of course not," Ava said earnestly.

"I mean, there's no one else *I* can tell because I don't really have any friends except for those few online and they don't really count. *You're* my best friend, Ava." Brooke smiled inwardly at Ava's delight in that announcement. Brooke had never said it before. She'd never had the need to. She had no need for anyone, at any time. But Ava was so gullible it was almost entertaining to watch as she soaked up every word Brooke uttered and smiled like she'd just won the friendship lottery.

"You're my best friend too. So the next time you get the insane idea to go visit Maria, give me a call first so I can talk you out of it. I'd hate to have to bail you out of jail labeled as a crazy stalker." Ava put her phone down and gathered Brooke into her arms for a hug. "We've got to get you out more."

Brooke didn't hug back. "I don't want to go out more. I'm happy doing what I'm doing. I just want my favorite ladies back together where they belong."

"Yeah, well, getting into a TV star's car while it has her baby on board isn't going to help that cause, is it?" Ava pushed Brooke gently toward the sink now full of water. "I can at least fix one mess you've caused today. How do you want your hair cut?"

"Can you style it something maybe like Maria's? I think that short style is pretty much all you could do to salvage the mess I've made." Brooke watched as Ava considered this and was surprised to see the precise moment the penny dropped.

"You had me pick up a color as close to Maria's as I could get, didn't you?" Ava narrowed her eyes at her.

Brooke smiled slightly, caught in her reasoning. "What can I say? I'm not tall or butch enough to look like Cole, but I think I could reasonably adopt Maria's cut and get that Nat Porter style. I might as well try for one win out of this debacle."

"Good thing for you I'm an excellent hair stylist." Ava began to gather up her shampoos.

Yes, I'm very lucky you're my friend, Brooke thought darkly the second Ava's back was turned.

I've just got to remember you're not as dumb as you look.

Chapter Nineteen

The golden pocket watch in Cole's hand shone in the bright lighting set up over the workbench. Everything was in place for the extreme close-up of her engraving it. The scene set in the jewelry shop was a brief one, shot out of sequence to accommodate actor Arthur Anderson's schedule. He was portraying Emily's father. The set they were shooting on was his worktable and it was here that he would teach Hollister how to mend watches by working on her own. They'd been rehearsing for over an hour, switching between the various scenes that needed to be captured all in one day.

Cole had received a crash course in engraving. It would be her hands seen etching her initials into the watch's casing. The initials Hollister had thought were her father's. The close-up shot of the engraving itself had been a lesson in patience. The intricate work didn't lend itself to having a camera trained directly onto nervous novice hands. Cole had gone through three pocket watch casings before her hand had stopped visibly shaking and she had carved the initials into the gold. They were to auction off the extra watches for a charity Mischa headlined. It would garner both positive publicity for the movie and raise money for a worthy cause. Cole had a watch from her earlier engraving lessons secreted away as her own memento from the movie. It had her own initials and Eris's etched out neatly along with the date they first met at rehearsals. A shaky but recognizable heart finished the personal sentiment. She'd asked to buy the watch but the jeweler supplying them had called her a hopeless romantic while waving off any mention of payment. He'd then made a veiled comment about supplying her with wedding rings. Since then she'd kept the watch discreetly hidden inside the secret padded pocket of her heavy leather motorcycle jacket.

The first scene filmed was a simple one. Edward Brown was training Hollister to take over his business. He had high hopes that Hollister would marry his daughter and the business could continue, run by a man. Hollister needed his help to mend the watch that had brought her back in time. Cole had already filmed the scene where Hollister tried to get the mended watch to work again, desperately trying to have it return her to her timeline and *her* Emily. The pocket watch, for all it had its innards replaced, would do nothing more than tell the time. For now, its magic was lost and had trapped Hollister in *this* time with a different version of Emily. She'd gotten the chance to start a life again with this woman, one who called to Hollister's lonely and lost heart. This Emily, whose heart beat out the same rhythm that her beloved wife's had.

Eris stood off-set, having a teaching moment with the director. Cole was so proud of her and how, amid the intense shooting they were doing, Eris still found time to listen and learn. Cole had no doubt Eris would take her place behind a camera and take up directing. She had an affinity for it, and her patience and friendly nature made her a joy to work with, before or behind the camera.

It had been an easy day on set. Arthur was an amazing actor to work with, and he told the best stories every time they had to take their seats off stage while the set dressers changed the scene for them. It amused Cole how enraptured the old man was with Eris. He treated her differently than he did Cole. He acted like a father to her on and off set with his genuine concern and his teasing comments. Eris played along with it. Their relationship in the movie was going to stand out on the screen for its authenticity.

For what felt like the millionth time, Cole felt her phone vibrate in her pocket. It was on silent, but the incessant buzz against her leg was starting to annoy her. She told herself she'd have to switch the thing off completely not to be distracted while filming her scenes.

Within a few minutes, it buzzed again and Cole let out a frustrated sigh and dug to get the phone out from under her many layers.

"What's wrong?" Eris frowned at her as she walked over to join Cole on a break and could see how agitated she was.

"I need to switch this damn phone off. I've got it on silent, but it's vibrating a rumba rhythm through my leg." She finally freed her phone and stared at the screen. "What the hell? I've had seven missed calls and someone messaging me every few minutes. I rarely get more than a message a day, and that's usually just Pizza Hut's daily offers." Cole scrolled through the twenty plus messages that were demanding her attention. They were all from Charles Walsh, her costar on *Fortune's Rise*. Cole quickly scrolled back to the first message.

Call me.

She had three more with that message, the last one in capital letters. Then it switched.

When you get a break from filming, call me ASAP.

"Is something wrong?" Eris leaned closer, shielding Cole from view as she opened more texts.

"I swear to God, if he's pestering me again about what he should wear to the premiere I'll block his number." She opened a few more. "What the hell is wrong with him?" She began reading them aloud so Eris knew what she was reading.

Don't make me write this in a text. Call me.

If your phone is uncharged like it usually is I will come over there and kill you. Answer your phone!

Please answer this text.

God damn it, all hell's breaking loose here. Reply when you read this.

Cole started typing back.

I'm here. What's wrong?

It didn't take long for a reply to come whizzing back. Cole's blood ran cold as she read it.

A fan just tried to kidnap Maria's son.

❖

Cole prided herself on being professional. She pushed herself to finish the day's filming without anyone on set noticing how worried she was. She'd asked Charles to keep her informed on any more news concerning what had happened to Maria. She'd handed her phone over to Eris when she wasn't filming to keep an eye out for any new texts Cole might receive. Cole had sent a text to Maria asking for her to call as soon as she was able. It hadn't been until after filming had stopped for the day that Maria finally got in touch.

Cole was back home in her apartment with Eris staying over when the call finally came.

"Maria, I have Eris here. Do you mind if I put you on speaker?" At her assent, Maria's voice sounded out loud and clear in the room.

"Cole, this really wasn't the way I wanted to meet the new lady in your life. Hi, Eris."

"Hello, Maria. We are so worried about you." Eris placed a can of beer in front of Cole and sat beside her, cradling a glass of wine in her hand.

"Yeah, well, it's been a stressful kind of day. Charles contacted you, right?"

"Yes. What the fuck happened, Maria? Just who is this woman that confronted you today?" Cole leaned forward in her seat. Eris gently stroked her back to help calm her.

"I was preparing to take Mateo to my mother's because I wasn't due on set until later this morning. I had literally left him a moment to go get his bag of toys from the front porch and when I came back there was a woman sitting in the back seat of my car right beside him. She started off so friendly. It was like she didn't realize that her being in my car wasn't the place for her to be. It was so unreal. Mateo was crying. I have no idea what she'd done to him before I got back, but the doctor I had examine him said he hadn't been touched so that's a blessing. I know Pudge was on the floor of the car so I'm guessing he was crying for him."

"Pudge?" Cole asked, frowning.

"Mateo's teddy bear. He won't go anywhere without him." Maria was silent for a moment. "Sorry, I have his baby monitor beside me and I have to keep checking that I can hear him breathing.

The kid snores. It's cute, except when he's sharing your bed and it's right in your ear. At the moment, hearing that sound is reassuring me he's asleep in his bed and he's safe and sound. Rico's outside. He's supervising the installation of a new high tech security system. There's going to be sensors and lights everywhere. No one will ever be able to just walk right up to our house again without us knowing."

"Do you know who the woman was? Have we met her on set or at a convention or anything? We used to have that group of women who'd congregate outside the studio lot and would be there whenever we came out. They were always so lovely though. I hope she's not one of them and she was right in front of our faces every day for months." Cole sat back and reached for Eris's hand. She desperately needed her contact. She had a horrible feeling this fan was one of those who'd caused her to lose her ex and was part of the catalyst for Cole to leave the show altogether. She'd thought that what she'd gone through was bad enough, but for someone to go after Maria and her son was even more terrifying.

"I can't honestly place her. You know how many people went by us at the last convention we did. They were a conveyor belt of faces. We just had time to say 'hi, how you doing? Thanks for coming,' sign their photos, and move on to the next. I don't remember her, and I didn't recognize her. But I could sure as hell remember her now after having her drag me away from trying to shield my son. She got right up in my face. It was all about that damned Morter ship, Cole. The fucking relationship they follow that doesn't even exist." Maria's anger was apparent in every word she spat out. "She wants you back on the show so we can be together again. I know there's a large fan base for that ship. Hell, we *courted* them back at the con because they generate publicity, and at the end of the day we need the viewers. We all know that if you fuck over the fans you can lose their viewership and kiss your ratings good-bye. We've known too many shows that have stuck their middle finger up to the viewers and said 'no, we're doing it this way whether you like it or not,' and their viewers have walked and the shows have tanked. *Fortune's Rise* can't take that kind of a hit. We've already lost thousands because you've left."

Cole shared a surprised look with Eris. "*Really*?"

Maria scoffed at her. "What did you expect? You were a popular leading character on the show. You have your own set of devoted fans, Cole. You left; they went too."

"But the show hasn't even aired the last episode when I leave yet."

"Some don't want to see you go." Maria sighed. "I know how they feel. I didn't want you to go either."

Cole stayed silent. Eris leaned into her and cuddled close for support.

"I know why you left, Cole. They broke up your relationship with that skinny blonde."

Cole had to smile. Maria had hated her ex from their first meeting.

"You know I didn't think she was good enough for you, but she didn't deserve to be scared away with their hate posts, death threats, and the warnings of bodily harm that should never be posted by a fan. For God's sake, it's just a damned TV show. Then Rico weighed in and blew up over the stupid cheating rumors they stirred up about us. I know I wasn't the friend you deserved through all of that, and I can't ever apologize enough for letting you down at the time you needed me the most. And Rico realizes now he made it a thousand times worse being such an ass, trying to soothe his wounded pride over the fact that people would rather see you and me together than my being with him." Maria paused. "But, Cole, this woman, this *fan of ours*, she found my address, came to my house, sat in my car, screamed at my child, and threatened me. She said she'd stop at nothing to get her endgame. That's you and me together in the show. Or off it. She confronted me about Eris being in your life as if you were cheating on me with her. This is crazy. We're not a couple, but she didn't seem to see it that way at all."

Cole's blood froze. This fan was involving Eris. Her head screamed to keep Eris safe. She had to ensure the so-called fans never had another chance to involve Eris in whatever stupid scenarios they concocted. She wondered what it was about this select few that they just couldn't leave Cole alone to live her life the way she wanted to. Eris was a no-go. Cole needed to stop this right now.

Eris seemed to know exactly what Cole was thinking. Her face hardened and she took Cole's chin in her hand and tugged on Cole to face her. "She is not scaring me away. I'm in the same business as you are, Cole. I've known some intense fans. Mostly men who would be willing to 'fuck me straight' and were happy to announce that to my face."

Cole's fury ignited. Eris gripped her chin a little tighter.

"I am not going anywhere. They are not ruining what we are starting here. And they are not stopping you from living your life with someone who adores you."

Silence fell over the room as Cole just stared into Eris's intense face. Finally, she nodded. "Okay," she said, her voice quiet so as not to break the moment between them.

"Eris, I *really* can't wait to meet you," Maria said. "Cole, you have the drawing of this woman that I was able to give the police. The show is posting it online tonight along with a video from the *Fortune's Rise* producers putting out the message to the fans for them to stop terrorizing its actresses and their families. They're also telling them to call the police if they know who came after me."

"Wow, that's a bold stance from them. Where was that response when my girlfriend was receiving rape threats because they felt she was in the way of you and me getting together?"

"I think they've learned their lesson, Cole, and are finally hearing what we'd been telling them for months. This kind of fanatical fandom isn't going to just slink away into the night because they aren't getting the content they want to see. They are generating bad press for the show and they are coming to our doors. We have to speak out now and tell them enough is enough."

"I wish it hadn't come to this, Maria."

"I know, Cole. I know you thought that if you took yourself out of the show that things would die down. This fan isn't letting anything get in her way for the kind of storytelling she demands to see. And she expects us to give her the Chris and Nat, or Cole and Maria, happy ending she's demanding."

"There's always been a fine line between fan and fanatic," Eris said.

"And this fanatic has had contact with us. She had the nerve to tell me she'd had her photo taken with me at the con as if I'd recognize her immediately and understand her actions. That I'd just sit down and chat with her about her grievances with the show over a cup of coffee." Maria sounded exasperated.

Eris interrupted what Cole was about to say. "Wait. She had a photo taken with you at a con?"

"Yes, the last one we did, apparently. Called herself my biggest fan because she'd had numerous photos with us. Every fan is our biggest fan. I just wish I could remember her."

"Call the convention team that ran that con. They could still have photos up on their site for people to buy or have copies on their files of every one taken," Eris said. "If they do, you can just search through the faces until you find her. You said you wouldn't forget her face now. Then look for her. She gave you a clue to who she is. She went to the con. They'll have her name and address as an attendee." Eris planted a kiss on Cole's cheek. "Maybe you can find her that way and put a stop to what she's doing. Then you can both sleep easier at night."

Maria laughed softly. "Oh my God, Cole. You struck gold with this one."

"Believe me, I know it." Cole said, looking at Eris in wonder.

The sound of papers rustling came from Maria's side of the call. "I'll get my manager on it straight away and get the police involved. I have the direct line to one of them. I'm not letting her get away with terrorizing Mateo. If I see her anywhere near him again? I'll kill her."

"That wouldn't help the ratings," Cole said, trying to defuse Maria's rage. "Let's get the police involved. Damn, I wish I'd just done that when it all started, but my manager said it would blow over in time and not to antagonize the rest of the fandom."

"You need a new manager," Eris said, her face darkening with annoyance.

"I know. I'm thinking of asking Mischa to recommend me a new one."

"I forgot you're hanging out with her now," Maria said. "Is she as larger than life as the rumors suggest?"

"She's all that and more. You'll see for yourself when you come to the premiere."

"You're inviting *me*?" Maria sounded tentative and disbelieving.

"We were caught up in a crappy situation, Maria. I'd like to think our friendship could withstand that."

"And Rico? Can you ever forgive him?"

Cole made a gagging face at Eris. Eris covered her mouth to mask her laughter.

"In time, I'm sure. Bring him along. When he sees how beautiful and talented a leading lady I have on my arm, both on and off set, maybe he'll quit spreading lies about me concerning his wife and me."

"Oh, believe me, I put him straight on that months ago. He realized how close he came to losing me over running his stupid mouth and slandering both of us in the process. He came off looking like a clown to acquaintances. He's still putting those fires out now among his drinking buddies to try to get a good reputation back."

"I'm glad to hear it." Cole felt a weight lift from her shoulders. Rico's lies had been a burden that had dragged her spirits down. He'd been a friend before all the shit had hit the fan. "Maria? If you need me, I'm just a call away, okay?"

"I know. I'll keep you informed on what the police find." Maria paused a moment. "And, Cole? Please stay safe out there. This woman is crazy."

Cole looked at Eris. "We'll be careful, I promise."

"When the police catch her? Dinner is on me," Maria said.

Eris laughed. "My sister owns a restaurant. We can keep the celebration going all night there."

"Deal. You can definitely count me in for that. Be safe, you two. Watch your backs."

"We will. Speak to you soon." Cole ended the call. "So the police are involved now. I feel like I can breathe a little easier at last."

The twinkling lights from the buildings outside drew Cole's gaze to her windows and out into the city that stretched endlessly for miles.

Cole sent a message into the night. *I hope this is the last night you sleep peacefully in your bed, bitch, unaware that someone is hunting you down like you did us. We're coming for* you *now.*

She stood and reached out a hand to Eris, unable to stop keeping her near after all that had happened that day. She hated feeling so needy, but her emotions were flying in every direction and she needed the calming influence of Eris to center her. "After today, I feel like I could sleep a whole month away. Take me to bed. I need to hold you close and have you hold me. It's been one hell of a shitty day."

"Tomorrow will be better," Eris said, leading Cole toward her bedroom, playfully swinging their hands between them. Cole knew she was deliberately trying to defuse the intensity of the day.

She just hoped Eris was right.

Chapter Twenty

It was so subtle at first that Cole didn't realize someone was trailing in her footsteps. It took a couple of days for her to stop dismissing it as her being paranoid. Cole finally flipped when she caught sight of a man watching her with Eris in her trailer. She stormed into Aiden's office, ready for a fight.

"You hired a bodyguard for me?" Cole leaned over the desk at Aiden.

Aiden just sat back in her seat and pointed for Cole to sit down. Cole did so.

"You're really having me tailed all over the set by some no-neck bruiser of a guy? Do you really think I'm in danger at work?"

"If your former costar can have that woman walk right up to her on her doorstep, then you'd better believe I'm taking no chances where you're concerned."

"I don't need protection."

"Then don't see it as me looking out for a friend. See me as protecting my investment in you as the lead in my movie. I can't afford to have some mad woman come after you while we're still in production." Aiden stopped for a moment. "Sounds cold and calculating, doesn't it, when I put it like that? But either way, you've got a shadow until Brooke Harman is apprehended."

"That fucking woman is still on the run. Maria was able to identify her from the con photos, but it still wasn't enough. She'd already packed up and left." Cole was furious the police had arrived too late to catch her at home.

"She had a trophy wall though, didn't she? All her photos and the cuttings, all helping to create the world she saw you two inhabiting."

Cole nodded. "There was even a photo of her with me at the airport the day we left for London. I can't believe she was there or that I spoke to her." Cole remembered what the police had reported. "She'd deliberately cut Eris out of the picture. I think that creeps me out the most."

Aiden ran her finger along a line in the wood of her desk. Her mind was obviously elsewhere. "Bernett had a wall for Cassidy. For some fans, they are reminders of characters they love. For others, it's a wall dedicated to their obsession and a visual reminder of what they want and can't have." She looked up, her face brooking no argument. "You have someone watching your back. Learn to live with it. He'll go as soon as we know you're safe from her. Maria's manager has assigned one for her too."

"Why was I not informed?"

Aiden frowned. "I was under the impression you'd received a text from the security firm telling you to expect a shadow."

Cole pulled her phone from her pocket. She checked her messages and found it, unopened. Cole looked at Aiden sheepishly. "I totally missed it. In my defense, I've been a little distracted lately. I'm sorry I overreacted. It won't happen again."

"What? Do you think what you've just done would have me kicking you off the set? I live with Cassidy Hayes. Believe me, I know over-dramatics when I see them. And I know the difference between anger and fear. I understand, Cole. Everything that is happening is bound to have you on edge."

"Do you know how far he goes to keep tabs on me?"

"He follows you home."

Cole digested this. "What, is he like sitting outside my apartment door checking out everyone who gets off the elevator?"

"No, I believe he waits in the lobby with the guy at the front desk checking that the only ones who come in are who they say they are. There's apparently only one way into your building and that means he can give you your privacy but still be on the lookout for Brooke Harman."

"How do *you* know all this?"

"Because *I* read *all* my texts." Aiden smiled smugly. "The security firm sends me updates seeing as it's my production team paying for your guard."

"Aiden," Cole whined, wishing she didn't have to do this for her. She willed herself to calm down and finally asked the question she hadn't had the strength to speak out loud yet. "Do you really think I'm in danger from this woman? This Brooke Harman?"

"You're asking the survivor of a man who went to a convention one day armed with the intention to kill my lover and anyone else who got in his way? He nearly killed a man who was guarding Cassidy. Bernett nearly killed me." She rubbed at her chest. "He didn't come armed with a photo for her to sign, or want a photo taken. He came with the clear intent that on that day he would kill Cassidy because he saw her as *his*. His to do with as he pleased. He held the power of life and death over her. And he chose death because he could see no other way to prove his ownership of her." Aiden smiled sadly over the desk at Cole. "As for you, you're someone who has had her private life constantly tampered with and who has been forced to leave a show that you probably would have worked happily on until cancelation…what do you *honestly* think?"

"To be honest, I'm not worried about me. I'm more worried about Eris. The fans managed to get my last girlfriend to leave. Admittedly, she wasn't someone I envisioned growing old with, but they deliberately targeted her with a barrage of hate. She left because she didn't feel safe anymore from them. I don't blame her. What they tweeted and emailed her was disgusting and it screws with my mind. They are *grown-ups*, for God's sake, not little children being spiteful over toys. Women, men, old enough to know better, who are forcing their way into my life and telling me who I should be with. And if I fail to comply, they deliberately make my life a living hell. I know other actresses who have gone through the same things. They land a role and suddenly they're not what a small but noisy element of the fan base wants after all. Judged and found lacking on everything from how tall they are to how much cleavage they show. The fans don't like their boyfriend, or their girlfriend, or who they hang out with off the set. A group of petty minded judges and juries who sit at their computer screens, laying out the law to people they don't really know." Cole rubbed at her face, tired of the constant trial by fire people in the acting industry had to face.

Aiden nodded. "I know. It's the nature of the business we're in, Cole. That's why I wanted to do things *my* way. Start my own business and create the kind of things I want to watch." She shrugged ruefully. "But I still can't control the way that media is received. I can't stop someone from reading my book and wanting Hollister with another woman. I didn't write it that way, but they can be adamant that Hollister should be with someone other than Emily."

"That's sacrilege," Cole said.

"Exactly, but whatever is written or shown becomes a different thing to every single person who interacts with it. I mean, I ship Batman with Selina Kyle. Not Vicki Vale, not Julie Madison, and definitely *not* Wonder Woman. I know what I like to see. But I don't refuse to watch the others, I just have my preference. Some fans can love a couple, even when they're not canon, and just be happy with that preferred coupling. They create their own little world where these characters are king and they don't hurt anyone. But the stans who demand that what they want they should get are the loose cannons in any fandom. It's the fine line between dressing as your favorite character for fun but also dressing as the actor and trying to take on his life for your own. Look how many people we've seen have plastic surgery to look like someone famous." Aiden got up from her seat and sat on the edge of her desk, closer to Cole. "I'm still one who can immerse myself in a fantasy world and be at peace there. I'm not lonely anymore. I have Cassidy, and a wide circle of friends. But I can easily lose myself in rich, imaginative worlds where I can leave reality behind and live the story told. I know people use my books to do the same thing, to be in a different place, be a different person, to have a sense of joy when real life sucks and you just need the escapism. For some, that's enough. But there's always that one who can't let go of their dream couple and it becomes an obsession. They *need* them together, nothing else matters or can fill the ache if something breaks that couple apart. We are a world full of lonely people, all desperate for something that makes us feel." She leaned over to rest her hand on Cole's shoulder. "The trouble is, sometimes for *them* to feel, they have to hurt others in the process."

Eris knew Cole had been sorely tempted to open up the throttle on her motorcycle and deliberately lose the bodyguard tailing them. They'd ridden at a more sedate speed though, mindful of the evening traffic, and pulled up in the parking lot of Andinos with the guard in tow. Cole had been uncharacteristically quiet all afternoon. Eris was waiting her out. She knew she'd find out eventually what Cole was fighting with, as they had few secrets between them. It made for a refreshing partnership. Eris was loving the freedom it gave them to express themselves and explore the intense feelings they shared. It wasn't like any other relationship she'd had before. It was as unique to her as Cole was.

Reluctant to let go of her hold around Cole's waist, Eris sighed and eased herself off the motorcycle. She left her helmet in place, knowing they didn't have the luxury of privacy in the middle of the parking lot. The grainy photo of her and Cole kissing still doing its rounds in the media was proof of that.

Jones, their guard for that evening, pulled his black car alongside them. He got out and gazed longingly at Cole's Harley Davidson.

"That's a beautiful machine."

Cole ran her hand along the leather seat. "Rides like a dream too."

Eris tugged Cole away. "Quit drooling over it, you two. It's just a bike."

Cole stopped dead in her tracks and covered the cycle's mirrors as if stopping it from hearing Eris's scurrilous words. "Just a bike? Just a *bike*? You take that back!"

Eris rolled her eyes at Cole's playfulness.

"I could guard the *bike* too," Jones said, his voice just a little too hopeful.

Cole waggled her keys at him. "Not a chance, Jones. The keys are coming with me. You're not tearing up and down the highway on my baby."

Eris felt sorry for him. "Will it help you feel better to know my sister has a place set up for you between the kitchen and the hallway and that whatever you want off the menu is free?" She laughed at how quickly his sad face turned into a shocked one then into a very hungry one.

"Really? I could never afford to dine in a place like this." He followed their lead into the restaurant.

"Don't be fooled by how grand this place looks, Jones. The prices are very affordable if you know what to order."

"Suddenly, I'm glad I got the late night posting." Jones rubbed his hands together. "Although if this is a recurrent theme, I'm going to need to buy a bigger suit."

"It's all a thanks for you watching over us when there's probably no need." Cole removed her helmet and ran a hand over her short hair as if checking for a bristle out of place.

"Best to be careful though, Ms. Calder. I've been in this business a long time. Cases where we're rarely engaged are few and far between." He followed them upstairs to the apartment above the restaurant. "I'll just do a sweep and then I'll leave you to your evening."

Cole leaned against the wall and watched him conduct a thorough search of the rooms through the open front door.

"It's like having an overprotective parent following us around, checking our bedrooms in case we have boys over," Eris said, leaning into Cole's side and peering around her to watch him.

"Well, that's not happening any time soon," Cole said. She turned away from the door. "My parents pretty much left me to my own devices when I was young. They were always too busy. I wonder sometimes why they even bothered to have a child."

Eris cuddled in closer. "I'm thankful they did. I'm warning you now, when you meet my mom and dad they will probably make you wish for a little less interest. But I'm sure you'll cope just fine. You've already endured my sister's third degree."

"Yeah, I was surprised how easily she got me to spill so much information, short of my shoe size or cup size."

"Oh, she'd have worked that out by just looking at you. She's spooky like that. She can size a boob within seconds. I've told her she should have been a lesbian."

"She should have been an interrogator." Cole nodded as Jones came out of the apartment and deemed it safe.

They entered and quickly removed their coats. Eris hung them up on the rail by the front door, toed out of her shoes, and padded around the kitchen in her socks.

"Melanie was on track to being a policewoman so her interviewing talent would have served her well. But while she was in college she met Georgio. He was an exchange student over in London at the time. One look and both were head over heels. Georgio was the heir to Andinos and Melanie moved to America to start training to be a chef to work by his side." Eris checked her phone. She replied to the message that had just dinged as Melanie welcomed her home. "I'm not knocking her choices because I get fed regularly and with quality produce, all while having a roof over my head while I pursue my own dreams. By the way, what do you fancy tonight, Chinese, Mexican, Indian, Italian, or a steak dinner perhaps? Oh, Melanie says they have fish in too if you're in the mood for white meat."

"Italian sounds great. I could seriously go for lasagna."

Eris tapped that into her phone and asked for the same. She put her phone away and continued as if there'd been no interruption. "I know she's happy here, and blissfully happy with Georgio, but I can't help but wonder."

"What?"

"I wonder what kind of life she'd have had if she'd followed her own path."

"I believe everyone comes into our lives for a reason. Everyone has a lesson to teach us, be it good or bad. I guess it depends on whether you believe in fate placing someone in your path to direct you to a happier outcome." She gestured toward the bathroom. "I'm going to quickly wash up, and when I come back we can discuss this further." Her phone rang while she was walking away. "Damn it, who is this now?" She answered the call as she walked into the bathroom.

Eris tried to sort out the jumble of thoughts and feelings going on inside her head. Why was she so adamant to stick to her guns and doggedly follow the path she had marked out for herself from the minute she'd started drama school? Was a part of it because she'd never fully understood Melanie changing her whole life in order to walk by Georgio's side and help him fulfil his dream? *Have I been trying so hard not to follow in her footsteps that I've limited my own life's experiences? Have I been so focused on my work and determined to be happy on my own that I ignored that, if I found the* right *woman, I could be happy with someone else in my life too?*

Eris's gaze went to the bathroom door. *Is Cole my Georgio? The one who is offering me a life outside of the work that has consumed me for years now? Do I let her do that?* Can *I let her do that? Is she the one to finally make me believe that I might have found a soul mate all of my own?*

Cole returned, rolling up her shirtsleeves which never failed to derail Eris's thinking.

"So, where were we?" Cole took Eris into her arms, but she looked shaken and distracted. The sudden change in her demeanor was startling. To Eris's keen eye she looked almost *frightened* but was trying desperately to hide it. "What's going on inside that brilliant mind of yours?"

"I was wondering what would happen to me if I chose a different path than the one I've been diligently walking for so long." Eris deliberately continued their conversation as if nothing was wrong.

"Well, that's the wonderful thing about paths. They have all sorts of turns and branch-offs that can lead you to new places. But that main path doesn't disappear. You can always go back to it and continue your journey from it if you choose." Cole rubbed her cheek against Eris's hair. "Have you ever thought that maybe you're the *Georgio* in your life's journey? The one who holds out *her* hand to someone who is traveling on a different path? Yet with just one look from you they'll alter their life's course to follow you in *yours*?"

"I can't say I've ever thought myself worthy of having someone trust me so much with themselves."

"I'd trust you with my life."

Though the sentiment was heartfelt and earnest, what Eris saw reflected in Cole's eyes made her heart still for a moment. Time froze as Eris stared and saw a bleakness there, hiding behind Cole's sincere words. *Something is dreadfully wrong. She looks like she's going to say good-bye*. Eris knew it as clearly as if Cole had just spoken the words out loud.

"I would never ask you to give up your dreams for me. I'd want to stand by your side and watch you succeed in everything you do. I know you'll be a director someday and you'll be fantastic at it. I don't ever want you to put your dreams on hold for…" Cole stuttered to a stop.

Eris continued to stare at her. "What's wrong?" Her chest ached at the agony that flashed over Cole's face. She could feel Cole shaking in her arms. It made Eris grip tighter. "What?" she asked, her voice soft over the sound of her own heart breaking at Cole's distress.

"I just got a call from the police. They haven't caught Brooke Harman yet. They have no leads at all so they're scaling back the search for her. She's not their highest priority." Cole's tone grew angry. "But she's still out there and every hour she's not found, you're in danger."

Eris digested every word Cole gave her. Cole's voice was breaking and her body trembling as she tried to keep herself together, but she was shattering and crumbling and all Eris could do was watch.

"You're the one they think she'll target, Cole, not me. You don't have to worry about me. We need to worry about *you*."

"But she can use you to get to me, hurt you to hurt me. I can't do that to you. You don't deserve what people like her are willing to do to discredit you all over social media. You don't deserve to have to deal with that kind of shit from the crazy followers I seem to attract. I don't want her near you."

"I won't let her do anything to me, Cole. The police will find this woman, you and Maria can breathe a sigh of relief, and you and

I will star in a blockbuster movie that will be a force for change in LGBTQ cinema."

"I can't help but feel you'd be better off without me, especially now—"

Eris cupped Cole's face in her hands. "Don't ever say that. Don't you realize how long I've been waiting for someone exactly like you to come stand right in my lane and refuse to let me pass unless we take the rest of the journey together?"

Finally, without hesitation, Eris made her choice.

"I want to walk my life's path with you, Cole. I want to walk beside you, or skip ahead of you urging you to follow me. I want to carry you when you think you just can't take another step and I want to walk our grandbabies along it and point out all the cool things their grandmas did together because they never walked alone again. I want our paths to merge so we don't miss another moment of being together." Eris watched as tears streamed down Cole's face. Her eyes misted as her own tears formed and fell.

"I love you, Eris." Cole sniffed inelegantly, making Eris laugh at her. "I really do."

"I love you too, Cole." Eris reached up to kiss her. Their kisses were salty from their tears but far sweeter for the words they shared. "Don't ever think you have to leave me to keep me safe. I'll always be safest here, right beside you." Eris smiled into Cole's shining eyes. "I always thought when I fell in love I'd be expected to lose so much of myself. I never realized that, instead, you'd give me the one thing I never thought I'd have."

"What's that?" Cole wiped away a stray tear from Eris's face and brushed at her cheek, caressing her as if she couldn't believe she was real.

"The confidence that my grandad spoke the truth."

"That soul mates exist," Cole said, knowing exactly what Eris was going on about.

"And that I'm worthy of having one."

Eris's words hung heavy between them. They both jumped at a soft chime that sounded. Frowning, Cole pulled a pocket watch out of her jeans pocket and popped open the lid to reveal the time.

"What are you doing with Hollister's watch?" Eris kept her voice barely above a whisper as they crowded over the pocket watch, as if keeping it from prying eyes.

"It's not Hollister's. They don't allow that one to be removed from the set except by its handler. This is one I got to work on when I was practicing my calligraphy. I was very kindly gifted it by the jewelers." Cole shrugged, her face reddening a little with embarrassment. "It's not like they could ever sell it once I'd engraved my own initials into it." She turned the watch over in her hand. Eris gasped when she saw her own initials there too, intertwined with Cole's, and a heart drawn in the gold as a permanent reminder.

"Who knew you were such a romantic soul, Cole Calder?" Eris traced the writing on the case then drew her finger along the shape of the heart. "Does the chime go off every hour?"

Cole frowned at the watch. "No, in fact it's not designed to chime at all." She flipped the watch over in her hand, trying to make sense of it. "It must have been my phone. Funny though, I automatically reached for the watch and not the phone."

Eris felt tears begin to well up again. She looked up and smiled.

Message received, Grandad.

Chapter Twenty-one

A Pocket Full of Time Instagram Live, 2 p.m. Q&A with actresses Cole Calder and Eris Whyte, producer Aiden Darrow, and director Olivia Todd.

Cole felt physically sick just looking at the placeholding screen that advertised the hour Aiden had earmarked for publicity purposes. Her stress levels were rising daily the longer Harman was missing. Q&A sessions only made Cole more nervous as they were so unpredictable. Cole had wanted to cancel it, but Eris had talked her out of that. Eris was right, they couldn't let one fan spoil things for the rest. Cole had reluctantly agreed. That didn't stop her from feeling anxious. This would be a perfect opportunity for Harman to show she was still watching. That thought alone made Cole's skin crawl. She really wanted her life back and to just be able to breathe again without worrying who was counting her every breath.

Aiden squeezed Cole's shoulder as she settled in beside her. Aiden and Olivia were to sit on either side of them. Aiden had brought in her assistant Gabby to have her finger on the screen so that if anyone started kicking off she could block them immediately. Cole knew Aiden wasn't taking Brooke Harman's silence for granted. She'd been here, done this before when Cassidy's stalker broke cover. The movie had to court its audience, and the publicity machine couldn't grind to a halt because of one woman's antics.

Eris took her seat and leaned into Cole deliberately in order to chat with Aiden.

"It's weird doing a movie where you're not quite sure what constitutes a spoiler because everyone has read the book."

Aiden laughed. "Oh, I can guarantee we'll get people worried their favorite scene has been left out. You can't translate a whole novel onto the screen unless you expect your audience to sit for countless hours. This is why I wanted to produce it myself and write the screenplay. I know the material by heart, and having been a screenwriter on other movies, I know what you can afford to lose without spoiling the plot or really disappointing the devoted reader."

"I think it's bringing the book to life," Cole said. "I can't wait to see the finished product myself."

Olivia rushed in, bearing bottles of water for everyone. "Sorry, I had someone feel *now* was the moment they needed to ask me something." She doled out the bottles and looked up at the clock in the conference room. "Phew. I have enough time to catch my breath before we see if anyone is watching us."

For a moment, Cole wished the internet feed would disconnect and they'd have to call it off. She didn't feel in the mood to be cheery and talkative about this project when all she could think about was that woman, out there, watching *her*.

Eris captured Cole's hand lightly in her own. "Breathe in, breathe out…" She repeated the mantra softly until Cole followed her instructions and felt herself relax.

"You nervous about being live, Cole?" Olivia took a swig from her bottle and dribbled a bit down her chin. "Oh fuck. That's a great start!" She mopped at her chin with her sleeve.

"More nervous about who will be out there asking the questions."

Aiden shook her head. "Don't be. There's not just us watching over this feed. Mischa pulled a few strings again. If Harman makes a move on here, the tech police are watching and will be chasing her through the web. There's no way I'm throwing you to the wolves, Cole. Trust me on that."

Cole nodded and took comfort in Eris's comforting smile. "You ready to answer all those invasive questions, babe?"

Eris's grin widened at the nickname that fell unconsciously from Cole's lips. Cole wasn't usually one for using such monikers, but it felt so natural to call Eris something personal. She *was* a babe. She was also *Cole's* babe. Judging by the look Eris was giving her, she liked it just fine.

"I'm ready for 'Yes, my corset is gorgeous, and thank God I can still eat while wearing it.' 'Yes, Cole is a dream to work with, and no, I won't tell you if that was us in *that* photo. We'd rather keep you guessing.' Or perhaps 'Yes, the movie has been an utter joy to work on and a big yes, Cole *really* is as handsome as she appears now that her hair is less girly.' Or there's 'Yes, I know I'm very *very* lucky to be acting with her.'" Eris leaned deliberately closer, teasing Cole in order to get her to loosen up. "And 'Oh God, yes, she kisses like a dream.'"

Aiden chuckled beside them. "Hopefully, they'll ask less personal questions because Cole can't hide that blush of hers if she tries."

Embarrassed, Cole hid her cheeks in her hands and gave Eris a stern look. "I'd better get asked some questions about you to even the score," she warned.

Seated just out of view of the camera, Gabby slipped Aiden a list of questions that had already posted on the chat. "There's quite the audience waiting, boss. Lots of eager people with lots of questions for you all."

Aiden poised her finger over the button to start the live feed. "Are we ready?" Everyone nodded. "Let's do this movie proud." She hesitated. "And if you see the nametag *BigMommaM*? That's one of Mischa's so consider yourselves forewarned."

"Oh God," Cole muttered. "Like I'm not nervous enough."

"I'm sure she'd go easy on us." Eris sounded like she didn't believe that for a second.

"Showtime, people." Aiden turned on the live feed and the numbers of the viewers started flickering rapidly as more and more joined to watch.

"Good afternoon, everyone!" Aiden began, and Cole, Eris, and Olivia followed suit saying hi. "I'm really happy to see so many of you online with us. Rest assured we have someone who's been collecting your questions already so you won't miss out for being so quick off the mark. Welcome to the *A Pocket Full of Time* Q&A here on Instagram Live."

❖

Cole had relaxed the more the hour wore on. She'd enjoyed listening to Olivia telling everyone how much fun she was having teaching Eris a thing or two about working behind the camera lens. Eris had answered some questions about the period costumes and she'd included Cole who was able to describe how hard it was running with a top hat perched precariously on your head.

Aiden had been noticeably quiet for a while and Cole surreptitiously glanced in her direction. Gabby was tapping away on the smaller tablet. She was blocking names from a sheet Aiden had slipped her. Cole hadn't been reading the messages scrolling up the screen as Aiden was picking through them. She'd been happy to just join in on whatever someone else commented on, and Eris always passed the question she had just answered on to her. She paid a little more attention to the chat feed on the screen and finally saw what Aiden was blocking. It was the same question, over and over, coming in thick and fast from multiple different names.

When are you coming back to Fortune's Rise, Cole?

Answer this. When are you coming back to Fortune's Rise, Cole?

Answer MY question. When are you coming back to Fortune's Rise, Cole?

It took all of Cole's acting skills not to react to seeing this missive streaming past at a fast pace. The question featured predominantly every ten to twenty postings, in between fans saying how excited they were for the movie, sending love to the actresses, or asking questions about them shooting in London.

Brooke Harman says hello.

Cole couldn't help herself. She flinched and hastily tried to cover it up by shifting in her chair. Eris kept talking, purposely drawing Cole in on the question too and keeping Cole's attention firmly on her.

Of course Eris had seen the questions earlier and had been deliberately distracting me from reading them, Cole thought.

You'll answer my question, Cole Calder, if it's the last thing you do.

Cole watched the threat disappear from the stream as more questions pushed it up and away. Fans who had seen that message started sending Cole their support and writing in capitals to "yell" at Harman, if it was her, for being such a crazy stalker. Cole knew that wasn't going to end well.

All four of them studiously ignored those questions and focused on wrapping up the hour. They urged everyone to keep an eye on the website for further updates from the movie set and thanked them for all their continued support. When the stream cut, Cole let out a ragged breath.

"How long was she on there?" she asked, looking over at Gabby who was still tapping away on her tablet.

"At least the last ten minutes in force. The same question started to spool in from about ten different addresses all at once. If this was Harman, she'd obviously set up spambots to keep hitting the feed with her question," Gabby said. "The tech police should be following the IP addresses to see if she can be traced."

"I noticed some *Fortune's Rise* queries on and off throughout the feed, but that's only natural. Then the same names started popping up and the frequency of the posting really started to rise." Aiden picked up her own tablet. "I'll go liaise with the tech guys and see if they have anything we can use."

"Maybe I should have answered her," Cole said, wondering if that would have helped or just made matters worse. Aiden shook her head.

"Bear in mind, it might not have been Harman. Nothing brings the internet trolls out from under their bridges quicker to stir shit up than a situation like this. If it was her though, she was threatening you at the end, Cole. Take my word for it; you can't ever reason with crazy. I don't think anything you could say now would appease her."

Cole nodded. She had that feeling too. This woman was too far gone to listen to reason and too lost in her fantasy world to see reality as it really was. Cole dreaded to think what she'd do if she came face-to-face with this Brooke Harman. She really hoped she'd never have to find out. What could you do for someone who saw you in a whole different light than the one you walked in? Who saw you as something and someone you would never be? What could you honestly do for a fan who truly believed the character you played was *real*?

As an actress, that was the highest compliment to be paid.

As someone stalked by a fan who couldn't see past the performance, it was terrifying.

Chapter Twenty-two

Eris had brooked no argument from Cole. She had them go back to the restaurant after the Q&A session, with Jones in tow. Cole parked her motorcycle in its usual place and allowed Eris to lead her through the back of the restaurant and up the stairs to the apartment. Eris could see how stressed Cole was. If nothing else, Eris was determined to get Cole to eat and then hopefully sleep. They had a busy day planned for the next day on set. They were filming the final scenes for the movie. It was going to be draining in so many ways. They had an early call because they were due in the makeup chair to be aged dramatically with the aid of prosthetics. Their application would take hours. Then it was just going to be the two of them on set bringing the movie to its close. Eris needed Cole in a better frame of mind to tackle those last scenes. Unfortunately, everyone had left the Q&A in a state of high alert.

Damn you, Brooke Harman and the crazy fan train you rode in on, Eris thought, furious that this woman could cause so much trouble. Not just for Cole and Maria now, but for the production of the movie and the *Fortune's Rise* set that was on alert, too. All because one person couldn't separate fantasy from reality. Eris knew that was the nature of the business, the escapism of every book, show, and movie, to suspend disbelief and open up a new world for the viewer to step into. Sadly, not everyone wanted to step back *out*.

"I'm really not hungry," Cole said, taking off her coat and settling on the settee. "I just want to sleep. When I'm asleep I don't have to think about her. She doesn't exist there. I'm free of that fucking Harman woman and her stupid uber-fan antics."

"Well, I'm hungry so you might as well have something too, then I'll take you to bed." Eris climbed onto Cole's lap and straddled her. She braced her hands on the back of the settee on either side of Cole's head and leaned down to kiss Cole long and hard. She felt Cole react and return each kiss with a fervor of her own.

"God, you're addictive," Cole muttered, wrapping her arms around Eris's waist and pulling her down more. "Make me forget everything but the taste of you on my lips, the feel of you in my arms, and the fullness of your fingers inside—"

"Hi, guys, just checking to see what you want to—oh!" Melanie walked into the living room and swiftly turned her back. "Wow. I can't believe it took this long for me to finally walk in on my baby sister making out with a girlfriend."

Eris eased back from Cole and they shared an exasperated look. "Yeah, well, I wasn't as wild and spirited as you were, Melanie." She sighed. "You can turn around. We hadn't started ripping each other's clothes off yet."

Melanie looked at them. "Are you going to order food off the menu or are you just gonna eat…" She gestured between the two of them. Eris shot her a glare, but Cole just laughed.

"What's on the menu tonight?" Cole asked, helping Eris dismount and sit beside her. She reached for Eris's hand and held on tight.

"Georgio has been perfecting his vegetarian/vegan burrito range all day. Would you two care to be his guinea pigs on those? I had one earlier." She rubbed at her baby bump. "Baby Andino gave it a thumbs up." She paused. "Or it might have been a baby thumbs up at the sponge pudding and custard I craved after it. Or the cookie dough ice cream after that."

Eris stiffened. "You haven't eaten all my ice cream, have you?"

"No, ice cream hog. Your tub of ice cream is exactly where you left it. Hidden beneath the broccoli in the freezer where you think I'd never look."

"Your cravings are a nightmare."

"Your ice cream is my favorite too. You can't blame a pregnant woman for needing to give her child the nourishment it craves."

Eris snorted at her. "I'll be glad when you can't play that card any longer."

"Yeah, then I'll just deal out the new pack of 'postpartum crazies' and we'll see how that works out!"

Eris looked at Cole helplessly. "Do you have any experience with pregnant women?"

Cole shook her head. "Not unless you count my working with Maria while she was pregnant. I just remember her getting bigger and them having to raise the fence between us on set because it wasn't hiding her rapidly changing shape."

Eris stared at her sister. "Burritos it is, please. And stay away from my ice cream."

Melanie childishly stuck her tongue out at her. "I'll go get your meals. You two," she waved a hand at them, "can go back to what you were doing, but I will be back so no getting past second base. Sensitive pregnancy hormones here."

"Melanie, there's nothing sensitive about you at all," Eris muttered.

"Don't think I won't tell Mom about what I walked in on you two doing."

"Don't think I won't finally tell Mom what I walked in on you and Georgio doing on her dining room table."

Melanie narrowed her eyes at her. "You'd better not teach your nephew or niece any of your mean little sister tricks."

Eris grinned. "I'm going to be the cool auntie. I will impart *all* my wisdom to that little peanut you're growing."

Melanie huffed. "I'm going to spit in your burrito."

"Don't make me call health and safety on you."

"Cole, corral your woman!" Melanie begged, frustrated she wasn't getting the last word.

Cole just laughed at their silliness. "No, I don't think so. I happen to like her wild and free."

Melanie threw her arms in the air. "God help me. With you two as their aunts, I don't stand a chance." She waddled out the door, leaving Eris laughing but Cole struck oddly silent.

Eris looked Cole over. "What's wrong?"

"I'm going to be an *aunt*?" She looked stunned.

Eris felt her heart soften at the incredulous look on Cole's face. "Well, of course you are if you're going to be with me. The baby will get us as a packaged deal. Auntie Eris and Auntie Cole."

Cole's smile grew. "I've never been an aunt." She sounded tickled by the idea.

"Not even to Maria's kid?"

Cole shook her head. "No, Rico pretty much did the lion guarding his pride thing. I can't say I blame him now. The rumors the fans started were a nightmare. They tangled us all in them and it ruined our friendship."

Eris leaned in closer. "My family is crazy, but you're more than welcome to create a little space for yourself in it."

Cole smiled softly. "I'd like that because I don't intend to be anywhere without you."

"I like the sound of that." Eris rested her head on Cole's shoulder, and for a moment they just sat in a contented silence.

"How long do you think it will take before our meal is brought up?" Cole asked.

"Not long enough for what you have in mind."

Cole sighed gustily. "Can I at least have you for dessert?"

Eris smiled. "I'll be sure to put a sock on the door to stop my sister from interrupting us again."

"God, I'm so lucky to love a smart woman."

"I swear you guys had better be decent in there!" Melanie's voice rang out from the stairwell.

Eris sighed. "Want to run away from all this, just you and me?"

Cole nodded. "My Harley is downstairs. We can go anywhere you want."

"I'll remember that. Just you and me, an open road, the thrum of the engine between our legs."

"I knew the cycle would be a turn-on," Cole said smugly.

"Yeah, but not as much as you are." Eris leaned in for a kiss just as Melanie walked in. Their lips barely touched before Eris pulled back. "Later," she promised, loving the hungry look in Cole's eyes that had nothing to do with the food Melanie was bringing to the table.

Cole got up and pulled Eris up after her. "You going to join us, Mel?" she asked, taking in the abundance of food Melanie was spreading out.

"Thank God, I thought you'd never ask!" Melanie sat down gratefully.

Eris didn't think she could love Cole any more as she watched her make up a burrito for Melanie and listen intently to her chatter.

I'm never letting her go, Eris thought as she took her seat at the table and listened to the stalker-free stories her sister was regaling them with.

Grandad? I take back all I ever said. I think I've found her. I think I've found my one and only. My soul mate. Just like you said I would. But only when I *was ready and when* she *was ready to be found.*

The lean length of Eris's back had become a canvas for Cole's fingertips to trace across. Eris lay face down on the sheets, her skin hot and sweaty from their first round of lovemaking. That had been all lips and tongues and a way to take the edge off so that the second round could be more open to exploration. They'd bought their first sex toy together online and both had been eager to try it out. It spoke of permanency, intimacy. They'd addressed it to the restaurant since someone was always there to sign for mail. Although both of them knew it might be more prudent for them to wait until they were alone at Cole's apartment, once they'd opened the box neither of them wanted to wait.

Cole drew a line from each freckle she found on Eris's flesh. She kissed haphazardly along a meandering path she marked out down Eris's spine. She playfully took a bite at a fleshy butt cheek. Eris squealed then moaned as Cole soothed away the sting with broad swipes of her tongue. Cole shifted from where she stood at the foot of the bed. She checked the straps of the harness that held their new toy in place and reached for the bottle of lube to liberally coat the silicone length.

"I love watching you do that. You get this really intense look in your eye and I know I'm going to enjoy every minute you're inside me, fucking me." Eris looked over her shoulder, watching Cole stroke the clear liquid from top to bottom of the cock.

Cole didn't answer. She climbed on the bed, stretching up to kiss Eris's smiling lips before Eris turned away and laid her head on her arms. Cole slipped down farther, easing between Eris's spread legs and lay on top of her, pressing Eris into the mattress. She let her weight incapacitate Eris for a moment. She didn't miss the moan that escaped Eris.

"God, you feel so good," Eris whispered, shifting her body as if to feel all of Cole everywhere.

Cole laid her lips near Eris's ear. "You want to get on your knees for me?"

"No, I want you to take me like this. Your body on top of me, as close as we can get. I like feeling you all over me. I like the feel of your breasts pressing into my back while you move." She shifted her head a fraction but kept her eyes closed. Eris spoke quietly as she laid open her soul to Cole's. "I like the feeling of being under you and that you're not doing it to overpower me or make me weak. I love having your head close to mine as you gasp with every press of your body inside me. That thing may not be real, but when you wear it? It becomes a part of you and I can't get enough of it."

Cole let more of her body settle on top of Eris and she began to move, simulating the rhythm she was going to employ inside her. "You ready for me?"

"Always."

Cole slipped a hand between them, making sure Eris was wet enough for her. She grinned at the abundance of moisture that her fingers found. She shifted and slipped gently inside, letting Eris get used to both the size of the rainbow striped cock and the length. Eris tensed then relaxed beneath her as Cole pressed farther then eased back a little. She only pushed forward again when she felt Eris relax even more to welcome her in. Each press of her hips, she got a little deeper and Eris's moans got a little louder. Cole waited for a second then pulled nearly all the way out and deliberately kept Eris in suspense.

"Oh, fuck!" Eris rubbed her face into the sheet. "No teasing. I am so desperate for you."

Cole dug her elbows into the bed and, with a pump of her hips, the cock slid in and out of Eris's wet warmth with ease. She could feel Eris's body move in perfect sync with her, their bodies so firmly in tune with each other. The drag of her nipples along Eris's back tortured Cole and her hips sped up a notch as her own arousal spiked and sparked. Focused on bringing Eris nothing but pleasure, Cole pushed aside the ache from her straining muscles and sought Eris's breaking point. Cole's own insides clenched in sympathy when Eris began to tremble and moan, as her inner walls began to clamp down on the cock. Eris was fisting the sheets in her hands, holding on tight as Cole moved harder, faster, and deeper inside her. Cole could feel the sweat building on their bodies. It made her movement easier, slicker, the heat of their skin matching the heat building inside Eris as Cole took her higher with every thrust.

Eris's body started to shake as Cole found the rhythm and the angle that drove Eris wild.

"Like that! Just there! Oh my God, Cole, yes!"

Eris's gasps grew louder and mixed with Cole's huffs of exertion as she pumped her hips harder against the tightening resistance inside. Eris's whole body tensed and then shattered with a body-wracking orgasm that triggered Cole's own release. She gripped onto Eris tightly as her climax rolled through her and left her wasted. Cole barely had the forethought to pull out of Eris before she slid off her to lie boneless on the rumpled sheets by her side. When she finally caught her breath, Cole reached out a hand to touch Eris's shoulder.

"Wanna go again?" she teased and heard Eris giggle in response.

"Sure, just let me get some feeling back in my legs in the next ten hours or so. Maybe you can help me find my eyes too because I think they rolled right out of my head!" Eris turned to face her. "Oh. My. God. You are a sex goddess!"

Cole laughed at her. "*We're* amazing together and we picked a really good toy." She looked down at the appendage sticking up at her. "I really need to get this off at some point, but I think my coming slipped a disc because I can't seem to get my muscles to work." Cole started to laugh at her predicament. She felt positively drunk on the happy sex endorphins flooding her system and high on her love for the beautiful Eris, who lay beside her, laughing along with her in her own state of euphoria.

"Have I mentioned how much I love you?" Eris asked, slapping a hand on Cole's belly and rubbing at her skin soothingly before reaching down to try to undo the buckles holding the harness in place.

"Yes, you have and I love you too." Cole managed to drag herself up just enough to plant a kiss on Eris's face before sprawling on her back again to look blindly at the ceiling. "God, you're so fucking sexy. I've never come from the feel of someone else coming before. The way your body moved against mine just set me off to follow you right over the edge. You bring a whole kind of special magic to my life, Eris Whyte, do you know that?"

"I hope I do." Eris's smile was tired yet happy. "Are you sure you're not going to stay over tonight?"

"I think I'd better go home and try to get some sleep in preparation for tomorrow's early call. If I stay here I'm going to be tempted to do more than just cuddle with you, and I think tomorrow's filming will be draining enough without us both being out of it because we've fucked all night."

Eris pouted prettily. "I'm going to miss you though."

"I'm going to miss you too. I don't like sleeping alone now that I've spent so many nights in your arms." Cole eased herself up, groaning as her stomach muscles screamed at the exertion she'd put them through. "I'll go take a quick shower. I don't want Jones giving me any funny looks because I smell like sex."

Eris sighed and finally turned over so she lay on her back. Cole fought back a groan. At the sight of Eris's sweet body Cole just wanted to dive right back in. In her head she was already kissing those sweet lips, teasing Eris's nipples to rigidity, and then working her way down to lick away all the remnants of their arousal that hung heavy in the room. She pushed herself off the bed before temptation got the better of her.

"Uh-oh," Eris said, shifting a lazy arm to rest it across her eyes. "What's wrong, babe?"

"I sense a *Code Red* emergency."

Cole paused at the doorway to Eris's bathroom. "What's that?"

"I need to sneak like a secret agent and go grab my ice cream out of the freezer without my sister spotting me and demanding half the tub."

"She's already had ice cream today. She said so."

"Like that is going to stop her?" Eris lifted her arm to squint at Cole.

"Do you want me to go grab it after I've taken my shower?"

"No, I'll lie here trying not to think about the water running off that gorgeous body of yours then shuffle downstairs when you leave so I can console myself with a tub of ice cream and some mindless TV."

"You know I wouldn't be leaving your side if it wasn't necessary."

"I know. Still sucks though. Go, wash our marathon sex session off your sexy bod, and then go back to that sister-less apartment of yours. Just text me all night, okay? I hate it when you're not here."

Cole paused for a moment, deep in thought.

"How can your brain possibly still be working after what we've just done?" Eris said.

"I'm trying to work out if we'd be better living together in my apartment or living here. My apartment gives you privacy and the place is pretty much soundproof so we can get down and dirty as much as we want, *anywhere* we want." She grinned at Eris's playful glare. "But if we lived here there's the attraction of endless free food and you'd be closer to help your sister with the baby when it comes." Cole was surprised to see Eris tear up at her words. "What?"

"You have no idea how damn special you are."

Cole knew she was blushing under Eris's adoring look. "Well, now that I'm going to be an aunt too I'd at least like to be close enough to see the little rug rat all the time. You know, to get some practice in, for preparation for all those grandbabies I see in our future."

"Go hurry and turn that shower on. I'm coming in there with you." Eris hauled herself upright.

Cole didn't need to be told twice.

Chapter Twenty-three

The uniforms for the serving staff at Andinos were surprisingly simple to copy. A white shirt, black dress pants, and a short black vest all finished off with a natty red tie. Brooke just walked right in, weaving her way through the customers, and no one paid any attention to her. She quickly found her way through to the private area and readied herself to go upstairs. Cole had parked her motorcycle in its usual spot so Brooke knew she was there.

She spotted the security guard she'd been waiting for. He sat at a small table purposely set up for him, finishing his meal. Brooke smiled as she walked toward him.

"Hi! Chef wants to know what you want for dessert." She reached for his empty plate and didn't miss how quickly his face changed when he realized who she was. Without hesitation, she brought the heavy plate down on his head, watching with a detached fascination as he staggered to his feet, clutching his bleeding skull. He still tried to raise the alarm, shouting and reaching for his gun.

"Oh no, there'll be none of that." Brooke pulled out a Taser from her purse and aimed it straight at his groin. The barbed darts delivered a voltage that floored him immediately. He hit the ground so hard Brooke winced in sympathy. While he was incapacitated, Brooke worked quickly to tie his hands with plastic restraints and stuck a strip of tape across his mouth. She looked around and was grateful to spot a utility closet nearby with its door ajar.

"I see a closet with your name on it," Brooke said, dragging the guard inside and dumping him on the floor. She ripped the darts from his body causing him to scream against his gag. "Now hush. Don't make me come back for you to silence you completely." She bundled the Taser back into her purse. She stilled at a noise that came from the stairs above. She listened as Cole shouted her good-byes to Eris and then heard the sound of a door closing.

Brooke congratulated herself on her forward planning. She pulled the gun from her purse and tucked herself into the shadows under the stairs.

"Jones?"

Brooke guessed Jones was the guard she'd just delivered a high voltage of electricity directly to his junk. She cautiously stuck her head around the edge of the wall and saw Cole open the back door and stick her head outside.

"Jones?"

With Cole standing with her back toward her, Brooke made her move. She rushed up behind her, wrapped an arm about Cole's waist, pinning one arm, and stuck the gun barrel firmly into Cole's neck.

"Hi, Cole," Brooke said, tightening her grip as Cole struggled against her. Almost delirious at having Cole in her grasp, Brooke breathed in the faint aroma of a mint shampoo and an underlying vanilla scent that clung to Cole's skin.

"Brooke?" Cole froze in Brooke's hold. "What are you doing?"

"I'm way past the point of being polite, Cole. You and I are going for a little drive, somewhere we can sort this thing out once and for all." Brooke tightened her grip around Cole's waist. "You can come with me without making a fuss or I can tie you up and leave you in my car while I come back into the restaurant and gut Eris's very pregnant sister. Then I'll go upstairs and carve up that pretty face of Eris's. The choice is yours." Brooke watched Cole's face as her threats sank in. The struggling ceased immediately.

"Don't hurt them. I'll do whatever you want."

Brooke was elated. She nudged Cole forward with her body, pressing the gun harder into Cole's flesh so she didn't do anything stupid.

"Where are you taking me?" Cole asked, walking slowly out into the parking lot once Brooke had deemed it safe to do so. The lot was empty; everyone was inside enjoying their meals.

"Somewhere we can be alone. I was watching you at the Q&A today, Cole. You deliberately ignored me. You can't know how much that hurt." Brooke opened her car door and shoved Cole roughly into the back seat. She brandished a plastic tie. "Put your hands together in prayer." When Cole did as bid, Brooke pulled the tie painfully tight and incapacitated Cole's hands. She grabbed a sleep mask and put it over Cole's eyes. "It's a shame to hide those gorgeous eyes of yours, but I don't want you seeing where I'm taking you. It would ruin the surprise." Brooke snapped the seat belt across Cole's chest, locking her in place. She ran around to the driver's side and got in. She looked over her shoulder at Cole, congratulating herself on a job well done, before starting the engine.

"It shouldn't have had to come to this, Cole. But maybe *now* you'll have time to answer my questions."

Eris padded down the stairs in search of her ice cream. Cole hadn't been gone more than ten minutes and Eris was already feeling the loss. She shook her head at her self-pity.

Grandad, you never said how needy this soul mate thing was.

She reached the bottom of the stairs and noticed the door that led to the main exit was wide open. Cole was always very careful to keep that shut. Something glinting on the floor caught Eris's eye. It was Cole's keys.

"Why are these here?" She didn't touch or move them as a horrible feeling of dread engulfed her. She called out. "*Cole*?" She heard nothing. Eris went to the exit and looked out into the parking lot. "Cole?" Her motorcycle was still in its space. Eris realized someone else was missing. "Jones?" She rushed back into the restaurant and found the table upturned and a dinner plate cracked in two. A blood stain marked the white china.

Eris ran toward the kitchen, screaming for Melanie.

"Geez, Eris, calm the fuck down," Melanie grumbled, wandering into view when Eris stormed into the kitchen. "I haven't touched your damned ice cream."

"Is Cole in here?" Eris asked, frantically looking around the kitchen before sticking her head out the doors to scan the restaurant itself. She met a sea of curious faces, all startled by her shouts.

"No. I thought she was with you."

"She was going back to her apartment tonight. She left ten minutes ago, but her Harley is still here and her keys are lying on the floor in the hallway." Eris wrung her hands together. "And I can't find Jones."

Georgio joined them as they all hurried back to what Eris had found. They jumped in unison when a loud thud came from the utility closet. Georgio motioned for Eris and Melanie to stay back as he cautiously opened the door. Inside, Jones lay bleeding on the floor, his leg raised as he prepared to kick at the door again.

Eris got her phone out and called for the police and an ambulance.

"What the hell is going on?" Melanie asked, trying to help staunch the blood pouring from Jones's head with her apron.

Georgio very carefully pulled the tape from Jones's mouth. Jones gasped for air when he was finally able to breathe properly.

"Harman was here. Her hair's a different color and she's not wearing glasses, but it's her. She was dressed as if she worked here."

"Did you see Cole?" Eris could feel her anxiety begin to rise to a fever pitch.

"I didn't see anything after she smashed the plate into my skull then tasered me right in the balls." He and Georgio shared a pained look. "I went down like a ton of bricks and she was able to tie me up and drag me in here."

Eris's mind swirled with fear. "She's got Cole." She felt Georgio's strong arm wrap around her shoulder.

"We'll find her," Georgio said, squeezing her before hurrying outside to search more.

"We have to. She's my soul mate." She smiled wanly at Melanie.

"You finally realizing what I knew from the moment I saw you two together?"

Eris nodded at her.

"Good. Then use that connection you're building to find her and bring her home."

Eris closed her eyes and called out to Cole in her mind. *I'll find you. I'll get you back home, back to the safety of my arms.*

Chapter Twenty-four

Cole was aware the car had stopped somewhere very quiet. Disorientated by the drive, she struggled against Brooke's manhandling of her out of the back seat. She tried to escape the hands that ran over her clothing, searching her pockets and apparently coming up empty for what Brooke expected to find. Cole's ears strained for any clue as to where she was, but all was deathly silent. She fought against a growing fear that threatened to engulf her as she walked on hard gravel that crunched with each step. Brooke kept her upright as Cole walked unseeing, her eyes still covered by the mask.

Kidnapped.

That one thought rattled around her head. Cole couldn't forget the cold steel of the gun that Brooke had pushed against her neck. The threat had been obvious. She's escalating, Cole thought. And I'm her last hope.

The sound of a door opening brought Cole's attention back to the present. Brooke pushed her inside. The air was different and Cole guessed she was in some kind of big building because their footsteps echoed out.

Eris. She sent out a desperate plea to her. *Please find me*.

Brooke remained silent as they walked through the building. A light switched on. It filtered through the fabric of Cole's mask. Finally, Brooke directed Cole to sit on what felt like a fold out chair. A handcuff snapped around Cole's right wrist and she heard the sound of a chain being dragged across the room and then the snap of it being fastened somewhere else. She resisted the urge to test her bindings. She had the horrible feeling Brooke had just tethered her like some rabid dog. Cole's nose wrinkled at the smell surrounding her. Everything smelled old and damp and neglected.

There was the feel of sharp steel against Cole's wrists, and she froze.

"Hold still," Brooke said, cutting through the plastic tie that bound Cole's hands.

The release of the tight plastic was a blessed relief, and Cole flexed her fingers and shook out her hands to try to get the circulation flowing back in them. The noise from the chain reminded her she wasn't in any way free.

Brooke removed Cole's mask, and for a moment she stared into Cole's eyes. Cole fought against an instinctual flinch from the intense stare. She warned herself to remain calm. Brooke was a fan. A *crazy* fan but a fan of hers nonetheless. Cole had a feeling she needed to put on her best performance to survive this. She had no idea what Brooke had in store for her, and Cole needed to be ready to face any and every situation. She knew enough Hollywood horror stories. Crazy fans meeting the objects of their obsessions didn't always end up happily ever after.

She tried desperately to channel Hollister Graham, the cool-headed woman who had disappeared in time and fought to find her way home. Just like Hollister, Cole was determined to reunite with Eris. And if that meant living through all shades of hell with this Brooke, then she'd do her best to survive.

"I'm sorry for having to treat you like this, and thank you for not fighting. I'd have hated having to sedate you in order to make you compliant."

Cole was surprised how normal Brooke sounded.

Cole couldn't rein her sarcasm in. "Well, thank you for that, I guess." Her mouth dropped a little when Brooke got closer. "My God, you almost look like Maria," she blurted out.

Brooke smiled and preened at her hair. "Do you like it? I had it done especially. I needed a change and this style just screamed 'try me.'" She frowned at Cole. "Your hair doesn't suit you like that though. Chris Moore would never shave her hair off so drastically. Nat wouldn't like it."

"It's just for the movie. It will grow back quick enough when the role is over." Cole watched Brooke cautiously. She seemed calm enough, but Cole remembered how Maria had described how threatening she got. How she had shifted from rational to almost demonic in a split second. She'd heard that shift in tone herself when Brooke had threatened bodily harm to Melanie.

Brooke dragged her own chair over to sit in front of Cole. She deliberately left a space between them. Cole wondered at her cautiousness when Brooke had Cole chained to the wall and was armed with both a gun and a knife.

"Will you answer my questions now?" Brooke said, smiling at Cole as if she were a child. She waggled a bottle of water at her, enticingly. "Don't worry, this isn't drugged."

Cole wasn't entirely sure she believed her, but she was desperate for something to drink. She accepted the bottle gratefully and twisted off the cap as best she could with one arm curtailed by the heavy chain and a handcuff that was already digging into her wrist.

After a long drink, Cole shrugged at her. "So, ask away. I'm a *captive* audience, after all." Cole prayed she could get through this. She had no way of stopping her if Brooke got violent. Cole was angry and frightened and really not happy at this enforced Q&A situation she found herself in.

"When are you coming back to *Fortune's Rise*, Cole?"

"As soon as the movie is done and they can find a way to write me back into the show." Cole barefaced lied. She watched the surprise on Brooke's face swiftly turn to something darker.

"You're lying." Brooke still sounded hesitant though, hope bleeding through the distrust.

"No, I'm not. I realized as soon as I made my grand exit that I had been stupid to leave so I'm currently in negotiations to get back on the show."

"And Chris and Nat? What about them?"

"It's early days yet, but let's just say I'm in negotiations for them too." Cole gave her a little conspiratorial smile.

Brooke stared at her. "You'd better not be lying to me. Telling me what I want to hear."

Cole sighed. "Brooke, you have held me at gunpoint, kidnapped me, and brought me God knows where to question me about that damned show you love so much. If I sat here and told you the show and its people can all go to hell because I've moved on, would you be any happier to hear that?"

Brooke shook her head harshly.

"Then believe me when I say I finally listened to the fans and have more talks scheduled once the movie is done." Cole watched Brooke digest this and added, "Maria is fighting for me to come back too."

Brooke grinned and punched the air. "I knew she would." Her demeanor changed again on a dime and as bright as her face had been it now grew dark and angry. "What about you and Eris? There are rumors circulating you two are together."

"It's purely a fabricated romance for the sake of the movie. It's not real. Celebrity gossip affords us a ton of free publicity. Two leading ladies finding love on the set of their latest movie? Sells more tickets because it draws in people interested to see whether they can spot those sparks flying in the movie."

"You don't love her?"

Cole shook her head and made a derisive sound. "No."

"Do you love Maria?" Brooke leaned forward, desperate to hear the answer.

"I've always loved Maria."

"What are you going to do about her husband?"

Cole hesitated, wondering what lie she could fabricate for this. "I think Maria needs to choose between us once and for all."

Brooke nodded. "She'll choose you. Who wouldn't?"

Cole took another drink, deliberately taking her time to stop Brooke from asking something else. "Why didn't you just come talk to me, Brooke? Why threaten me and have to haul me out to…" She looked around the room they were in to get some idea as to where they were. Peeling posters rotted into the brickwork. They seemed to be advertising ice cream. Cole had a flash from just hours earlier of her and Eris. Joking over ice cream. *Code Red.* She shook that memory away and drew a blank at her mysterious surroundings. "Wherever the hell we are."

"Somewhere remote and empty enough that we won't be disturbed here. Any letters I sent to you or your manager went unanswered. You're rarely on Twitter or Instagram anymore, and my posts on your accounts mysteriously end up deleted. You're a hard one to reach, so I thought I'd try a different route. I tried to talk to Maria." Brooke grew agitated. She stood and began to pace. "I didn't go after her son, Cole. That was all a lie. I just wanted to talk to her. Just to have a rational conversation like we're doing."

Cole couldn't help but wonder at how rational Brooke thought it was to kidnap someone, chain them up, and hold them hostage all for a "little chat." She finished off her water and handed Brooke the bottle. "Please tell me that there're still working bathrooms in this place. I really need to go."

Brooke nodded. Cole wondered if she could punch her hard enough with her less dominant hand when Brooke got within range.

The gun Brooke pulled from her pocket quickly put a stop to any violent actions Cole was conjuring in her head.

"There's no need for that." Cole couldn't take her eyes off the weapon in Brooke's hand.

"It's just added assurance that you won't try anything stupid." Brooke unlocked the handcuff from Cole's wrist and gestured with the gun for her to get up and start walking.

Cole finally got some sense of where she was as they walked through the derelict building. She surmised it had been a factory at some point. Through a large cracked windowpane, Cole saw nothing but trees surrounding a huge parking lot. There were no sounds at all of traffic or people. She spied a large sign hanging broken from its post. The sign was covered in dirt and moss, but Cole could just about make out the writing.

McCoy's Ice Cream.

She was captive in an old ice cream factory. "Hmm, ice cream," she muttered. "I like ice cream."

"This place has been abandoned for years," Brooke said, directing Cole into the women's room and to a specific stall. "Seemed too good an opportunity to waste when I needed somewhere we wouldn't be disturbed."

Cole stared at the obviously wiped down and cleaned up stall. "Did you clean this up for me?" She leaned against the wall and patted the toilet's tank. "That's really sweet."

"I can't see anything you can use to escape so I'll just wait outside and give you your privacy. Don't take too long." She handed Cole a pristine roll of toilet paper and a bottle of hand sanitizer. "I came prepared."

Cole took them both. "Thank you."

She waited for Brooke to leave before hurrying to do what she needed to do as quickly as she could and clean herself up. Then Cole reached inside the hidden pocket in her leather jacket that Brooke had patted over but missed. Her pocket watch lay inside, and Cole checked the time. It was nearly midnight. She wondered if Eris was aware of what had happened to her yet.

Cole got her phone out of the same pocket and started to quickly type a text to Eris. Her hands shaking with nerves, her fingers hit all the wrong keys and the phone autocorrected every damn thing that actually made sense. Frustrated and hearing the footsteps of Brooke coming back into the room for her, Cole finally managed to type out *Code Red* and hoped that the signal was strong enough to send the message out. She shoved the phone back in her pocket and came out of the stall just as Brooke was going to reach for the door. Brooke had the gun pointed at her face. Cole flinched, raising her hands to shield herself. Brooke lowered it a little.

"You ready to go back?"

Cole nodded, handing over the toilet roll and sanitizer. The walk back was in silence. Cole searched for any signs of an escape, but there was no way out that she could see. Back in the main room, Brooke handcuffed Cole again and retook her seat opposite her.

"So, what are your thoughts on how Chris and Nat should finally come out and fall in love?"

Brooke's tone was entirely conversational and genuinely interested. They were just two women chatting about their favorite TV show. The only problem was one was bound while the other sat cradling a gun in her lap.

Cole feared it was going to be a long night.

The police dusted Cole's keys and anything else Brooke could possibly have touched for fingerprints. The restaurant's CCTV footage was pored over and taken away for more analysis. Jones argued about leaving his post but was bundled in the back of an ambulance to get an x-ray on his skull and to have other places checked for damage. The camera footage had revealed all. The police knew who had kidnapped Cole, they had no idea where she could be, and time was now a precious commodity.

Eris sat at one of the tables in the restaurant watching the police interviewing the staff. No one had noticed Brooke. She'd seamlessly blended in, accosted Jones, and taken Cole. Eris shivered at the realization that Cole had been kidnapped just feet away from where she'd been. She'd never heard a thing. She hadn't even heard Jones's fight. And she hadn't *felt* Cole leave.

Melanie leaned into her. They were both nursing cups of tea. Aiden and Cassidy sat opposite them. Eris had called Aiden immediately after she'd called the police. They'd all just watched the camera footage that very plainly showed Brooke leading Cole at gunpoint from the restaurant into a waiting car. It had been surreal.

Melanie slumped against her. "Melanie, you need to go to bed. You can't do anything more for now. The baby needs rest. Georgio will look after me, and I have Aiden and Cassidy too."

Melanie shook her head stubbornly. "I'm not leaving you at a time like this. I'll take power naps. Just make sure I don't drool in front of your bosses." She smiled weakly at Aiden and Cassidy. "I'm so glad you two are here for her."

"We wouldn't be anywhere else," Aiden said.

"Just be grateful Mischa has been informed but decided to stay by the phone instead of coming out." Cassidy spoke in an aside to Aiden. "You know she'd have wanted to see where Jones had been tasered." She mimicked Mischa's voice. "Strictly for research purposes, darling."

Her irreverence made Eris smile for a moment before the devastation and loss overwhelmed her again.

"It's got to be hard though, after what you went through." Melanie took a sip from her tea and grimaced at the taste. "Needs more sugar." She spooned in another generous amount to dissolve into the already overly sweetened tea. Everyone coped in their own way.

Cassidy nodded. "Cole's situation is kind of similar to what I had with Bernett. That's the weird thing about fans, their love of you and your work can flip like a switch. They can be your biggest fan one day, then the next day hate on you for an innocent comment you make or a role you take. And you have no idea what *they* are doing yet they know everything about *you*. You just go on with your day-to-day life not knowing what someone is planning for you." Cassidy grimaced at Eris. "I'm so sorry, sweetie."

"She knew Cole was here," Eris said. "She was literally leaving when Brooke jumped her. It's driving me insane wondering how close she came to missing Cole had Cole left just a few minutes sooner." The guilt was eating Eris alive. *If* Cole hadn't come back with her to the restaurant, *if* they hadn't spent hours making love, *if* Cole had stayed…

"We can't guess what *would* or *could* have happened. Those kind of thoughts don't get us anywhere," Aiden said.

Cassidy's attention seemed distracted by the crowd that had started to linger outside the restaurant. "There's quite the little gathering out there."

Eris looked over her shoulder. "I have no idea how the hell the fans find out about these things. It's like they're one step ahead of us every time."

"The police have put out a missing persons alert for Cole. Word of that would have spread like wildfire as fans these days search for any mention of their favorite's names all over public media," Aiden said.

A voice shouted out from the crowd. "We love you, Eris!"

Eris felt tears sting her already burning eyes. "I need her back. I need to know she's safe and that woman isn't going to hurt her."

More voices began ringing out, sending Eris their support. Eris began to sob. Melanie gathered her up in her arms and let her cry.

Another voice began to shout above the rest. Agitated, frantic, calling out for Eris and Aiden. "Aiden Darrow! I need to talk with you! Eris, please! It's about Brooke."

Eris wiped at her eyes and lifted her head to see who was shouting. Officer Jodie Campbell, a tall, serious looking blonde who was acting as the liaison between the police and the women around the table, started toward the door.

"I'll go quiet them down," she said.

"Officer?" Eris's voice slowed Campbell's determined gait. "Let her in, please. At this point I'll listen to anyone and everyone if it will help Cole."

Campbell nodded and slipped out the door. Eris watched her call forward a woman who was pushing her way through the line of fans.

"She could just be a nosy fan wanting her five seconds of fame for hanging with us in here, you know," Cassidy said, her gaze firmly fixed on the harried young woman Campbell was escorting into the restaurant.

"If she is, baby bump or not, I'll kick her ass black and blue," Melanie said, shifting in her seat as if preparing for trouble.

Eris patted her arm. "Calm down, slugger. Let's hear what she has to say."

The woman looked frantic, her hair was a mess, and she looked like she'd dressed more for speed than for looks. "Oh my God, I am so glad you're all here. I didn't know which police station to go to and then my twitter feed blew up with the news about Cole being abducted and I knew I had to get *here*." She took a deep breath as she reached the table they all sat at.

"Who are you?" Melanie asked.

"I'm Ava Riley. I'm a big fan, Eris, but I really wish I wasn't meeting you like this." She took her phone out of her purse and handed it to her. "I think you need to see these."

Eris stared at the screen. The photo was of Cole, blindfolded, in the back of a car. She was obviously unaware photos were being taken. Ava reached over and flicked the screen to another shot. A close-up this time, of Cole's face, half hidden by the sleep mask. Another flick and there was Brooke Harman, taking a selfie, with Cole behind her.

"I think my best friend Brooke has just done something really stupid."

Chapter Twenty-five

Cole was taking slow sips from a new water bottle Brooke had given her. She was tired and grumpy from working all day and not getting the sleep she so desperately needed. It was draining her energy having to be mindful of every word that came out of her mouth. Brooke had her at one hell of a disadvantage. Every time the chain rattled when she tried to move her right hand reminded Cole of that. The handcuff was tight around her wrist, affording no wriggle room. When she tried to twist her wrist, the bite of the metal stung and threatened to break the skin.

"You know, you could have just spoken to me in the parking lot. I would have stopped and talked to you. You didn't have to resort to this. Any of this."

"I just needed to talk with you, and after Maria..."

"You fucked up with Maria. You should never have gone near the kid."

"I didn't do anything to her kid." Brooke's tone changed. It got harsher, defensive.

"I know. But you invaded her private life." Cole closed her eyes as fatigue swept over her like a tsunami. "And God knows what you thought you were doing kidnapping me. This isn't normal, Brooke."

"I didn't really think beyond getting you alone so I could talk to you."

"Not thinking before you act." Cole hummed a little. "I bet that drives your girlfriend insane." At the silence, Cole opened her eyes again. "What?"

"I don't have a girlfriend."

"Really?"

Brooke ran a hand through her hair. "I don't want to talk about it."

Cole nodded. "I get that. But if you *wanted* to talk about it, I'm a good listener. Get it all out, lay it bare, and unburden yourself. I'm not exactly an expert on relationships, but I can listen. You brought me here to talk, so talk."

Brooke was silent for so long that Cole's mind began to wander. She wondered what Eris was doing and if she'd had her ice cream. Was she sitting, absolutely fuming, wondering why Cole hadn't texted her yet? Was she calling all the hospitals in case Cole had taken a spill on her ride home? Did Eris know Cole hadn't even gotten as far as her motorcycle? Maybe she should call her. *Hi, honey, sorry I didn't call you earlier. I'm just a little tied up at the moment.*

"I don't have a girlfriend because my mom would kill me if I did."

"Oh." Cole pondered this for a moment. "Religious reasons or just good ol' homophobia?"

"I'm supposed to be the dutiful daughter like all her friends had. The good girl, one who brings a nice boy home, gets married in a church, and breeds children by the hundreds."

"You could do all that with a girlfriend. Being gay doesn't make your baby making equipment disappear." Cole made a face. "I wish it would though. Periods are such a goddamn pain."

"If I told her I was gay she'd be furious. She'd be so disappointed in me. Then she'd disown me."

"What would she think of you publicly harassing one actress and kidnapping another?" The tired part of her brain pushed the words out of her mouth and waved them off with pride. The other half, trying desperately to remain cool, was screaming at her to stop antagonizing the crazy chick with the gun.

"I don't know. She doesn't use the internet, so hopefully she's missed seeing my face splashed all over it for that damned misunderstanding with Maria."

"And how are you going to explain this with me?" Cole stared at her. "What are your intentions with me, Brooke? You have me in a secluded place, chained to a wall like a dog." Cole finally asked the one question her brain had been screaming since this nightmare began. "Are you going to kill me?"

Brooke shook her head emphatically. "No! I need you alive to have you back with Maria on *Fortune's Rise*. I'm not a monster, Cole."

"Then what exactly is your endgame in all this?"

"*Endgame*." Brooke leaned forward in her chair. "That's the point exactly. That's why I'm doing all this. To get my endgame."

"For Chris and Nat."

"And you and Maria."

"What is it about those two characters that's got you so determined to see them gay?" Cole saw Brooke's face darken. "No, let me finish. I'm fascinated to hear because I just play Chris as written. I know she's supposed to be straight and so is Nat. What is it that *you* see that makes them lesbian?" Cole didn't want to antagonize her further so she desperately tried to temper her words. "I need to know, so I can go back to the studio and say 'this is why they should be together.' Help me, Brooke, because you can't say they're representation because they aren't actually gay. Neither of them has a back story that was particularly fleshed out enough for anyone to identify with." Cole sighed. "I watched a show recently where they brought in a guest star for just a few episodes. She had more back story in her role than Chris and Nat had in every season put together. And they wrote this character for a specific viewership in mind that gave them representation *and* their story on the screen. I'm not saying my portrayal of Chris is one-dimensional, but she doesn't dress or act in the least bit gay, and she has never displayed any romantic feelings toward Nat. So I'm real curious, Brooke. What is it that *you* see? There are other shows with proper lesbian characters in them. Why fight to change two straight women?"

"Because the other shows don't have you and Maria in them. You two are perfect together. You strike sparks off each other. You're the perfect 'enemies to lovers' trope. You have *chemistry* without even trying." Brooke laughed derisively. "Those other shows? I can't tell you how many have straight actresses trying desperately to play gay but instead come off looking like roommates who sometimes have to touch. I've gone through so many shows trying to find my representation there. I've seen one lesbian death after another. Breakups written and handled abysmally by straight men. Producers taking the lesbian characters' screen time away because they overshadowed the boring straight lovers who were supposed to be the romantic lead in the show." Brooke stood up, slipping the gun into her pocket. "But then I watched you two. You have so much charm and wit. There's an unmistakable fire between you both. Maria's character is work driven with no private life worth mentioning. I *relate* to that. She's cool, calm, collected, until she starts arguing with Chris and then she's electric and *alive*. I *want* that. I want those two together." Brooke wandered over to look out the window into the night sky. "I can't have that kind of relationship myself, but I can at least live it through you two. Every week I can see the kind of life I want—being out, being gay, and flirting with the woman of my dreams over the fence." Abruptly, she turned away from the window and shifted her gaze to Cole. "It's your fault I'm doing all this."

"Mine? How?"

"You said 'Never say never' at the last con you did. That's what I'm doing. I'm never going to say good-bye to Chris and Nat. I'm going to do everything I can to get my endgame. I want Chris and Nat as a couple, and I want you and Maria together in real life like you deserve to be. I've been to all the *Fortune's Rise* conventions. I've been right there from the start, cheering you two on. You have something between you, it's blatantly obvious. I know it's true love. She just needs to realize you're the one she needs."

Cole nodded dumbly. *Oh God, I am so screwed here. She has zero grip on reality.*

"It's been so easy trying to get you two together. Maria's husband was such an easy mark with an intimate picture or two of you pair mocked up in Photoshop. He did most of my work for me, running his mouth off around town, inadvertently fueling rumors about an affair between you and Maria. Then that ex of yours proved how little she cared by running at the first sign of dislike directed at her on Twitter. I didn't have to work hard to lay the foundation for you and Maria to take comfort in each other's arms. Your lives were so simple to manipulate."

Cole felt sick. The warm water she was drinking turned sour in her stomach as it mixed with all the fears and terrors Cole had faced for so long by Brooke's hand. She was literally sitting before the woman who had orchestrated every terrible thing in her life. She gagged and Brooke quickly picked up a trash can and shoved it under Cole's chin.

A soft hand brushed over Cole's head as she retched.

"You just need to grow your hair out to look like Chris again. Then we can all get back to normal and you can be on TV where you belong. With Nat *and* Maria." She rubbed at Cole's back. "Endgame, Cole. *You're* my endgame. I might not be able to have what I want in real life, but I can live it vicariously through the show. I *can* and *will* have it with you two. You made me believe I could have this."

Brooke trailed her fingertips across Cole's shoulders and around her neck. Her grip tightened just enough to make Cole freeze. A loud voice echoed in Cole's head, warning her she wasn't safe. Cole was too busy throwing up to pay it any attention.

Brooke leaned in close to Cole's ear and whispered in a singsong voice.

"*Never say never*."

Eris couldn't take her eyes away from the phone that was now in the hands of the police. They were flicking through the pictures of Cole and talking among themselves while Officer Campbell interviewed Ava. Eris was so grateful to her. She could have kept this knowledge to herself. Brooke was her best friend, after all. But Ava had sought them out in the night to help them find Cole. Eris could tell Ava was nervous answering so many questions so she reached over and took her hand. The pitifully grateful look Ava gave her made Eris know she was right to trust this woman.

"How long have you known Brooke Harman?" Officer Campbell's pen was poised over her notebook.

"Since Clexa."

Campbell frowned. "Clexa?"

"I got to know her on a forum online for the show *The 100*. We shipped the ladies in it, Clark and Lexa? We got on well and found we lived really close to each other so met up in the real world. She's been my best friend through all our ships."

"Ships?"

Ava sighed. "We like the same ladies in shows and we fangirl over them. It's harmless fun." Ava grimaced expressively. "At least on my part it is. Brooke started to take it really seriously when *Fortune's Rise* came on the air."

"What was it about that show that made her less fan and more fanatic?" Eris asked, desperate to know what had been the spark lighting the unstable powder keg Brooke had become.

"She has a major thing for Cole. Cole's her dream girl. Seeing her with Maria, knowing Cole is gay in real life, was all Brooke needed for her fantasy of shipping Cole and Maria together." Ava looked embarrassed. "Sorry, Eris."

Eris squeezed her hand. "It's okay. You're doing great. You're a fan of Cole and Maria too, right?"

"I love them both, but I don't ship them together. Cole has never shown any interest in Maria personally, and Maria is straight and married. I don't do real-life shipping, it's pointless."

"But you do like Chris and Nat together?"

"Yes, they'd be a fantastic couple. But I understand that the show hasn't written them that way so I'll just stay happy in my fantasy bubble and gorge on the fan fiction my friends write."

"You wouldn't go as far as Brooke, then?" Campbell asked.

Ava almost shouted her answer at her. "Hell no!" She quieted down quickly when everyone's eyes turned to her. "I'll fill in online polls and tweet the show to ask if they'd consider pairing the couple up, but to go after them in real life? No. No one should do that. They are playing *characters*, it's not *real*."

"But Brooke doesn't see it that way?" Campbell asked.

"She was getting angrier with every episode when she wasn't seeing enough of what she wanted. She started to make stuff up for each scene Chris and Nat had together, saying it oozed subtext. It didn't though. But she got enough fans behind her who were desperate for that kind of content too. They all deluded themselves they could see it as well." She took a moment. "Then Cole announced she was leaving the show and Brooke *changed*."

"You know Cole was having problems with her fans?" Eris asked.

Ava nodded. "We all knew. Some of us tried to step in when others got too possessive or aggressive about her, but there isn't a lot we can do. In hindsight, I think Brooke was behind a lot of it. I didn't want to think she was capable of such a thing, but she took such a delight in Cole losing her girlfriend and in the rumors Maria's husband had been furious over their supposed affair. God, he was such a jackass about the shit the fans stirred up. I understand his anger. They deliberately targeted him. But to not believe his wife? His very *straight* wife? And poor Cole who had never, ever alluded to any kind of attraction to her?" Ava sighed then muttered, "He was such a dick, but the fans who stirred all this up are ten times worse."

"Brooke kidnapped Cole from this restaurant this evening. Do you have any idea where she could have taken her? Do you have any idea where Brooke is at all? According to our reports, she's been missing from her home for days and she hasn't shown up at work." Campbell looked up from her notepad. "Has she been in contact with you?"

"After she confronted Maria, she called me over to do her hair. I really should have realized then something was seriously wrong. She was harsh, agitated, but then Brooke isn't exactly sweetness and light. I'm used to her being sharp and abrupt. She had me cut her hair and color it in a style just like Maria's."

Eris groaned under her breath. "She was changing her appearance to something Cole would recognize."

"She said she wouldn't go after Maria again, that it was a spur-of-the-moment thing, a dumb idea. I never in a million years thought she'd go for Cole. She *loves* Cole. Then a day or so later, she stayed at my house for the night. Said she needed to be with a friend. I'm guessing she used me to hide while the police were searching her house after her picture was released." Ava rubbed her hands over her face. "God, I was such an idiot. I thought she was just an intense fan. Unerring devotion is part of being a fan nowadays."

"You haven't seen or heard from her since?" Campbell asked.

"No. Not until tonight. I was getting ready to go to sleep when my phone went off. I saw the photos and couldn't believe my eyes. I texted her back asking her what she'd done, but all I got back was 'Endgame.' I got up, dressed, and rushed out the door. I wasn't even sure where I was going to go, but Twitter was awash with the news about Cole disappearing from the restaurant so I drove down here as fast as I could." She looked at Campbell. "Without speeding, I promise."

"You rushed here but checked Twitter first?" Campbell looked puzzled.

Ava stared at her as if Campbell was decidedly dim. "Yes. Don't you know that's the best place to keep up with the news? The Morter fans were all over Cole's kidnapping. They got me up to speed fast. They're posting what they're seeing and hearing from outside here right now. Reporting live to Cole's fans all around the world."

"Social media," Campbell muttered, shaking her head.

"It led Ava straight to us with photographic proof that Cole is with Harman," Aiden pointed out.

Eris squeezed Ava's hand. "Do you have any idea where Brooke could have taken her? Does she have a special place she goes, another house maybe?"

Ava shook her head. "She only has her apartment and she goes to her mother's, but she wouldn't take Cole there. Brooke can't even be herself when she goes to visit that woman."

Eris was getting more and more frustrated and frightened. Where the hell had Brooke taken her?

Another officer returned her phone. "We've removed the photographs. Did you post them online anywhere?"

Ava looked aghast. "No, I didn't! I would never hurt Cole in any way and there is no way I'd have used those dreadful photos simply to get *likes* by sharing them online." She huffed. "I'm not that kind of fan."

"I know you're not." Eris put an arm around Ava and hugged her. It was clear how upset Ava was. "Thank you for protecting Cole."

"I'm sorry I didn't see this coming, Eris," Ava said. "I'd have done anything to have stopped her."

"You've been amazing. You could have stayed at home. Let's face it, you could have just ignored the messages and gone to sleep." That thought alone terrified Eris.

Another officer walked over to the group. "We're having trouble trying to locate the signal off Cole's phone. It might be she's been taken somewhere where signals are weak or it could be her phone is turned off."

Eris shook her head. "Cole's phone is always on. Especially since Harman was still free." Eris grimaced then jumped when her own phone pinged. She dug her phone from her pocket.

Code Red.

Eris stared at the screen until the words seared onto her retinas.

"Eris?" Cassidy asked quietly, reaching across the table to her and shaking Eris out of her stupor.

"It's a text from Cole's phone."

Everyone crowded close to read it.

"What does Code Red mean other than a reference to your previous show?" Ava asked, peering at the screen.

Eris shrugged, at a loss. She began to rack her brain for what the message could mean. She ran through everything she could think of that Cole had ever said about the show and her. Everyone left her in silence while Eris tried so hard to decipher Cole's cryptic text. She stared at the screen, willing it to say more.

If it even came from Cole in the first place.

Eris threaded her fingers through her hair and willed herself to think while the police renewed their effort to trace Cole's call again. A message from it meant the phone was active now.

"Do you think *Brooke* sent that message to taunt you?" Cassidy asked.

"I don't know. But if it's Cole, what is she trying to tell me?" Eris bit back the sob that threatened to escape her chest. Cole was still alive.

"As a kid, the only time Brooke said she was ever happy was when she was with her dad," Ava mused out loud. "Her dad used to work at this big ice cream factory. Brooke would go with him sometimes, watching the machines work their magic. She said they always had plenty of ice cream in the house, but her mom limited Brooke's intake because 'men don't want fat girls for their wives.'" Ava rolled her eyes. "She was about five at the time. That woman is just a mean ol' bitch. It's no wonder Brooke is so screwed up."

Eris's thoughts slipped back to her last moments with Cole. They'd been so happy, delirious after their lovemaking, hesitant to part, and Eris teasing her about needing ice cream.

Ice cream.

A Code Red emergency.

"Oh my God," Eris gasped. "Ice cream. Last night I wanted ice cream. I called it a Code Red emergency because I was going to have to be sneaky like my secret agent from the show and get to it without Melanie seeing me." She gave Melanie an apologetic smile.

"That's just mean," Melanie grumbled.

"Could that be what Cole is referring to?" Eris asked. "That was the last time Code Red came up in our conversation."

"Do you recall the name of the factory, Ms. Riley?" an officer asked Ava.

"Mc something, like in McDonalds. He'd lost his job years before he died so I bet the place is long gone…oh my God." Ava's eyes widened. "Brooke's note. How could I forget that? I found it on the kitchen table when I came home from work. She'd left without saying good-bye. It made no sense at the time. It said '*Staying with family for a while. Don't worry about me, I'll be happy there.*' It makes perfect sense if she's at the factory. It's the only place she was ever truly happy because she was out from under the controlling hand of her mother."

An officer held up their phone. "McCoy's Ice Cream. It's east of here, out in the middle of nowhere in a lot with two other abandoned businesses. It's been derelict for years."

"The perfect place to hide out with someone you've kidnapped," Cassidy said.

The police started moving and Eris got to her feet. "I'm going to beg them to let me go with them. I have to be there for Cole when they find her."

Ava stood too. "I'll come with you."

Eris gave her a look. "Do you really want Brooke to know you were the one who told us where she was hiding?"

Ava sat back down with a thump. "When you put it that way, no, I don't think so. I think, after all she's done, our friendship is well and truly over."

"Ava can stay here with us until we know what's happening," Melanie said. She pulled Eris in for a hug. "You keep me informed, okay? And you be damned careful out there. This woman isn't sane."

"I know. But if Cole is there, I need to be there too. I need to know she's all right."

"Go bring her home, Eris." Aiden stood and hugged Eris close. Cassidy did the same.

Eris ran out after Officer Campbell. After much discussion, Campbell finally allowed Eris to sit in the back of her police car after her promising not to get in the way of their investigation.

Eris gazed out the car window as the city passed by at breakneck speed. They drove out from under the glare cast by the bright lights and tall buildings, out toward an older part of the city where buildings lay undisturbed and unused. They had been lost in time as the city moved onward and upward. The old businesses just couldn't keep up with the modern day demands.

Eris just prayed she was right and that Cole's two worded message was pointing them in the right direction to find her alive.

Chapter Twenty-six

Usually, Cole enjoyed discussing her career with her fans, chatting about the characters she'd played, and what part of herself she'd brought to each one. She loved seeing their intent faces as they listened to all she had to reveal from behind the scenes and watching their joy as they told her what the characters meant to them. It made all the long hours on set worthwhile. She could see the same intent look on Brooke's face now, hanging on every word Cole managed to utter.

Cole had no concept of time there. She only knew she was deathly tired, terror draining her energy. She hoped what she was saying was what Brooke needed to hear. She kept testing her bindings, but the chain was unyielding and the handcuff cut into her skin. The room only had one door and Brooke, with her gun, sat between Cole and its escape.

In the lull between questions, Cole voiced her fears again. "I don't want to die, Brooke, okay?"

Brooke shook her head. "If I kill you, Cole, how will I get to see you and Maria living what I dream about?"

"You have a gun."

"It's an old one my dad kept as token protection in the house. Forget it, Cole, please. I'll keep you safe here. I won't hurt you. Haven't I looked after you well?"

Cole had to agree she had. "You've been the perfect host here in this delightfully deserted factory, miles from anywhere else, where you brought me after kidnapping me."

Brooke stared at her a moment and then laughed. "I love your sense of humor. You're so funny. It's no wonder Maria is so in love with you."

Cole closed her eyes and flopped back in the chair, too tired to have to deal with Brooke and her crazy notions about her and Maria.

I want Eris, Cole thought mournfully. My endgame is with her, not Maria.

"Cole, I need you to stay awake."

Cole shook her head. "Let me sleep. It's way past my bedtime and I have an early call tomorrow." She opened her eyes and glared at Brooke. "I'd better not miss the shoot. It's the last scenes and I have to be there."

"Just another hour or two together and then I'll drive you home. Okay? I don't want this evening to end."

"You know where I live?"

Brooke shrugged. "I know everything about you."

"Isn't that comforting?" Cole muttered, not in the least bit mollified.

"Please. Talk with me. I've waited so long to have this opportunity."

At Brooke's pleading tone, Cole struggled to be more alert, seemingly unable to do anything but obey. She froze as a bell chimed. An incoming text on a phone sounded loudly.

"Who the hell would be texting me at this time in the morning?" Cole said without thinking.

Brooke was beside her in a flash. "You have a phone? I patted you down before we got in the car and I couldn't find one on you anywhere." She began pulling at Cole's clothes.

"Quit that!" She fought against Brooke's hands with her only free one. "Stop it!"

"Give me that fucking phone, Cole. Now!"

"I don't have one on me," Cole lied, knowing that if Brooke found it she'd see the last text Cole had sent to Eris.

Brooke held out her hand. "Give it to me."

Cole glared at her. "No, because I don't have it with me."

Brooke backhanded her across the face. The blow was hard enough to rock Cole back and tip the chair over. Cole landed flat on her back where she lay trying to comprehend what had happened. Her right arm hurt where it strained against the shortness of the chain holding her captive. She rolled back up and ran her hand over her cut lip. "Goddammit! I still have close-ups to film!"

"Then give me your fucking phone."

Cole grumbled under her breath and managed to right herself.

"Listen to me. I don't have my phone with me because it's still in my backpack at the restaurant because I forgot to pick the damned thing up as I left." Cole got up on her knees. She was angry and tired and rapidly losing her patience. "And I didn't get the chance to go back in to get it because you grabbed me, stuck a gun in my neck, and fucking kidnapped me!" Cole shouted the last accusation right in Brooke's face. The show of anger earned her another slap that caused her head to snap back and her jaw to ache.

"Hitting me isn't going to make my phone magically appear for you. You've checked my pockets and haven't found one. It had to be your phone going off because MINE. ISN'T. HERE!" Cole screamed at her and half expected to find herself knocked out in Brooke's ire. Instead Brooke turned on her heel and stormed off after her bag. Cole shakily ran her fingers over the hidden phone and pocket watch in her jacket. She pictured the heart etched on the watch and sent out a prayer that, if things got worse, Eris would always know that Cole had loved her with all her heart and soul.

Brooke pulled her phone out of a side pocket and stood reading her message. She purposely didn't look at Cole.

"What? Did you get a bank statement? A bill reminder? A two-for-one offer at Taco Bell?" Cole ran her hand across her chin and stared at the blood that covered her fingers. "Is this what you really wanted? To see me bleed?" She held her hand up for Brooke to see.

Brooke made an angry noise. "No, it's not my intention to hurt you, but I thought you'd hidden your phone from me. You can't hide things from me, Cole. They can trace phones. That's why I brought you out here. The signal is terrible and intermittent at best, and I just needed some alone time with you."

Cole got to her feet and righted the chair. She sat back in it and wiped the blood off her hand onto her jeans. She stared at the stain for a while. "So much for not hurting me."

"You made me angry, Cole. I lashed out. I'm sorry." Brooke tossed her phone back in her bag. "That was one of my online friends asking if I'd heard the news of your kidnapping. I'd turned all my notifications off for the internet, but she has my phone number." She padded back to Cole, knelt in front of her, and reached out to touch her face. Cole drew back. "No, I won't hit you again. I just…I just get so angry sometimes. It's like this red mist falls in front of my eyes and I lash out." She touched Cole softly. "I'm sorry I hit your handsome face."

She got a strange look in her eyes that Cole reared back from. "Are you seriously thinking of *kissing* me right now?" Cole asked, incredulous that she'd even try.

Brooke blushed bright red and stood up. For the first time that evening, she looked flustered.

"You could just pretend I looked like Maria," she said. "You said I did."

Cole felt the urge to throw up again. "You need to let me go home. Please, take me home now before this gets any worse."

Brooke nodded. "I guess you're right." She pulled the handcuff key out of her pocket and brandished it at Cole. "Can I trust you not to try to play the hero if I release you? I still have my gun."

"Just get me out of this cuff and get me out of here."

Brooke took one step and stopped. Suddenly on high alert, she scanned the room then shot to the window to peer outside.

"What?" Cole asked, watching as Brooke rushed to the door and disappeared. "You'd better not leave me here!" she shouted after her. Cole tried to wrench the handcuff from her wrist again. It still wouldn't budge and instead just cut deeper into her wrist. Cole waited impatiently for Brooke to return. She was surprised when Brooke ran in as if the hounds of hell were at her heels.

"We have to get out of here. Someone's outside. I can hear them."

Cole held her arm out and shook the cuff and chain. "Hurry up, then."

Brooke fumbled with the key and finally snapped open the cuff. Cole shook out her aching arm and surveyed her bruised and bloodied wrist. Before she could wind up to take a swing at Brooke and pay her back for the blows she'd been dealt, Brooke had run back across the room to grab her bag.

At that moment, the door flew open and police officers swarmed in, guns drawn and shouting. Brooke screamed and tried to run back to Cole, but an officer grabbed her and began reading her her rights.

A female officer rushed over to Cole. "You're okay. You're safe now."

"Is Eris okay?" That's all Cole wanted to know.

"She's fine, if a little frantic. She's waiting outside for you in my patrol car."

"TRAITOR!" Brooke screamed like a banshee and wrenched herself free from the officer's grip with an almost superhuman strength. When he reached for her again, she whipped around and elbowed him straight in the throat. He fell to his knees, gasping for air. Brooke ignored him as she glared at Cole. "You told me Eris meant nothing to you!" She pulled out her gun and began to fire.

Pandemonium broke out. Cole's line of sight with Brooke disappeared as the police officer threw herself in front of her for protection. Cole watched in horror as shock and pain exploded on the woman's face the second a bullet struck her. Cole barely had time to register it before something hit her with enough force to knock her off her feet. They both fell to the ground, the woman moaning in pain while Cole lay beneath her, dazed and confused and wondering what had hit her.

She'd fallen sideways and was able to see the police piling on Brooke to bring her to the ground. One officer quickly kicked the fallen gun out of her reach. Another handcuffed her and hauled her up and out. She struggled against him, looking back at Cole with crazed eyes.

"I'm sorry! I'm sorry! Forgive me!" she said, her voice pleading and desperate.

"Let me guess, you 'didn't think.'" Cole gritted her teeth against the pain, throwing Brooke's lame excuse back at her one last time before looking away, dismissing her. Brooke's screams echoed around the empty factory.

"No! No! Cole! You can't let them take me! I love you! I'm your biggest fan!"

A paramedic rushed over to Cole while another went for the policewoman. "Can you tell me where you were hit?"

"My ribs, I think." She squirmed under his invasive touch.

The paramedic checked her face first then inspected her jacket. He lifted it away from her body and moved Cole's hand that curled protectively over her ribcage. Cole grunted at the pain as he prodded and probed. "Did that crazy bitch actually shoot me?" Her anger rising, she fought to get up. "I'll fucking kill her!"

The paramedic pushed her back down and lifted Cole's shirt. He looked a little surprised, but when he touched Cole's skin she flinched from the pain. He cast a quick glance at what was going on beside him. "Is the officer shot?"

"I have a through and through here." The paramedic nodded as he examined the woman's bloody arm.

The paramedic lowered Cole's shirt and tugged at her leather jacket. "Someone was watching over you tonight, ma'am." He grinned at her. "You literally dodged a bullet."

Eris started tugging frantically on the door of the police vehicle the second she heard gunshots shatter the quiet. She'd watched a few minutes earlier as the police, including Campbell, descended en masse on the factory. Lights and sirens were off so as not to give themselves away or to warn Brooke the factory had been surrounded. There was an almost oppressive silence, and then all hell broke loose.

A police officer held up a hand to Eris to signal for her to wait, but Eris wanted out and she wanted to get to Cole right this second.

"I need to go to her," she told him through the glass.

"Once the coast is clear. Until then, you stay in there out of harm's way."

Eris knew he was just doing his job. Her running in while they were taking Brooke down would be incredibly stupid on her part. That didn't mean she wouldn't do it in a heartbeat to get to Cole.

The sound of gunfire stopped. Eris strained her ears to hear what was happening. She distinctly heard someone yell for the paramedics and her heart seized in her chest for a long, terrifying, beat.

Cole.

Eris rapped on the window again and the officer gave her a "don't make me tell you again" look that made her furious. Her fury turned incandescent when she saw Brooke all but carried out from the factory, kicking and screaming.

"Let me out now! I'm going to beat the shit out of her!" Eris demanded. The officer let out a bark of laughter then quickly schooled his face back into as serious a visage as he could muster.

"I wish I could," he said, eyeing her speculatively.

Eris believed him.

Watching the main doors for any sign of Cole, Eris began to get more and more worried as time ticked by. She was getting ready to kick the glass out of the police car when someone came to the main doors and gestured to her officer. He opened the door for her, and Eris almost knocked him over in her haste to get out. She rushed past the man who'd given the okay for her to go inside and quickly followed the line of police. She skidded to a halt at the entrance of the room where Brooke had kept Cole prisoner.

Cole sat on a deck chair. Officer Campbell was next to her having her arm seen to by a paramedic. Eris pushed her way through the police who were checking over every inch of the room, taking photos and gathering evidence.

"Cole?" Eris was suddenly terrified at what she'd find the closer she got to her. Another paramedic stood and moved out of the way for her.

Bloodied and battered, Cole Calder was still the most gorgeous woman Eris had ever laid eyes on. She fell to her knees beside the chair and pulled Cole to her, holding on tight, letting Cole know she'd never let her go. Cole's arms were equally tight around Eris.

"Eris," Cole said as her voice hitched in Eris's ear. "God, I thought I'd never see you again."

"I'm here, sweetheart." She pressed kisses all over Cole's face, her heart bursting at the look of relief on Cole's bruised face. "You know, there are easier ways to get out of an early morning set call," she said, trying desperately not to cry but tears escaped anyway.

"Am I in trouble with the crew?"

"No, of course you're not. As excuses go, I'd say you've outdone anything Mischa could ever come up with." Eris pressed a kiss to Cole's forehead and reluctantly eased back when she realized Cole was in pain. She ran her hands over Cole, trying to find the source of Cole's discomfort. "What happened to you? Where are you hurt?"

"I got shot," Cole said.

"You're shot?" She took her hands from Cole's body, terrified she would hurt her.

"Yeah, I got shot but I'm *not* shot."

Eris stared at her. "Did that bitch drug you? You're not making any sense." She turned on the paramedic. "Why haven't you got her in an ambulance already?"

"The bullet never penetrated to flesh. Officer Campbell here shielded Cole and took the bullet for her. However, the bullet went right through her arm and impacted on Cole."

Cole laughed shakily, unmistakably in shock. "Apparently, I'm like Superman. Bullets bounce right off me."

"But how?" Eris was at a loss. She was concerned by how Cole was reacting and confused by what had occurred.

Cole patted her jacket beside her. On it lay what was left of her phone. The case was broken into a thousand tiny pieces and the screen cracked beyond repair. "I think I need a new one," Cole told her.

"Understatement of the year, my love," Eris muttered. "The bullet bounced off this?" Eris couldn't get her head around the damage she was seeing.

"No, but it helped," Cole said. She opened up her right hand that had been clutching something tight, obviously reluctant to let it go. "This is what stopped the bullet."

Eris felt tears well up as she saw the remains of Cole's golden pocket watch. It was barely recognizable. The casing was misshapen and all the fine workings inside were obliterated from the impact. All that remained of the back case was the heart etched out by Cole's hand. What was left of the bullet lay embedded in the gold, buried deep. Literally stopped by time.

"Hollister's watch saved you." Eris shook her head in disbelief. She put her hand over her mouth to hold in the sob that threatened to escape. "Oh my God, you could have died. I could have lost you."

Cole pulled Eris closer and held on tight. "I'm here. I'm a little sore from the impact, but I'm okay. Officer Campbell being hit slowed the bullet for when it hit me. I owe that officer my life for her actions." She smiled at Eris shakily, then looked at the destroyed watch in her hand. "Hollister Graham and her damned magic pocket watch. Hollister's watch stopped her from leaving in order for her to live out her life with Emily. In reality, this one just did the same for me for *you*." Cole kissed Eris gently. "We could call it fate, destiny, or some kind of damned crazy luck. Your grandad would probably argue it's so his granddaughter and her soul mate can experience what he did in life with your nan. Whatever you want to call it, it wasn't my time to leave you, Eris. It wasn't my time." She clung to Eris tightly, shaking in her arms.

Eris's tears fell faster as she realized how close she had come to losing her. "Don't ever leave me, Cole."

"Not in this lifetime or the next," Cole promised. "Can you get me out of here?"

"Your place or mine?"

"Either one. As long as you're with me I'm home."

Chapter Twenty-seven

The application of prosthetics to rapidly age an actress was something Cole had never done before. She sat in the makeup chair, her eyes glued to her reflection in the mirror. Fascinated by the whole process, Cole watched as the team applied layers to her face to add wrinkles and a softer edge to her jawline that came with maturity. Then they repeated the same on her neck and hands. Next, the team applied the makeup to blend it all in seamlessly to emphasize the fragility of her now older looking skin. Cole had watched her face age before her, fifty years added effortlessly. Cole couldn't believe her eyes. She knew the makeup team was amazing, but they had truly created magic.

"Wow," Cole exclaimed. She was tempted to blink a few times to see if the illusion shattered and it was just her younger face staring back at her in the mirror instead. "My God, I look like my father. That's a little sobering."

Cole was glad that the cuts and bruises on her face she'd suffered from Brooke's violent actions were fading. Her wrist had healed too, but there were faint scars left as a reminder. Aiden had made her take time off to recover, arguing over Cole's insistence that she was ready to get back to work as soon as possible. Reluctantly, Cole had seen a doctor to make sure that a rib hadn't been broken and then had been booked into a therapist to talk about her ordeal. Cole had talked privately with Aiden who convinced her to give therapy a go. It was helping. She couldn't forget what had happened, but she *could* control how much power it had over her life. Aiden *and* Cassidy had taught her that. It helped talking about how frustrated she'd felt about not being able to fight back and break free. She knew it wasn't her fault, but the guilt over Officer Campbell being hurt protecting her was hard to shake off. Cole had paid a visit to the young police officer, only to find that Mischa had gifted her with the best physiotherapist in his field to aid in her recovery. Cole had been grateful for her doing so but still had to ask Mischa why.

"Because you're a friend, darling, and I always look after my friends. Besides, Marco is a friend who owed me a favor so that's one debt wiped clean. I also intimated that if Jodie can't return to police work, I'm sure we'd be happy to employ her as security for our productions. Never hurts to know someone that's dedicated to their job." She'd patted Cole's cheek. "And she proved that saving you."

Cole's attention returned to the present at the sound of scissors making one last round on her hair. They had dyed it a fetching salt-and-pepper gray that Cole was secretly hoping was how her own color would manifest itself. She stared at herself in the mirror and saw herself years from now—older, and hopefully wiser.

She turned to make a comment to Eris who was receiving the same treatment in the chair next to her. She'd been quiet for a while. Cole realized that she'd fallen asleep while they'd been fixing her wig of long white hair. Cole let her rest. Eris hadn't been sleeping well since Cole's kidnapping. Neither of them had. Eris had admitted she was frightened too in case Cole disappeared again. Cole had begged her to go to therapy and had been relieved when Eris had agreed without a fuss. It had become obvious Eris needed help processing the terrible ordeal. Her recovery was just as important as Cole's and they were taking time to savor their time together and to come down gently from the heightened state of fear they had both suffered.

The studio had issued a statement to inform both media and the fans that Cole was safe. Cole didn't want to give interviews. She didn't want to constantly relive what had happened or keep a crazy fan's name in the press and give her any notoriety. She just wanted to get back to work. Brooke Harman was going to receive a lengthy jail term for kidnapping, attempted murder, and shooting a police officer. They'd added stalking and child endangerment too, so her release wasn't going to happen anytime soon. Cole had spoken to one of her own lawyers to make sure that, once imprisoned, Brooke would have no internet access at all to stop her from following her favorites. It would also curtail any interaction she had with equally delusional fans who thought she was some kind of celebrity and role model. Additionally, there would be no watching anything on TV connected to Cole, Maria, or even Eris. Her "ship" was well and truly sunk, as was she.

Eris began to wake up. Cole watched as Eris's eyes comically opened wide as she caught sight of herself in the mirror.

"Yes, you really did sleep that long, Rip Van Winkle!" Cole teased her, reaching out to clasp Eris's hand in her own. She finally got to have a good look at Eris's makeup. "My God, if this is how you're going to look when we're chasing those grandbabies around then I'm going to be more inclined to chase after you instead!"

The makeup team all aww-ed at Cole's sincerity and Eris's sweet laughter. They fluttered around Eris, fixing her hair just so. Cole knew this last scene was going to be hard to film, but as she looked at Eris, aged, pale, and drawn for her character, she knew the emotions would be true.

"You ready to get this last scene in the can?" Cole helped Eris up from her chair. The white nightgown Eris wore floated around her feet. It rested on top of her Nikes, which was a strange combination of old and new. Cole was in full Hollister wear. The clothing looked more worn, a little duller. Bright and shining still, Hollister's pocket watch hung from its chain on Cole's waistcoat. She held it a moment, feeling the cold of the gold plating slowly warm in her palm. For a moment, she mourned the loss of her own version. It sat in police evidence, but she'd begged for its return once they were finished with it. Aiden's adopted father, Frank, had said he would salvage what he could and rebuild it for her, with Aiden's help.

Eris tugged her from her introspection. "Ready to close this chapter, Mr. Graham?"

"Ready when you are, Mrs. Graham." Cole loved that the characters had been married in the story. No one had revealed Hollister's true gender and they had lived a full and happy life together, eventually.

But all good stories must come to an end.

Chapter Twenty-eight

The convention hall was ready to be filled with people intent on spending the weekend meeting their heroes and watching the panels. Aiden was debuting the first screening of the trailer from *A Pocket Full of Time*, and advance ticket sales of that screening had shown them there was a huge audience waiting for this release.

Cole wandered through the empty hall dedicated to *A Pocket Full of Time* and stopped in her tracks before the publicity posters hung like tapestries from the ceiling. One had her and Eris looking down at the pocket watch in Cole's hand. Another beside it had them in a romantic embrace. Cole loved that one more.

"Ohh, I want that poster in our bedroom," Eris said from beside her.

"Me too," Mischa said with a cheeky grin as she sauntered past them.

Aiden and Cassidy stopped to look up at the artwork too. Aiden's eyes shone with excitement. "Wow, those are fantastic," she said. "I'm going to need a whole other room to display all the merchandise from this movie."

Cassidy nodded. "We really should start looking for a bigger home together. This movie is just the start. You'll need a proper area to display all your goodies from all *your* movies."

"Oh! With a bigger house you can hold bigger parties," Mischa said, clapping her hands excitedly.

Cole noticed Aiden looked horrified at that thought.

"But no one can throw parties like you can, darling," Cassidy said, patting Aiden's arm as if to say "I've got this" and left her with Cole and Eris.

"Well, that's a given." Mischa preened and held out an arm for Cassidy to link hers through. "I've been thinking about the parties we need to throw for the premieres. We're going to need top class catering and I was thinking Andinos fits the bill here." They started talking among themselves, plotting and planning.

Aiden just shook her head at them and turned her attention to Cole and Eris. "These posters alone will sell the movie. God, you look amazing together."

Eris blushed but Cole agreed. "Can we get smaller versions of these pictures? You know, something a little less the size of a small skyscraper?"

"Don't worry, I'll get Gabby to sort you out with all the good stuff. The proper posters will be a much more manageable size to frame. Which reminds me," Aiden looked a little abashed, "I need to get all the cast to sign one for me so I can hang it on my Inspiration Wall."

Cole had seen that room for herself. She loved how Aiden's collection of movie and superhero memorabilia was her pride and joy. Cole and Eris had conspired and commissioned a statue to be made of Hollister and Emily. They had posed for it and left the artist with plenty of photos as source material. It would be an original, one-of-a-kind piece for Aiden's collection, a thank you for her giving them their first movie roles. It would be ready in time for the US premiere of the movie, and Cole couldn't wait to see Aiden's face when they presented it to her.

Cole slipped her hand into her jeans pocket and felt her pocket watch sitting safely in there. It was new and shiny but housed salvaged pieces from the one that had saved her life. It even had the original heart that Aiden and Frank had carefully melded onto the watch's casing. It took its place under the new initials that Cole got to etch onto the case. Cole totally understood Aiden's love of things of significance. She owned one now.

Eris hugged herself and let out a squeal. "I'm so excited! I've done a few conventions, but not for a movie where *my* face is up on the frickin' huge posters! Melanie is going to freak when she sees them."

Cole knew that Melanie and Georgio would be stopping by later that afternoon to watch them on the panels and to get a professional family photograph taken for fun. "She's probably going to cry," Cole said, now used to the baby hormones that were controlling Melanie's emotional status. The baby was due soon and Cole was just as excited as Eris was for the arrival. Cole had gained a new family and she couldn't wait to welcome the latest addition to it.

"Just so long as she doesn't go into labor here I don't care." Eris pointed to their *Gone With the Wind* pose. "Look at us. God, if I wasn't a part of that couple I'd ship us on that picture alone."

Cole laughed at Eris's exuberance but caught Aiden regarding her quietly at the contentious word that had slipped so innocently from Eris's lips.

"I'm okay, boss," Cole assured her. "Though I'll admit I'm nervous with it being my first time out in public and back before the fans. In *Fortune's Rise* I was one of many. *This* movie rests on my shoulders and Eris's. That's a big responsibility." She shrugged a little. "I don't think I'll ever be able to completely lose my mistrust of fans after what Brooke put me through. But this is the business I choose to work in. It comes with some crazy things attached, but it also brings so much joy." She pointed at the posters adorning the room. "*We* did this. You wrote it, you produced it, we star in it, and we get to share all that with the world. A lesbian story, written by a renowned lesbian author, starring lesbian actresses who just happened to fall madly in love on the set. *That's* the representation I want to be a part of. That's the kind of story I want to tell the world." She felt Eris's arm slip around her waist in support. "That's the spotlight I want to bask in."

Cassidy's voice sounded out from across the hall. "Guys, they've set up a room for us back here. Mischa's had wine and soda and a veritable feast delivered for us." Cassidy hung around the door at the back of the stage. "Oh, and there's beer for the more uneducated palate."

Cole grinned at Cassidy's blatant dig. "Thank her for me, please!" She took one more look around the room while it was quiet. "This is so cool. Today is going to be amazing, if a little overwhelming."

"The five of us on stage together, talking about the movie." Aiden grinned. "That really *is* the kind of thing dreams are made of."

Eris took out her phone and held it out to Aiden. "This is definitely a photo opportunity for publicity's sake."

Cole and Eris posed before the posters and then Cole waved Aiden over and they took a selfie that quickly joined the others online on the official site.

The sound of staff starting to get things ready for the day filtered into the room and the three of them left to meet back up with Cassidy and Mischa to prepare for the madness ahead.

The deafening roar of welcome Cole received as she walked on stage blew her away. The audience stood and cheered and shouted their love for her. The sea of faces before her was a blur as tears filled her eyes at the outpouring of genuine support. She waved to everyone and quickly took her place next to Eris who was standing at the table. The noise didn't stop and Cole was totally overwhelmed by it all. She automatically reached for Eris's hand and the audience cheered at that too. Cole knew she was blushing, but she didn't care. She laughed with Eris and the others at their enthusiasm and waved at them to sit back down while she took her own seat behind the long table on the stage. They adjusted the microphone in front of Cole and she waited for the noise to calm down before she spoke.

"Wow! I wasn't expecting that kind of a welcome!" She didn't let go of Eris's hand under the table, needing her strength and stability to keep her together. "Thank you. And can I thank all the fans who have been sending the positive tweets and messages to me. I've seen them, and I appreciate them. Thank you for showing me what the *true* meaning of a fan is."

Her insinuation didn't go unnoticed. The crowd erupted again.

Cole looked out over the audience as they finally took to their seats. In the front row she could see Melanie and Georgio waving to Eris. Beside them sat Jodie Campbell. The police officer looked a little out of her comfort zone being in the audience and not guarding it, but she was gamely sitting next to Ava who was clutching a piece of paper ready to ask her questions the minute the mics opened. The media coverage had deliberately left Ava's name out at her request. She hadn't wanted any association with Brooke at all. Cole liked the fact Ava had gotten close to them all but she never abused that connection. She was a fan who respected the boundaries. Aiden had made sure Ava and Jodie would be at the premiere as honored guests. Cole appreciated that kindness. Without either of them, Cole's outcome could have been so much different. She'd never know exactly what Brooke had planned for her once the questions had dried up. She did know that, without Ava exposing her and Jodie literally putting her life on the line, Cole might not have been sitting where she was today. And she wouldn't have missed today for the world.

Aiden addressed the audience. "To start this panel off we have the first official showing of the trailer for *A Pocket Full of Time* for you all to see." The audience screamed. "Our leading ladies haven't even seen this yet so it's quite the reveal. Oh," Aiden built up the suspense, "as an added extra, for all your wonderful support throughout this production, we have an actual scene from the movie too. Just enough to hopefully whet your appetites before the movie's release. So enjoy!"

The room let out excited whispers and laughter as the lights went down and the screen behind the panel changed from the view of the guests to the movie's logo. That alone drew out squeals.

Everyone on the panel turned in their seats. Cole didn't know what to expect. She was excited and nervous. Eris moved in closer to her.

"I'm so excited I could throw up!" she muttered. Cole knew exactly what she meant.

A beautiful, rich swell of music started, and Cole and Eris watched in stunned silence as the trailer began with Hollister's disappearance. The effects employed to create that scene were more than Cole had ever dreamed of and her jaw dropped. It pretty much remained like that throughout the whole trailer as top-hatted Hollister met Victorian Emily and their story unfolded through a series of scenes that showed the premise of the plot without revealing it all. The audience screamed at the show of an intense romance, and they squealed their excitement at every shot Cole and Eris appeared in together. Eris was wiping her eyes by the end of it, but Cole was spellbound. She couldn't wait to see the whole movie. Cole wanted to experience it for herself, as a viewer, to lose herself in the telling of it now that her part in the making was completed.

The bonus clip was Hollister meeting Victorian Emily for the first time. It immediately transported Cole back to England. She could almost feel the cobblestones beneath her feet. The audience was agog, oohing and awwing at all the right places. Cole remembered watching Eris behind the camera there. Cole was determined to support her in every endeavor she took on. If this movie did well, there would be the chance of sequels to follow. Cole wondered if one of them would see Eris both on screen *and* behind the camera, directing the continuation of Hollister and Emily's stories herself. She really hoped so.

The audience's appreciation of what they'd seen filled the room. Cole soaked in the excitement. Surreptitiously, she ran her hand over her leather jacket hanging from the chair. It had become a talisman for her. She'd had the bullet hole in the leather repaired, but Cole knew exactly where it had been. Tucked inside her inner pocket was a small felt covered box. Cole had been nervously checking that it was there all day. So much so that Eris had asked if she was okay. Cole loved that Eris could read her like a book, but she didn't want to spoil her surprise, so she had to take the coat off to stop herself from patting her chest every five minutes. Cole had a secret meal planned, with the help of Georgio, for when they returned to the restaurant. Cole had ordered the exact same meals she and Eris had shared at Captain Jack's Restaurant in England. She had it all thought out. The kidnapping had taught her a valued lesson. Life was short. And love was rare. Cole knew that she and Eris were soul mates and she didn't intend to waste a single moment they were together. She'd picked out a ring with the help of Cassidy and Mischa. Cassidy, because of her unique sense of style, and Mischa, because she knew the best jewelers. As much as she was loving the fun of the convention, Cole was more excited for the night ahead. She envisioned a lengthy engagement, but she wanted Eris to know her intentions were true. Together forever, in this life and the next.

The audience loved what they were seeing, and Cole could see her friends Aiden, Cassidy, and Mischa basking in their reactions. Eris's gaze was on Cole though.

"Look at what we can do together," Eris said, marveling at the screen and the audience's enjoyment. "We create magic."

"In everything we do together," Cole agreed.

"I'm so glad I found you," Eris said, her meaning clear and full of love.

"Me too. I'd have been lost in this life without you."

"You and me, forging a new path together. We're going to be a force to be reckoned with." Eris kissed Cole's cheek without thinking and the audience's immediate reaction to the display made them both laugh.

Cole looked at Eris and knew, with all her heart, that there was no one else she wanted to share the spotlight with.

Epilogue

Snow fell outside the window of the jewelry shop. The street was deserted and everyone hunkered down inside their homes, waiting for the wintery weather to ease. Hollister sat watching the snow drift on the wind. It had been a cruel season and she wished desperately for spring.

She feared Emily wouldn't see it though.

Every shallow breath Emily took pierced Hollister's heart. Emily was sleeping now. She'd been exhausted after a coughing fit that drained her of what little energy she had. The doctor had left hours before. He didn't have comforting news for Hollister. Emily wasn't recovering from the bout of pneumonia that had left her bed bound and weak. The doctor had warned her it wouldn't be much longer. So Hollister had dragged a chair to their bedside and sat vigil, watching her sweetheart fade away.

"Tell me again our story," Emily said suddenly, startling Hollister from her thoughts. Emily's voice was raspy from all her coughing. She turned her head slowly on the pillow and fixed Hollister with a look that saw through her very soul.

Hollister did as bid. "I traveled through time for you, sweet Emily mine." She gripped Emily's hand in her own and held on as tightly as she could. To keep her tethered to her, to this time and place, just for a moment longer. "This impossible pocket watch brought me from the future, landed me on your doorstep, and brought me home to you. I recognized you immediately. *My* Emily.

Exactly like the love fate tore me from when the watch opened and took me away. You were my only constant in a time not like my own. *My* Emily. I had to be with you, I couldn't live without you."

"You courted me like a proper gentleman." Emily smiled at the memory.

"All the time hiding my true nature."

"I didn't care, when I found out." Emily raised a weak hand to Hollister's face. "You were my soul mate. Sent through time to save me from a life of loneliness and despair. My father was ready to marry me off to any young man that he could find willing to take me. Then you arrived and blessed me with a husband that loved me." Her smile was beautiful still. "Even though you really were my *wife.*"

"I tried to return home though, but the watch was damaged and refused to work. Your father helped me mend it and, in doing so, taught me his craft. I built the watch here, engraved my initials on it, and yet in my time, this was the watch I found." Hollister shook her head. "I'm not sure how or why that could be. It all sounds like some crazy fantasy. It's far beyond my knowledge of how the universe runs." She drew Emily's hand to her lips and pressed a kiss on her knuckles. Emily's hand felt cold to the touch. Hollister's heart clenched at what that meant. "But whatever magic was at work here, I came and I found you."

"And we lived a full and happy life."

"That we have, my love. Your father's legacy lives on and will pass on to Arthur who I've trained so hard to replace me."

"Do you regret we never had children of our own?"

"I don't know how we would have managed it. Though the thought of having little girls that looked like you filled me with hopeless dreams. But we took in Arthur, and raised him as our own. He's a good man. He'll carry the mantle of your father's work proudly for us."

"I'm not getting better, am I?" Emily's voice was fading and Hollister held on tighter.

"No, my love. I don't think you're strong enough to fight it this time." Hollister's voice broke and she tried desperately to hold back her grief. "But that's okay. I'm right here beside you. You're not alone."

"But I'll leave *you* alone." A tear escaped from Emily's eye. It traced a path down her cheek.

"Don't you worry about me. Just believe that I'll find my way back to you. Wherever you are, Emily, I will find you. I traveled through *time* for you. You can't get more fated than that."

"Promise me we'll meet again."

"You know we will. And every time we meet, in every life, I'll touch your heart and you'll recognize me. I'll find you. Not even heaven will keep us apart. Our hearts are bound. Our souls are one. I love you, Emily."

"I love you too, Hollister." Emily took a breath and was silent for a while.

Hollister held her own breath, fearing this was it.

"I recognized you, you know," Emily finally said, surprising Hollister with her words. "That first time we met? I didn't know you but I recognized you somehow. My heart felt pulled toward you, and although I didn't understand it, I knew you were important to me. I knew, deep in my heart, you were *mine*."

"You felt it too? You've never told me that before."

For a moment, Emily's smile was bright and vibrant, and Hollister could see past the older visage and back to the young and vibrant Emily she had met all those years before.

"I couldn't let you get too complacent."

Hollister laughed through her tears at Emily's smug tone. "You always have to have the last word."

Emily nodded. "You love it."

"I love you." Hollister leaned over to kiss her. She pulled back and smiled at the curve on Emily's lips.

"My wife," Emily said on a whisper.

"My life," Hollister vowed and watched Emily's chest rise one last time as her breathing stopped and she passed away in peace.

Hollister bit back a mournful wail as the enormity of her loss struck her. She was alone, out of time, out of place, and without the one woman who had kept her grounded in a reality that was never her own.

Hollister reached for her watch to record the time Emily had died. The hands on the watch blurred through her tears. The second she snapped the case closed, a familiar bolt of electricity slammed through her body. Hollister didn't struggle this time. She handed herself over to her fate willingly. Her eyesight started to alter, and she could see clearer than she had in years. Her body straightened and her aches disappeared. She was de-aging, her body returning to the form she had been when she first arrived. A cine reel started in her mind's eye. Countless memories flashed before her and she watched herself and Emily living through all the stages of their life together, taking her back to the moment they'd met. That memory hung for a moment before her as if captured as a still. Eventually, it dissolved away as did Hollister's body. She watched as their bedroom faded before her and she slipped from the lifetime of love she'd lived.

"Take me to Emily," she ordered as darkness started to crowd in around her. "Take me *home*."

The End.

About the Author

Lesley Davis lives in the West Midlands of England. She is a die-hard science-fiction/fantasy fan in all its forms and an extremely passionate gamer. When her games controller is out of her grasp, Lesley can be found seated at her laptop, writing.

Her book *Dark Wings Descending* was a Lambda Literary award finalist for Best Lesbian Romance.

Visit her online at www.lesleydavisauthor.co.uk or on Twitter @author_lesley

Books Available from Bold Strokes Books

A Woman to Treasure by Ali Vali. An ancient scroll isn't the only treasure Levi Montbard finds as she starts her hunt for the truth—all she has to do is prove to Yasmine Hassani that there's more to her than an adventurous soul. (978-1-63555-890-6)

Before. After. Always. by Morgan Lee Miller. Still reeling from her tragic past, Eliza Walsh has sworn off taking risks, until Blake Navarro turns her world right-side up, making her question if falling in love again is worth it. (978-1-63555-845-6)

Bet the Farm by Fiona Riley. Lauren Calloway's luxury real estate sale of the century comes to a screeching halt when dairy farm heiress, and one-night stand, Thea Boudreaux calls her bluff. (978-1-63555-731-2)

Cowgirl by Nance Sparks. The last thing Aren expects is to fall for Carol. Sharing her home is one thing, but sharing her heart means sharing the demons in her past and risking everything to keep Carol safe. (978-1-63555-877-7)

Give In to Me by Elle Spencer. Gabriela Talbot never expected to sleep with her favorite author—certainly not after the scathing review she'd given Whitney Ainsworth's latest book. (978-1-63555-910-1)

Hidden Dreams by Shelley Thrasher. A lethal virus and its resulting vision send Texan Barbara Allan and her lovely guide, Dara, on a journey up Cambodia's Mekong River in search of Barbara's mother's mystifying past. (978-1-63555-856-2)

In the Spotlight by Lesley Davis. For actresses Cole Calder and Eris Whyte, their chance at love runs out fast when a fan's adoration turns to obsession. (978-1-63555-926-2)

Origins by Jen Jensen. Jamis Bachman is pulled into a dangerous mystery that becomes personal when she learns the truth of her origins as a ghost hunter. (978-1-63555-837-1)

Pursuit: A Victorian Entertainment by Felice Picano. An intelligent, handsome, ruthlessly ambitious young man who rose from the slums to become the right-hand man of the Lord Exchequer of England will stop at nothing as he pursues his Lord's vanished wife across Continental Europe. (978-1-63555-870-8)

Unrivaled by Radclyffe. Zoey Cohen will never accept second place in matters of the heart, even when her rival is a career, and Declan Black has nothing left to give of herself or her heart. (978-1-63679-013-8)

A Fae Tale by Genevieve McCluer. Dovana comes to terms with her changing feelings for her lifelong best friend and fae, Roze. (978-1-63555-918-7)

Accidental Desperados by Lee Lynch. Life is clobbering Berry, Jaudon, and their long romance. The arrival of directionless baby dyke MJ doesn't help. Can they find their passion again—and keep it? (978-1-63555-482-3)

Always Believe by Aimée. Greyson Walsden is pursuing ordination as an Anglican priest. Angela Arlingham doesn't believe in God. Do they follow their vocation or their hearts? (978-1-63555-912-5)

Best of the Wrong Reasons by Sander Santiago. For Fin Ness and Orion Starr, it takes a funeral to remind them that love is worth living for. (978-1-63555-867-8)

Courage by Jesse J. Thoma. No matter how often Natasha Parsons and Tommy Finch clash on the job, an undeniable attraction simmers just beneath the surface. Can they find the courage to change so love has room to grow? (978-1-63555-802-9)

I Am Chris by R Kent. There's one saving grace to losing everything and moving away. Nobody knows her as Chrissy Taylor. Now Chris can live who he truly is. (978-1-63555-904-0)

The Princess and the Odium by Sam Ledel. Jastyn and Princess Aurelia return to Venostes and join their families in a battle against the dark force to take back their homeland for a chance at a better tomorrow. (978-1-63555-894-4)

The Queen Has a Cold by Jane Kolven. What happens when the heir to the throne isn't a prince or a princess? (978-1-63555-878-4)

The Secret Poet by Georgia Beers. Agreeing to help her brother woo Zoe Blake seemed like a good idea to Morgan Thompson at first...until she realizes she's actually wooing Zoe for herself... (978-1-63555-858-6)

You Again by Aurora Rey. For high school sweethearts Kate Cormier and Sutton Guidry, the second chance might be the only one that matters. (978-1-63555-791-6)

Coming to Life on South High by Lee Patton. Twenty-one-year-old gay virgin Gabe Rafferty's first adult decade unfolds as an unpredictable journey into sex, love, and livelihood. (978-1-63555-906-4)

Love's Falling Star by B.D. Grayson. For country music megastar Lochlan Paige, can love conquer her fear of losing the one thing she's worked so hard to protect? (978-1-63555-873-9)

Love's Truth by C.A. Popovich. Can Lynette and Barb make love work when unhealed wounds of betrayed trust and a secret could change everything? (978-1-63555-755-8)

Next Exit Home by Dena Blake. Home may be where the heart is, but for Harper Sims and Addison Foster, is the journey back worth the pain? (978-1-63555-727-5)

Not Broken by Lyn Hemphill. Falling in love is hard enough—even more so for Rose who's carrying her ex's baby. (978-1-63555-869-2)

The Noble and the Nightingale by Barbara Ann Wright. Two women on opposite sides of empires at war risk all for a chance at love. (978-1-63555-812-8)

What a Tangled Web by Melissa Brayden. Clementine Monroe has the chance to buy the café she's managed for years, but Madison LeGrange swoops in and buys it first. Now Clementine is forced to work for the enemy and ignore her former crush. (978-1-63555-749-7)

A Far Better Thing by JD Wilburn. When needs of her family and wants of her heart clash, Cass Halliburton is faced with the ultimate sacrifice. (978-1-63555-834-0)

Body Language by Renee Roman. When Mika offers to provide Jen erotic tutoring, will sex drive them into a deeper relationship or tear them apart? (978-1-63555-800-5)

Carrie and Hope by Joy Argento. For Carrie and Hope loss brings them together but secrets and fear may tear them apart. (978-1-63555-827-2)

Death's Prelude by David S. Pederson. In this prequel to the Detective Heath Barrington Mystery series, Heath discovers that first love changes you forever and drives you to become the person you're destined to be. (978-1-63555-786-2)

Ice Queen by Gun Brooke. School counselor Aislin Kennedy wants to help standoffish CEO Susanna Durr and her troubled teenage daughter become closer—even if it means risking her own heart in the process. (978-1-63555-721-3)

Masquerade by Anne Shade. In 1925 Harlem, New York, a notorious gangster sets her sights on seducing Celine, and new lovers Dinah and Celine are forced to risk their hearts, and lives, for love. (978-1-63555-831-9)

Royal Family by Jenny Frame. Loss has defined both Clay's and Katya's lives, but guarding their hearts may prove to be the biggest heartbreak of all. (978-1-63555-745-9)

Share the Moon by Toni Logan. Three best friends, an inherited vineyard and a resident ghost come together for fun, romance and a touch of magic. (978-1-63555-844-9)

Spirit of the Law by Carsen Taite. Attorney Owen Lassiter will do almost anything to put a murderer behind bars, but can she get past her reluctance to rely on unconventional help from the alluring Summer Byrne and keep from falling in love in the process? (978-1-63555-766-4)

The Devil Incarnate by Ali Vali. Cain Casey has so much to live for, but enemies who lurk in the shadows threaten to unravel it all. (978-1-63555-534-9)

His Brother's Viscount by Stephanie Lake. Hector Somerville wants to rekindle his illicit love affair with Viscount Wentworth, but he must overcome one problem: Wentworth still loves Hector's brother. (978-1-63555-805-0)

Journey to Cash by Ashley Bartlett. Cash Braddock thought everything was great, but it looks like her history is about to become her right now. Which is a real bummer. (978-1-63555-464-9)

Liberty Bay by Karis Walsh. Wren Lindley's life is mired in tradition and untouched by trends until social media star Gina Strickland introduces an irresistible electricity into her off-the-grid world. (978-1-63555-816-6)

Scent by Kris Bryant. Nico Marshall has been burned by women in the past wanting her for her money. This time, she's determined to win Sophia Sweet over with her charm. (978-1-63555-780-0)

Shadows of Steel by Suzie Clarke. As their worlds collide and their choices come back to haunt them, Rachel and Claire must figure out how to stay together and most of all, stay alive. (978-1-63555-810-4)

The Clinch by Nicole Disney. Eden Bauer overcame a difficult past to become a world champion mixed martial artist, but now rising star and dreamy bad girl Brooklyn Shaw is a threat both to Eden's title and her heart. (978-1-63555-820-3)

The Last First Kiss by Julie Cannon. Kelly Newsome is so ready for a tropical island vacation, but she never expects to meet the woman who could give her her last first kiss. (978-1-63555-768-8)

The Mandolin Lunch by Missouri Vaun. Despite their immediate attraction, everything about Garet Allen says short-term, and Tess Hill refuses to consider anything less than forever. (978-1-63555-566-0)

Thor: Daughter of Asgard by Genevieve McCluer. When Hannah Olsen finds out she's the reincarnation of Thor, she's thrown into a world of magic and intrigue, unexpected attraction, and a mystery she's got to unravel. (978-1-63555-814-2)

Veterinary Technician by Nancy Wheelton. When a stable of horses is threatened Val and Ronnie must work together against the odds to save them, and maybe even themselves along the way. (978-1-63555-839-5)

Bold Strokes Books
Quality and Diversity in LGBTQ Literature